Someone Better Than You

A Comedy of Manners

Barry Knister

BookLocker
Trenton, Georgia

Copyright © 2024 Barry Knister

Print ISBN: 978-1-959620-31-0
Ebook ISBN: 979-8-88531-780-1

All rights reserved. No part of this publication may be reproduced, stored in a retrieval system, or transmitted in any form or by any means, electronic, mechanical, recording or otherwise, without the prior written permission of the author.

Published by BookLocker.com, Inc., Trenton, Georgia.

The characters and events in this book are fictitious. Any similarity to real persons, living or dead, is coincidental and not intended by the author.

BookLocker.com, Inc.
2024

First Edition

Library of Congress Cataloging in Publication Data
Knister, Barry
Someone Better Than You: A Comedy of Manners
by Barry Knister
Library of Congress Control Number: 2024914326

To contact Barry Knister, please email him at bwknister@sbcglobal.net

"People seem determined to discover themselves in fiction, a version of narcissism that might repay study."

—Christopher Hitchens, "American Notes," *Times Literary Supplement*, September, 1987

FOR MY PACKAGE DEAL

1
2010: Southwest Florida International Airport

"I suppose you'll be all right."
Surprised to be spoken to, Brady Ritz turns quickly. "Of course I will," he says. "Your old stepdad's a hurricane survivor."
Your *old* stepdad is meant to generate sympathy, but Jane has already turned away. Now she's fiddling with the collar on Madison's preppy polo. Give the kid a puppy and a fishing pole, and she can model for the next L.L.Bean catalogue.
But what's really on Ritz's mind is how Jane has stopped calling him Daddy. He is her stepfather, and she's thirty-two, but Jane has always called him that. Really, he thinks, watching her, what would it cost you?
A voice goes on mumbling over the airport's PA system. A security guard glides by on a Segway. The soft, pliant voice and the scooter's smooth whirr remind Ritz of how nice he's been all week. How quiet and helpful, anxious-to-please. That's really all anyone wants from you, Ritz thinks. To be nice, homogenized. Denatured.
Thick black hair curtains her face as Jane adjusts Madison's barrette. The little girl is staring vacantly at planes outside the observation window. One of them will fly her and her family back to Michigan. Ritz's son-in-law is off to the

side, holding Madison's younger sister, Ashley. He is explaining something and points to the plane.

Ashley and Madison. God. But of course Dan is responsible for the grandchildren's trendy, gender-neutral names. He talked Jane into it, just the way he's lecturing his four-year-old. Dan points again, and Ritz studies his son-in-law's cornball mutton chop whiskers. His bored, all-knowing tone of voice. The graphic on his tee shirt shows projectile vomit landing on a kitchen floor, painted with the name of a band. *Blech.*

"Okay, that's us." The PA voice is still echoing as Jane lifts her daughter. Ritz reaches down for the canvas bag at her feet, but Jane grabs it and straightens. "It's easier this way," she says.

"All right."

Lounging now in the bucket seat formed by her mother's body, Madison turns to regard him. She knows something is wrong, but hasn't asked questions.

"Goodbye, Grandpa."

"Goodbye, Maddy."

When Ritz moves in for the parting hug. Jane hesitates. But she is conventional like her mother, and relents. As the three now form a clumsy embrace, Madison taps him on the neck. "You have a mole," she says. "Right here." She taps again below his right ear.

"Would you like one?" he asks.

"Like what?"

"A mole."

"No."

"I could get you one." Brady winks. "From the Mole Hole. A big one with red lumps and green slime."

"No!" He sneaks a peak. Is Jane suppressing a smile? "Grandpa's being silly," Madison says. "You can't buy moles."

"The Mole Hole is a store, honey." Jane steps back from him. "A gift shop in Naples. Moles are little animals that live in the ground. We'll read about them at home. Grandpa is just being grandpa."

Little animals that live in the ground, Grandpa just being his silly old self. Brady smiles and pats Madison on the head. Before, whether or not what he said was funny, Jane laughed her girlish, life-enhancing laugh. Not now, he thinks. This is the new Jane, the postpartum nanny. The schoolmarm mom who lost her sense of humor.

Dan has come from the window. He shifts the four-year-old on his arm and moves in for the second pro-forma hug. "Goodbye, Brady, thanks." Ritz's answer is muffled by mutton chop whiskers. They unclasp, and everyone starts moving toward security check-in. The week is ending without his having made a case for himself. But why should I need to? he thinks. Why do they always shoot the messenger?

As though she agrees with him, little Ashley starts whimpering. Without breaking stride, Jane reaches out to smooth her cheek. Unlike her preppy sister, Ashley is dressed for combat in a camouflage tee shirt and bib overalls. Ritz is sure she chose her costume this morning to fit whatever drama was still going on in the dream theater occupying her small, coppery head. *She* would say *Yes!* to a lumpy mole with green slime.

"Stop!" They all turn at the concourse. "No!"

"Come on, honey—" Dan holds her close and keeps walking in his slow, measured way. "You know we have to leave."

"No, Daddy, we *don't*." Ashley adds a theatrical catch in her throat. "You know we don't, Dad… You say nothing… is cast in stone… We don't have to leave… it's not cast in stone, it's *not*—"

The parents exchange knowing looks and keep walking. *Cast in stone.* Brady keeps pace behind them. A strong surge of gratitude passes through him for the only person who gave him the time of day all week. My precocious little ally, he thinks. My co-conspirator

"No! No! No!"

Not allowed beyond the rope, he watches her struggle. As Dan hands over his driver's license, Brady remembers her last Christmas in a church basement during a children's play. The arrival of Baby Jesus was followed by a small robed figure. Ritz's program described her part with political correctness as a "wise person." Ashley first pointed to the straw-filled manger, slowly lowered her arm, and faced the audience. "It's plastic," she said. "Not a real baby." *Perfect!* He started to clap, but Ritz's wife grabbed his hands. She held them fast as the Wise Person went on about the polyvinyl chloride reality of Baby Jesus, until a humorless Nice Person led her away.

Dan is cleared and steps to the moving belt for luggage. "Okay, 'bye." Jane sets down Madison.

Someone Better Than You: A Comedy of Manners

"Promise to call when you get home," he says.

"All right, I promise."

"You have window seats?"

"Always. The girls insist." Jane un-shoulders her backpack. "You always got us window seats," she says. "We loved it."

"We've had lots of good times, Janey."

"That's true, they were." Jane reaches down and again hoists Madison. "Good times."

"I like to think—"

As though ready for this, Jane reaches out with her free hand and places her palm on his chest. When he places his hand on hers, she slips free. She grabs up the bag and backpack, turns with her daughter and walks toward the TSA counter. Madison looks over her mother's shoulder, and waves.

2
Words Are Deeds

In fifteen minutes he is on southbound I-75, heading back to Naples. Ritz isn't happy, just relieved the visit is over. He can still feel Jane's palm pressed flat on his chest. According to his wife, promises made to the girls and non-refundable tickets are the only reasons they flew down.

Brilliant sun glints off cars zipping past on his left. Semis, pickups, stake trucks hauling pavers and mulch. How many grandfathers are driving home after taking grown children and grandchildren to airports? Some are basking in the warm afterglow of the visit, others de-compressing with a sense of relief. He wonders how many are driving home with a sense of regret.

Rising on both sides of the Interstate are the berms and retainer walls of golf communities. The remaining land in Collier County will almost certainly become more of the same. For more grandparents. Brady lives on a golf course, but he no longer likes the game. Even before everyone stopped playing with him, golf had gotten old. His former partners are still at the Monday-Thursday-Saturday regimen. He sees them from his second-floor balcony, tooling down the ninth fairway in Shriners-parade golf carts.

He adjusts the rearview mirror.

Yes, even before what he calls the Cold Snap, Brady is sure he was tired of golf. Tired of the right-wing, anti-Obama "humor" that went with it. Bored by endless talk of TV shows he never watched. The same stretch of fairway now led to the same emerald-green carpet of bent grass, followed by buffet tables and chafing dishes and tubs of iced beer. The same forced enthusiasm over good shots, or feigned anguish at robbed opportunities. No one plays with him now, but Brady is convinced he was already done with golf.

Expressway traffic is light and he is on auto pilot. Jane appears to him in her mommy jeans and jersey top. Cradling Madison, she grabs the canvas bag and straightens.

It's one thing to earn a modest living by pedaling tourists around Mumbai or Hong Kong. But here, in the First World? With blank-eyed children riding behind in a cart as the coolie mom pedals and talks on her cell phone about why she decided to shave her head? Doing all this in heavy traffic, with every other driver a texting adolescent, or a blotto senior citizen weaving his way home after Happy Hour at the American Legion?

He called the column "Suburban Pedicab Parents." Never mind that what he wrote is true: the carts *are* dangerous. So what? His wife says that's the column that broke the camel's back for Jane. When she and Dan ride their tandem bike, they pull the girls in one of the rickshaws.

Taillights are going on up ahead. Brady takes his foot off the gas, and slows to a stop behind a pickup truck. No more dad or daddy, he thinks. Jane is the only young person he takes seriously. How could someone so bright and talented turn her back on him over something so trivial? Being turned into a scapegoat by Republican retirees still in love with Ronald

Reagan, he gets that. At first, he sort of *got* his wife of almost thirty years leaving him out of embarrassment. But bright, talented Jane? Over a few jokes in two or three of his columns? No, that doesn't compute.

His phone buzzes. That will be Natalie. Before she left him, she made Ritz put a cell phone in his car. In "Arrested Development," he called cell phones a millennial substitute for teething rings and nipple pacifiers. He takes it from the dashboard.

"Did you get them there on time?"

"And hello to you, too." When his wife doesn't answer, he says, "No, Natalie, I sold them. A human trafficker made me an offer I couldn't refuse."

"What about fruit? Did you make sure they took home citrus?"

"There wasn't room. The white slaver said they could eat all the tomatoes they want out in the field. Tomatoes are fruit."

"You didn't remember."

"I remembered."

"No, Buzz. 'I had other things on my mind and forgot,' that's what you always say."

Yes, he forgot, but Brady says, "I did not. I got them there on time, I remembered everything. I remembered the kiddies' shells from Sanibel, I remembered the hats and stuffed animals I bought them at the zoo." Like *old stepdad,* stuffed animals are meant to gain sympathy.

"Did you get the fruit at Green Thumb? You didn't, you went to Publix."

"Natalie, for God's sake spare me the organic party line. There was no way they could take fruit. Organic or genetically modified. It looked like Ellis Island, people in steerage with everything they own."

"You always criticize their clothes," his wife says. "It's superficial."

"I'm not talking about clothes."

"'People in steerage'? Of course you are. You always say Jane and Dan look like the homeless. You say millennials have no sense of occasion or form."

Brady releases his seatbelt, and shoves up to see ahead. All the taillights are still glowing. He sits back down with an oddly strong wish his wife would believe him. Please just let it go, he thinks. Not so far back they still laughed at each other's jokes. They were good together. Now, it's all lectures and fault-finding.

"Not including whatever they checked, I counted four carry-ons. Backpacks, Bean bags—"

"You never appreciated what was involved in traveling with children. Every time we took the girls somewhere, you complained."

Brady clucks his tongue. "You're unpacking a little baggage of your own," he says. "Here we go with the only-child gambit, the know-nothing stepdad routine."

"Don't you dare, Buzz. I never said that except in jest and you know it—"

Natalie starts coughing, and covers the handset. She has sinus trouble every May and June. In the silence, Brady wonders whether she *did* mean it. Early in the marriage, she joked about "a certain privileged only child" who had never needed to consider others. Maybe she actually believed it, he thinks. Believed not growing up with siblings or raising "little ones" made you oblivious to others.

"All right, I'm back," she says. "So, they went home with no fruit."

"Everything but. Are you all right?"

"I'm fine, it's pollen. You should know. Alex died."

Ritz eases back with the phone pressed to his ear. The news shouldn't come as a surprise. Alex Brubaker's been sick a long time with prostate cancer. But it shocks him. As he has many times, Ritz sees his best friend's ravaged face inches from his own. We had unfinished business, he thinks.

"You might want to send Betty a card, or call," Natalie says. "She told me she enjoyed your early columns."

"Right. The ones before I got carried away, as you put it. I'm sure you two had a good talk. I'm sure you and Jane talked all week."

"Of course we talked, Jane and I talk several times a week. Why would we stop just because she's down there?"

"Talking about me," he says. "You know what I'm saying."

"It wasn't easy for her. You should be glad they came at all. I wouldn't have."

"You don't."

"That's different, and you know it," Natalie says. "If you want to know, I defended you. I told her Alex encouraged you to use your own name."

"And? What did she say?"

"Jane said—" His wife clears her throat "—she forgives you, but things can't be the same."

It disappoints him. Frustrates him. "That's her version of forgiveness?"

"I want to ask you something." Natalie's voice has dropped into the register she reserves for serious matters. "And I want you to think before you answer."

"My cognitive powers are on full alert."

"Why didn't you talk to her? Why leave it up to me?"

"Because I did nothing wrong," he says.

"That's no answer. You had Jane with you a whole week, and never explained yourself. Tell me why."

"Explain what? I did nothing wrong," he says again. "It's a simple matter of pride. I had a harmless hobby. I wrote a jokey column for a little magazine. I told the truth as I see it, and my 'best friend' sucker-punched me."

"I don't believe you." Natalie coughs. "You keep calling it harmless truth-telling, but you hurt people. And you know it. And please stop blaming Alex. It's your name on the book, not his. You're always talking about the real world, Buzz. That's the real-world reason you said nothing to Jane. For a whole week. Do you want to know what she said?"

Hurt people. Brady hates the word. "Does it matter?" he says. "You're going to tell me."

"She drew a comparison to Native Americans and photography."

"Uh huh."

"She said they feel their souls are stolen when someone takes their picture."

"That's unalloyed nonsense," he says. "What about all the shutterbug tourists visiting Indian reservations? Their casinos are wall-to-wall with surveillance cameras."

"Maybe they aren't Indians," Natalie says. "It doesn't matter, you're missing the point on purpose. People somewhere think you take their souls when you take their picture. Jane feels the same way. You took what was hers and made fun of it."

Brake lights are blinking off ahead. If his talented stepdaughter thinks he stole something from her, Brady regrets it. But he still can't see why a few words matter so much.

"Fine," he says. "I used a few details in something I wrote and didn't ask permission. Why can't she let it go? Why can't you? You say I'm critical, you call me petty. So are you, Natalie. So is Jane and everyone at Donegal. Why can't any of you just forgive and forget?"

He is already mouthing his wife's answer. "You don't understand and don't want to," she says. "*You're* the one who won't let it go. You criticize everyone and everything, and still don't get how hurt people feel—"

Memorized from many such calls, Ritz goes on miming his wife's words. Traffic is starting to inch forward. Good. When she calls, it still gives him an odd boost. Even when they fight, it restores a sense of connection.

Judgmental. Hurt. Feel. Bobbing his head to the rise and fall of his wife's voice, Brady puts the shift lever in Drive. In his view, American culture is buried under a steamy compost mound of emotion. Of soap opera feelings and self-pity. If I were God, he thinks, I would create a lexicological delete key.

The first word to go? Feelings. Just imagine—he nods in agreement——every reporter denied the word, each and every time he shoves a microphone in someone's face. Every talk-show host, every right-to-lifer or pro-choicer. *How does it—* and nothing. Just a blank space requiring thought.

"—because words are deeds, and they can hurt—" Good, *words are deeds* comes near the end "—and when those words are remembered, they hurt all over again." There it is, Brady thinks. Word Number Two on your cosmic delete list. Hurt. You hurt me, you hurt my pride, my ego is one big hematoma, my feelings are stuck all over with voodoo needles—

"Stop—" For no reason, *voodoo needles* triggers him. "Let's cut to the chase," he says. "Why are you still in Michigan? Five months, Natalie, this makes no sense. That's it, I'm flying up. What's actually going on?"

"No, Buzz, please don't. We went through this last week. It's something I have to work through alone. I'm not sick, please don't fly up. I keep thinking how long you kept your secret from me."

"Not that again," he says. "You can't be serious."

"Don't you see? What kind of marriage is that? I'm trying to get past it, but I haven't. Not yet. You weren't unfaithful to me with another woman, but you were unfaithful."

Last week she said the same thing. "Not telling you I wrote satire for a little magazine makes me unfaithful? Do you have any idea how drop-dead crazy that sounds?"

"I have to go," she says.

"You already did that, in January. One week after our anniversary. Our twenty-eighth if memory serves."

"No, Buzz, someone's at the door. He's here to tuck point the chimney."

"What's wrong with it?"

"Bricks fell off," she says. "It's lucky no one was hurt."

Brady takes his foot off the brake pedal. Another *Hurt*, he thinks. And still calling you unfaithful for not telling her about *Grumble*. It makes him furious, he has to move.

"Now I like that—" He checks his rearview mirror before swinging left and accelerating. "I like spending money to keep people from being hit by falling bricks. I get that, Natalie, I really do, a brick on the head actually *hurts,* you *feel* it, that's the real-world, life-threatening—"

She ends the call. He clips his phone on the dash and eases back on the gas pedal. Ahead on the right, a Jeep is nose-down in the culvert. Facing forward, Ritz remembers his wife on New Year's Day. She is standing at the glass door wall in the family room, looking out at the swimming pool.

Are you here by yourself?

It's a joke between them, the first words he ever spoke to her. But Natalie doesn't answer. She is holding his book, wearing the black silk pajamas he gave her for Christmas.

3
Cupid's Swizzle Stick

"Are you here by yourself?"

They were standing in the smoky lobby of *The Detroit Post*, and she was wearing black. She looked at him a second before turning to her left. Her right. Brady felt himself blush. "You got me," he said. "Except for these two hundred other life forms, you're here all by yourself."

"One of them is my date," she said. "Gwen Nolan from accounting. She broke up with her fella and asked me to come with her. My name is Natalie McTavish."

"Brady Ritz." They shook hands. He wasn't the kind who took the initiative with women, but he liked looking at her. And her use of a retro word like *fella*.

"How about you?" she asked. "Are you a life form all on your lonesome?"

Brady liked that, too. "Exactly," he said. "I'm another one of those fellas, but in reverse. I got my marching orders on Christmas Eve." Her neutral-on-first-meeting smile slipped away. "Don't misunderstand," he said. "I probably had it coming."

"I think that's mean." Now she was frowning. "Telling someone it's over on Christmas is wrong. Unnecessary. Whatever you did or didn't do, that's intentionally cruel."

Taking what he'd said so seriously left Ritz not knowing how to answer. They sipped their drinks, and waved away the smoke being generated by a crowd of two-pack-a-day newspaper types. *All on your lonesome* was not a common expression. Was she talking about herself being lonesome, or did she mean he looked lonesome? If she meant him, Brady Ritz looked to her the way he should: like a man dumped by the latest in a widely-spaced series of women who thought he was funny and liked him for a few months, then didn't. The latest had left him to attend the 1982 *Detroit Post* New Year's party on his own. On his lonesome.

"It sounds as though you speak from experience," he said finally.

"Yes, I've had some, but nothing very mean. I'm thirty-two, divorced, and have two children." She was now looking at him with a flat, no-nonsense gaze. "Experience has taught me it's good to get that out there up front," she said. "I manage the office for a group of lawyers. All of them are big on bow ties and Porsches."

"How old are they? Not the lawyers, your children."

"Five and three. Anne and Jane. Their father wasn't a bad man or a mean man. Just not a very reliable one. After we divorced, he went to Montana. He died in an accident."

It was a lot to digest in the *Detroit Post's* smoky, crowded lobby. Ritz had never met anyone so direct. So candid.

"And you?" she asked.

Aware now of her narrow waist and broad shoulders, Ritz followed her shorthand approach. He was thirty-six. He had grown up on the city's west side, gone to Mumford High School and on to U of M to study English, then to grad school. After he dropped out, a friend had gotten him in at the *Post*.

"What did me in at Michigan was grading papers," he said. "For a tenured professor who could almost write his name in the dirt with a stick. That, and teaching freshmen. You know you shouldn't teach when your students' elbows keep slipping off the desk."

It was a canned speech used before in similar circumstances. Alex Brubaker, his friend at the *Post* had gotten Ritz a flunky job as a gofer and mail sorter. Ritz had now worked for the paper for eight years. No siblings. His parents were both dead, and he hadn't been married.

"I assume you no longer sort the mail," she said.

"Correct. I'm a copy editor. Now I fix what reporters write. My nickname is Buzz, short for Buzz Cut. Because I make them shorten their stories."

Natalie smiled. "Are you good at it?"

"Compared to my teaching skills, yes," he said. "The younger reporters call me their fixer." She smiled again. "McTavish. You're Scottish?"

"I'm actually Polish with a dash of German," she said. "It should be Mazurkiewicz—" she spelled it for him. "Except the clerk on Ellis Island couldn't manage my great grandfather's name. According to family lore, the clerk said, 'D'name's McTavish, now move along, next in line.'"

Ritz laughed. She had given the Ellis Island clerk a convincing Brooklyn accent. "My great grandparents just assumed that's how it was done here, so they kept the name." He laughed again. McTavish to replace something unpronounceable, something much easier to record in a ledger. "I wonder—" She held out her empty glass and Ritz took it. "It's an Old Fashioned."

He headed for the bar. McTavish for Mazurka-something. Brady loved it. They gave you a new name in the New World, and if you wanted to stay here, you kept it. He passed a woman doing her best to look like a movie star. She was holding her wine glass in an affected way, picking up and putting down her aching, spike-heeled foot. Natalie McTavish knew better. No dumb shoes or makeup. No look-at-me clothes to mar what he already thought must be her very good body. Just a plain black cashmere sweater and slacks. Small hoop earrings. Women grad students at Michigan had all seemed to emulate the fashion sense of Emily Dickinson, or some notable figure from the Third World like Indira Gandhi. And her smile. He even liked what she was drinking, an Old Fashioned. No one knew what they were anymore, but she did. He got two, and elbowed his way back. When he neared her, Natalie's smile was one of welcome.

"Thank you." She took the drink. "Do you want the garnish? I never eat it." An offering, Ritz thought. An invitation. She pinched the stick with orange slice and cherry, and as she brought it out, Ritz reached for it.

"Oh God, I'm so sorry, I didn't—" Beneath the orange and cherry, the stick's pronged end had jammed under Ritz's thumb nail.

"No, it's me, I was clumsy."

"Please, Brady, hold still." She steadied his hand, then gently pulled the stick free. It hurt, but he sipped his Old Fashioned in a manly show of indifference to pain. She had spoken his name. A drop of blood oozed from his thumb. She peeled the napkin from the bottom of her drink and held out the glass. He took it and balanced it in his good hand with his own drink, then watched as she reached in her glass and fished out a piece of ice. Wrapping it in the napkin, she now pressed it in her palm around his thumb.

"Androcles and the lion," he said.

"What? Oh, yes, clumsy Androcles, I'm so sorry." She kept her fist wrapped around his finger. "I'd like my drink now."

By the end of the hour, Ritz was seeing them having dinner in his favorite restaurant. And she was funny. "The girls and I were in this ice cream parlor, next to a table of nuns. The twenty-something waitress comes to the nuns' table. 'Hey, guys, are we ready to do the deed and order?'"

At midnight, horns and buzzers went off. People cheered and began singing Auld Lang Syne. It wasn't at all like him to make the first move, but he stepped closer. Natalie didn't back away. They kissed lightly and parted, but he held her arms a moment before letting go. At the end of the night, she agreed to go out with him.

In the following weeks, Ritz and Natalie discovered they were compatible in terms of both their bodies and minds. Unlike other women he'd known, she was funny. Good with words. She was no prude and enjoyed sex, but preferred it with the light off. So did he. They liked the same food and music. Neither of them smoked. Equally important, Natalie told him her daughters liked him. "They declared you to be 'weird, but in a good way,'" she told him.

He took her to the Detroit Symphony (with cellist YoYo Ma), then to a Billy Joel concert. "Do you know what Chuck E Cheese is?" she asked on the drive home from Billy Joel.

Ritz shook his head. "Well, no, why would you? It's the girls' favorite place, but you need to understand. If we go, it's not your kind of thing. It's for families with small children. Think in terms of a stress test."

Before picking them up the following Friday, he prepped himself with vodka and breath mints. He had read up on Chuck E Cheese, and now knew what Natalie meant by stress test: a demonic pizza parlor built around an inflated, bubble-like structure full of elementary-school-age children being monitored by the damned, their stunned parents. As Anne and Jane ran off to find their circle of hell, he knew Natalie was watching him. Would he bolt? Have a seizure? It was a test he wanted to pass. He gripped the edge of the table and did his bug-eyed, dazed-by-sonic-overload look. She smiled with relief, then gave the look back at him, and mouthed *thank you.*

After ten months, she was still with him. How much this had to do with the practical needs faced by a single mother Ritz wasn't entirely sure. But on nights when he stayed over, Anne and Jane seemed glad to see him in the morning. When he asked Natalie to marry him, they were seated on a bench in a shopping mall. He treated the moment as a jokey retail transaction, to mask his fear of getting turned down. Natalie hesitated, and looked bleak. "Would you want us to have children?" she asked. "I know myself pretty well. I worry too much with Ann and Jane, and I know in my heart it would be a mistake to have another child."

Ritz had some recollection of growing up, but his parents were gone, as were his aunt and uncle. He had no brother or sister to compare notes with, and his memories of childhood were more like snapshots or postcards. But he remembered how protective and cautious his gentle accountant father and librarian mother had been in raising their only child. Remembered with remorse how much they had worried about him. And how he had exploited their fear to get his way.

"Why would I want a child?" he said. "You're a package deal." Natalie grabbed his lapels and kissed him. It was true. He had never felt a need to pass along the Ritz genes.

4
Paradise

He reaches Naples and exits the expressway. Soon, Ritz is passing bible-thumper churches, storage facilities. He glances at the new Chick-fil-A. In their marketing, the franchise makes much of being closed on Sundays. I hear they bless the french fries, he said the first time they drove past. No—Natalie shook her head. I'm too full of sin to eat there. He laughed at the idea. But not today.

At Davis Boulevard he turns right, and now begins passing the gated entrances to golf communities like his own. Cedar Hammock. Naples Heritage. Countryside. It's June, and the snowbirds have left. The Ritzes vacationed here, and when Natalie's father died, her inheritance made it possible to buy a house for the winter months.

He turns at the entrance to Donegal Golf and Country Club. Ritz waves to the guard house, and slows for the scanner to read the bar code on his side window. The gate swings open and he drives in. Ahead lies the sprawling clubhouse behind big, silvery Bismarck palm trees. To the left spreads the practice putting green. On the right, four HarTru tennis courts bake in the afternoon heat.

Marriage and parenthood require real change.

Ritz turns onto Donegal Boulevard. He hears that one from Natalie every time he brings up how predictable Jane has become. His wife is smarter than he is, but she often relies on catch phrases and conventional wisdom. Ritz doesn't think anybody changes. Not really. Being forced to adapt, yes, but that's entirely different. That's just knuckling under. In Ritz's view, the whole idea of change should get the Delete treatment, along with feelings and hurt. *I am not Michael Jordan, nor was meant to be. I was never going to slam dunk any layups, or ace a three-pointer at the buzzer. This I am sure was made certain when I myself was nothing but a microscopic basketball waiting for cell division.*

Golf carts are trundling along the path that runs parallel to the road. He stops to let them cross. Habitual cigar between his teeth, Tony Minetta is at the wheel of the second cart. Minetta is big-bellied, dressed in yellow shorts and matching golf shirt. Perched on his head is the signature pork pie hat that protects his hair transplants. He starts across the road, looks pointedly at Ritz, raises his gloved hand and jabs the air with his middle finger. Those in the next cart skip the gesture, but stare as they pass.

Ritz accelerates. He wrote that hair transplants make a man's head look like a cribbage board. Nothing he wrote had anything to do with Minetta. Not the sport—he used bocce ball instead of golf—not the player's physical description. Aside from the crack about cribbage boards, nothing.

On his right stretches a row of houses similar to his own. Some have circular drives, some make much of pillars. All are aggressively landscaped in the Florida style, with elephant ears and coconut palms. In keeping with Donegal's strict building regulations, all the houses have identical red tile roofs. Each time he and Natalie were shown another condo, she pointed to the ceiling. The day after we close—Ritz would finish her sentence—a flamenco troupe moves in upstairs. Right, she said. And Michael Flatley lives next door. But then they found a great house just being completed for someone who had walked away from the deal. It flattered his ego to think of living in such a place. Everything is taken care of by others.

At Glynnis Court, Ritz turns and swings up the second driveway. He switches off the ignition. Was Dolores here? She cleans once a week, he can't remember the day. He gets out and moves up the paver walk. Inside the screened entrance, he opens the heavy inner door and steps into the foyer. No, this wasn't her day. When Dolores comes, the house smells fresh.

With the door closed, he now hears a familiar thumping. Brady moves through the foyer, up the hall. At the far end, the house is all glass. The pool floats outside, and beyond the screened cage spreads the ninth fairway. He reaches the kitchen/family room, moves to his right and swings open the door to the garage. Ace Foley is thudding on the treadmill in front of Natalie's Buick. The spine of his T-shirt is stained with sweat.

Like Ritz, Foley is in his sixties, but he looks younger. Like someone in a diet book, or a TV commercial for an all-inclusive resort. Ace pumps iron, jogs, swims laps. Last year, he ran the Naples senior marathon. If Foley hadn't missed a turn, the odds are good he would have won his division. But he turned left instead of right at Gulf Shore Boulevard. That's when the new facts of Foley's cognitive decline led him down Gordon Drive to the enclave of Port Royal. A private security guard asked whether he could be of any help.

Brady steps into his field of vision. "Buddy! How they hangin'?" His neighbor smiles broadly. "You want it? I'm almost done."

"It's all yours. How long have you been at it?"

"Fifty minutes.... Let me finish the hour..."

The smile slips away, but Foley doesn't slow or falter. In the foyer of his own house hangs a four-by-six-foot poster blow-up. The original photo appeared on the cover of a financial-services magazine. Foley is pictured in a black-and-yellow wet suit. His chestnut hair is slicked back and reveals a youthful widow's peak. Ace is on water skis, hands behind his back like a speed skater.

This is it, the thing itself. But the modern retiree isn't like the poor, bare, forked animal in King Lear. *He's a water skier with the tow rope in his teeth. He needn't beware of the foul fiend Flibbertigibbet. Not in an age of designer drugs, organ transplants and titanium ball joints. He has plenty of money, courtesy of his financial planner, and he's in excellent health.*

Of equal importance, he knows nothing of dignity, or reflection. For as long as he lives—and these days it will probably be much longer—he will go on slapping over those waves and whacking that golf ball. Dead at the top, maybe, but hugely pleased with himself.

By that point, Ritz was using references to literature in his *Grumble* column. He made Foley's wetsuit blue, the skier bald. But it doesn't matter. People refuse to see what he wrote wasn't about Ace Foley, or Tony Minetta, or anyone else at Donegal. Or about Jane. It was about the times, and what Brady calls "the last trimester"—retirement. All he did was borrow bits and pieces to create characters. He never brutalized real people in the sacred name of *art* like Philip Roth. Nothing ambitious, nothing artsy craftsy. And certainly nothing unfaithful. He was just having fun for its own sake. But no one cares. As soon as Donegal residents learned he'd written a book, they began finding themselves in his essays. *Chose* to find themselves. And didn't like what they found.

As for Ace Foley, at least he isn't masturbating. After Deirdre Foley died, it became clear what kind of libido she'd been dealing with. Following her memorial service, one of the funeral directors found Ace jerking off in the coat room. A week later, Tom Gracy caught him at it in the port-a-potty next to the eleventh tee. It gave Ritz the title for a *Grumble* post ("Whacking-off: A Golfer's Handbook"), but by then the magazine had folded.

5
Life vs Art

When Foley comes in from the garage, Ritz is watching *CNN*. But not paying attention. He is still processing *You were unfaithful*. Natalie didn't mean it literally, but so what? What matters is that she's not here. Who then is being unfaithful? What is marriage, if not two people who've got each other's back? The one person he most needs has turned hers on him.

Toweling his head, Foley has stopped to watch. Ritz rocks out of his recliner and comes back with a glass of water. "Thanks." Foley drains it and hands it back. "When'd you get here?"

"Just now." Ritz sets the glass on the kitchen island. Does Foley mean *this* right now, or out in the garage? He has good days and bad.

He stops rubbing his hair and frowns at the TV. "Goddamn Arab terrorists," he says. "Look at them, jumping up and down like that. I say nuke 'em all. What do you think, Brady? What the hell, git 'er done. Sooner or later it's going to happen, everyone says so. Why screw around? Bunch of thugs. Look at that!"

Foley loops the towel around his neck and holds the ends. Like most Donegal residents, *CNN* is not what he watches. He keeps *Bang News* on all day, next to a second TV tuned to *ESPN*, the sports network.

"Nukes won't work," Ritz says.

"Why not? You can't reason with people like that." Foley shakes his head. "Bang did a show on what you're seeing. That?" He points. "Right there? There's a flea carries some kind of germ, it's in all of them. They get it from their sheep or goats. This bug goes right into the brain, that's what you're looking at right there—" He nods. "That thing with shooting off their rifles? It's the flea. When you have that kind of enemy, they don't leave you a choice."

It's pointless. Long before Foley turned the wrong way on Gulf Shore Boulevard, he was lost. But Ritz can't help himself. "Ace, come on," he says. "Nukes are crazy. What about fallout? You'd have radioactive—"

"Here we go," Foley says. "You mean Israel, don't get me started. That Israel lobby in Washington? They own us, Brady. I'm sorry, I have Jew friends up the wazoo, but that lobby owns the stars 'n stripes. We have to do something pretty soon."

Foley nods for emphasis, and heads up the hall. Ritz follows. At the entrance he opens the door. Ace gives him a friendly punch on the shoulder before stepping through the screened enclosure. Good, he's jogging toward his own house across the street. Ritz waits until Foley is inside before closing the door.

He turns in the foyer and looks up the staircase. At the top, a skylight forms a warm cup of pale yellow. Like the banister, the stairs are made of polished travertine marble, with a carpet runner. The Ritz house in Michigan has hardwood floors. Natalie says creaking up and down the stairs makes her think of pirate ships in a movie, just before battle.

Someone Better Than You: A Comedy of Manners

As he climbs in silence, Jane's paintings march up the wall next to him. First is a big close-up image of African violets, but not in bloom. He considers the idea brilliantly ironic. Enough with idealized beauty, the picture says to him. Here's what is real most of the time. The next is even more contrarian: sodden, broken peonies after heavy rain. Then a potted rubber tree. The waxy leaves seem to reach out to him from the canvas.

At the top of the stairs, the hall forms a gallery, and here the pictures are all abstract. Since the cold snap, Jane's work has served Ritz as an oasis. A refuge. He hoped coming down and once more seeing her paintings treated with respect would make a difference. He has always thought of this early work as an overture. A prologue. But Jane decided the world needed more people. Since Madison and Ashley were born, she hasn't painted.

Perhaps disappointment is what leads him so far back. He remembers himself at forty-one, Jane at nine. They are reading on opposite ends of the big leather couch in the Michigan house. Hundreds of times he's watched himself look up from his book. Snow is still falling outside the living room windows; logs are popping in the fireplace. Her older sister and Natalie are off shopping, but Jane is with Daddy. Is it corny? Hallmark sentimental? Ritz doesn't care. In some irreducible way, he is sure he was never happier. Jane now reads mostly about child development. Last Christmas, she gave him a book on nurture versus nature.

He passes the closed door to the guest bedroom, and stops at the open entry to his wife's study. The wall in front of her desk is covered with framed family photos. This is where Natalie did all the necessary, grown-up things. Paid bills for car leases and insurance, filled out tax forms, wrote thank-you notes and birthday cards. She has arranged for all the important mail to be sent to her in Michigan.

Whump

Ritz walks quickly to the end of the hall, into the master bedroom. He crosses, swings open French doors and steps out on the narrow balcony. Below on the left, Murray Grunwald is in his own pool cage. He is in his underwear, bent over and feeling for the flexible golf tee fitted into a square of AstroTurf. A canvas tarp hangs opposite on his pool cage.

If he is going to the library to get Murray more audio books, Ritz needs to leave now. But he waits for his neighbor to find the tee. With care Grunwald places the ball, takes his hand away, straightens. It looks like he has a three wood. Now he begins searching the AstroTurf with his bare feet, for the depressions that guide him where to stand. He finds them, and addresses the ball.

Ritz smiles. The only reason for all the pre-swing ass wiggling and club positioning is to show your foursome how serious you are. But Murray is by himself, and legally blind. As he watches, Ritz wonders: if you'd written about blind golf, would he still be talking to you?

Whump

His neighbor bends to place another ball on the tee. Ritz backs inside and softly closes the French doors. He crosses the room and sits on his side of the bed to change from sneakers to boat shoes. Out in the hall, Jane's paintings hang in shadow.

She promised to call when she got home, but didn't. He finishes with the shoes and straightens. Resting on his nightstand is a copy of his book. Your act of infidelity, he thinks. Your version of fooling around.

He reaches in his hip pocket and gets out his wallet. Ritz works through the business cards, finds one and pulls it free. Until now, he hasn't considered calling her, but he takes up the cordless.

6
Sunshine

He first saw her on Naples Beach.

Ritz was burning off frustration, swimming out into the placid Gulf of Mexico and back. Out and back. It was the day he woke convinced Natalie was sick up in Michigan. Maybe even gravely ill. Nothing else could explain her being gone so long. He had made his plane reservation before calling. I'll be up in two days, he told her. Instead of being relieved or even glad he was coming, she gave him her bogus you-betrayed-the-sacred-bonds-of-matrimony-with-your-word-processor speech.

As Ritz swam and once more heard his wife's voice, a book title came to him. He had taught it to his dozing students in Ann Arbor, Albert Camus' *The Stranger*. The hero Meursault kills a man on a beach in North Africa. He is convicted of murder, not for killing someone, but because the prosecutor proves Meursault failed to cry at his mother's funeral.

Different beach, same logic, Ritz thought.

He reached shore and slogged out. A young couple glanced at him, standing in the shallows. They were six feet apart and facing each other, both on cell phones. Breathing hard, he passed them, moved to his low-slung beach chair, and flopped down. Ritz watched them. Maybe they're talking to each other, he thought. Almost as stupid as the cockamamie idea that publishing a collection of essays was an act of infidelity. Not a harmless alternative to some *normal* hubby down in his man cave making bird houses. Infidelity.

A young woman passed before the still-talking couple. He watched her walk up the beach, and admired her figure. Instead of a come-and-get-it postage-stamp bikini, she had on a sensible one-piece similar to the bathing suits Natalie wore.

Three days later he saw her in Olde Naples. She was sitting alone during Happy Hour, at the bar in Vergina. The mood at his club was too hostile, but Brady had needed to be somewhere with human noise. He glanced down the bar at her. I'm sick of being all on my lonesome, he thought. Just another one of those fellas. On impulse, totally out of character, he picked up his drink, moved down and sat next to her.

"Hello, I'm Brady."

"Hello, Brady. I'm Sunshine."

His face gave him away, but she held his gaze. "Well," she said, "here we are in the Sunshine State, what else would it be?" That made him smile. Years before on New Year's Eve, Natalie had given him a similar straight-ahead look. "You're right," he said. "Why *not* Sunshine?"

Twenty minutes later, he asked whether he could buy her dinner. It was just a casual, mock-chivalrous gesture made by a retiree to a pretty young woman. But when she said yes, Ritz felt trapped. She didn't look like a prostitute, but what did he know? That's what she must be. Why else agree to have dinner with him? He had never picked up women before or after marriage. Furtive and vigilant as they were led to a booth, he felt completely out of his element.

But she was more or less well-spoken. When he described seeing her at the beach and the loony couple with cell phones, Sunshine laughed in a natural, relaxed way. Natalie still laughed, or had. Even after close to three decades. And was still funny. But she had left him. Not for a week or two to teach him some kind of lesson, but for months. And was now calling him unfaithful. When they spoke, all that remained of their old marital give-and-take was a humorless impatience.

The wine they were drinking fit with the nostalgic tunes coming from the restaurant's piano player. Wine and tunes he and Natalie had both liked. Abandoned over words, he thought. Left all on your lonesome for *writing*. When the waiter began to uncork the second bottle, Brady made a quick decision: after two hours of eating and drinking, it would be dark. He would be able to smuggle her into Donegal. As Ritz scanned the dining room for familiar faces, he noted that Sunshine had nice table manners. When she told him her last name, it further helped to relax him: Sunshine Urbanski wasn't much different from Zeno Kowalski. That was the fake name he had used for his column.

She said she was twenty-six, taking business courses at Naples Community College. If so, she was paying for books and tuition by "dating" older men. More specifically, much older men like himself. As she talked about an intro-to-marketing class, the piano player now began "Stella by Starlight." It was his wife's favorite jazz standard.

"My flat fee is three hundred for straight sex," Sunshine said. "I like to get that out there up front. More for add-ons. I also make use of a bonus system. If you like me and vice versa, three dates at the going rate earns you the fourth at half price. I got the idea from restaurants."

Get that out there up front. His wife's words from long ago joined "Stella by Starlight," along with Sunshine's strict retail approach to sex.

The waiter poured the last of the wine, set down the bottle and left. "I'm sorry, I can't," Ritz said. "I guess I misled you, but I can't."

Sunshine looked at him a moment before taking up her glass. She drank a sip and set it down. "That's all right, Brady. Maybe some other time."

She snapped open her purse and searched a moment before handing him a business card. "Let's you and me like think of this as R&D," she said. "You're funny, and I like the dimple in your chin." She winked before slipping out of the booth. Ritz waited until she was again seated at the bar before looking down at the card. In bold uppercase letters above her name and number, HUMAN RESOURCES

7
Amateur Philanderer

Back at six with Murray Grunwald's audiobooks, Brady runs upstairs to shower. The small, brightly lit room is made of more travertine marble; twin bench seats rest on blunt, fluted columns inspired by the Acropolis. Water pours down from a Frisbee-size shower head; jets pummel him from the walls.

He wonders what his modest, prudent parents would think of such an opulent bathroom. Let alone the house and pool. Parents whose lifelong fiscal caution was shaped by childhood memories of the Great Depression. He remembers his father doing chores, dressed in one of Walker Ritz's few concessions to weekends. Instead of starched white dress shirts, he wore sport shirts, but always with a tie, to put up storm windows, mow his own grass.

Brady shuts down the rain forest and steps out. Toweling off, he now sees himself two hours earlier in the library, searching among audiobooks. *You're that man.* He turned. The woman in the entry was dressed a lot like his wife, with reading glasses on a neck chain. *I have a friend at Donegal. I was in Barnes and Noble and skimmed a few pages. I asked myself, how does such a person live with himself?* By blinding puppies, Brady wanted to say. That's what keeps me going. But he kept quiet. It was better to let people think they'd said something too devastating for a reply.

Loading his palm with shaving cream, he counters the memory with Ashley Vanghent. That morning, on his way to the kitchen for more coffee, he saw her ahead, and stopped to watch. Somehow, she had managed to climb onto one of the stools at the kitchen island. He saw she was getting ready to salvage the unhealthy, forbidden toaster waffle that grandpa had left on his plate at breakfast. Madison and her parents were outside in the pool for a last swim. As Ashley gripped a grownup knife to apply butter, Ritz sensed a surge of shared rebellion. They don't like what you wrote, he thought. And Ashley can't have a damned toaster waffle. She put down the knife and used both hands to pick up the Log Cabin syrup. Very carefully she filled each depression. She set down the syrup, and took up a can before looking out to be sure no one was coming. Now she gunned whipped cream over everything, like fire retardant sprayed around a crash site.

Brady starts shaving, and the memory leads to one of the photos in Natalie's study. He is seven, three years older than Ashley. It's Christmas. He is seated between his doting parents, on the couch in their Detroit living room. His father has set the camera on automatic and come back to be in the picture. All three are smiling. He is a sweet-faced, round-cheeked boy, and on his lap rests his Christmas present, a dachshund puppy.

Six decades, he thinks, shaving his upper lip. Brady Ritz's firmly Protestant parents have been gone for thirty-five years, and their son no longer believes in heaven. But as he shaves, Walker and Irene are looking down, watching him get ready to meet a hooker.

***

The driveway from the parking lot to the clubhouse is on a slight incline. As Ritz trudges up, loud voices fall silent in The Bilge. That's what they call the covered porch behind the bar. The Bilge is the last outpost for Donegal smokers.

Very nervous, he passes without looking over. As Brady enters the lobby, two couples are just coming up from the dining room. The women are leading the way, both talking. The first takes the last step, and Brady holds open the door. "Thanks." She smiles and looks back down at her feet, but again looks up. Still talking, the second woman is right behind her, but seeing him, she brings a heavily ringed hand to her throat, and steps aside for the men.

Still holding open the door, Brady is sure the woman is covering her throat to hide jewelry. When no one moves, he lets go of the door, and continues down the hall. "Booze Cruising on the Cheap" he called it. Florida residents can pick up unsold cruise cabins at the last minute for next to nothing. *The premium beverage package includes a liver transplant.* He scoffed at the duty-free junk people bought, the oversized watches and what Natalie called the putana handbags. The gold chain necklaces sold by the foot. Inspired by Jane's paintings, he gave special attention to the ships' low-brow art auctions. He devoted a whole column to "the king of kitsch," Thomas Kinkade, to his greeting-card thatched cottages tucked away in snowy forests, or defying gravity on sun-drenched mountainsides.

Terry Condon is seated alone at the end of the bar. Good. Condon is one of the few club neutrals. Small, and always dapper in Aloha shirts, he takes seriously the reported advantages of drinking red wine. He is hunched over what will be a glass of merlot.

Ritz crosses the lounge, and voices drop. The only time he still comes here is in the late afternoon, after the golfers have gone home. He sits next to Condon, and the bartender comes down, a kid in his twenties.

"Mr. Ritz, how you doing?"

"Doing, Tommy. It looks quiet."

"Yeah, you know, summer." Tommy wipes the bar. He used to reach over to shake Ritz's hand, but the Donegal staff know what happened. They're still courteous, but more reserved. Ritz orders a Rob Roy, and Tommy gets started.

"So, Terry, how have you been?"

"Hi, Brady." Condon sips his merlot. "We've been well enough, considering."

"Considering" is usually code for what will follow: upcoming surgery or test outcomes. Ritz is more than ready to listen to biopsy or cat-scan results, but Condon says nothing more. As conversations resume behind them, Tommy puts down a napkin and the Rob Roy.

"I heard you want another assessment," Ritz says. "What's it for this time?"

Condon sits on the club's board of directors. "We think a contingency fund would be good," he says. "For hurricane season. That way, if cleanup and repair costs are high, the actual assessment won't tap people out."

"Interesting. That makes sense."

It isn't interesting, and doesn't make sense. Besides, Ritz already knew the answer from the club's monthly newsletter. But he is nervous and needs conversation. Right now, he would agree if Condon wanted to assess for a lunar probe. One board member didn't like how fast people were driving, and got a single speed bump installed in front of his house. Last year, the board's morbidly obese president managed to shame his colleagues into installing a hydraulic lift. It had nothing to do with the Americans with Disabilities Act, but each night he now rides the lift majestically down to dinner, next to the three steps to the dining room.

"Okay—" Condon drinks off the last of his merlot, and signals Tommy to bring the chit. He signs, slips off the stool, and gives the bartender a thumbs up. "Time to meet the missus."

"Say hello for me," Ritz says.

Condon nods, and turns away. Ritz's wife plays bridge with Judy Condon. In the fall, if Natalie is still in Michigan and wants to switch houses, her stock should enjoy a nice pop at Donegal. After she leaves the bridge table, the others will lean in to catalog his offenses. *I knew there was something wrong with him.* Yes, that's how it will go. Ritz sips his Rob Roy. With Natalie, they'll be solicitous and attentive. If you need anything (pepper spray? The name of a good locksmith?) or just want to talk (Suicide Watch? Attorneys?) us girls are here for you.

Sunshine appears in the bar's mirror, just as something hits the back of his bar stool. It happens again before Ritz can turn.

"What the hell are you doing here?" The man slams again with his walker. "This club is members only."

"I am a member." Ritz slips off the stool. "Six years in September."

The man glowers at him, arms braced on the walker. "You can't throw shit around in your club and still belong." He stares for emphasis, but when he turns away, one of the walker's struts catches Ritz's barstool. He starts to topple and Ritz grabs his arm, rights him. The man pulls free, and starts rolling toward the hall.

Sunshine has stopped in the entrance, and steps aside. "Hi there," she says. "It's Carl, right?" The man stops and looks at her before nodding. "Are you singing yet?"

"Can't. Doctor's orders."

"I'm sorry to hear that. Are you still on chemo?"

"For another month, but I have to wear the bag for a year."

"It's all worth it, Carl. Have a great day."

Carl nods again. He puts out his hand, and Sunshine shakes it good-naturedly. She waits for him to shuffle past before looking to Ritz. She winks, and comes forward. They have never touched, but she understands to hug him before they sit at the bar. The hug lifts a weight, he feels vindicated. Almost relaxed.

"I see you're on everyone's shit list," she says and crosses her legs.

"You know him?" Ritz asks. "Carl?"

"Not from work, from a visit. I know the Donegal bookkeeper. We stopped in for a drink on karaoke night. Carl was watching the singing. He told me his favorite song. Ready?

'You are My Sunshine.' So, like I'm going to remember Carl. He said his doctor told him no singing until he's better. It's probably colon or bladder cancer, he wears a bag. I didn't tell him my name. I thought it would like get him, you know, confused with the favorite song thing."

Brady imagines Carl sitting in the Oncology waiting room at Naples Community Hospital. The woman next to him is reading aloud from *Vanitas*.

The bartender has again come down. This time he's smiling, happy to be serving someone his own age. "Hi, Tommy." Sunshine puts out her hand and he shakes it. "Same as last time, Gray Goose martini, straight up with a twist. Put it on Mr. Ritz's tab."

Tommy nods, and turns to the premium brands.

She isn't beautiful, but definitely good-looking, with dark, wide-set eyes. Slavic cheek bones. Her auburn hair is up this time. She's wearing black slacks, a loose-fitting purple blouse. At dinner in Vergina, Sunshine told him she's been on cruises, but she isn't wearing any duty-free jewelry. Just gold hoop earrings, and a French knot pinky ring. Her nose is—a nose. Good eyebrows. As Tommy shakes the martini, Ritz admires her in the bar's mirror. He's seen her for all of three hours, but he already knows she has a great memory, and is very controlled.

Tommy sets down a napkin, the cocktail glass, and pours from the shaker. "Enjoy," he says. She raises the martini to him, then to Ritz. He gets his drink, and they toast.

"Old Lefty." She sips, and nods to the TV above the mirror. Phil Mickelson is getting ready to tee off. "He has this rivalry with Tiger Woods," she says.

"So I've heard."

"You're not so big on it," she says. "Sports. You didn't talk about it at dinner."

True. As Ritz has gotten older, sports now seem engineered. Over-exposed. He used to come here to watch, to be one of the guys. Ritz cheered with everyone else, or groaned and banged the bar in disappointment. *Back in the day, you didn't see the big moment repeated half a dozen times before the next commercial. If you didn't see the impossible cross-court backhand, or the over-the-shoulder catch, you didn't belong to the fraternity that ever after would remember the moment. Now, you can buy Big Moments on DVDs.*

"Want to leave?"

"Sorry." Ritz raises his glass, and they clink again. "How was your day? Or is that an add-on?"

Sunshine laughs. It's a good laugh. Not as good as Jane's or Natalie's, but good enough. "No," she says, "we're on your nickel. Isn't that what you say?"

"It is."

"Okay. My day—" She takes a sip, and holds the martini in front of her. "There was the big boil on Aunt Bessie's butt I had to work on. You know, those pesky bed sores. Then I picked up her oxygen—God, that shit's expensive, keep that in mind. Traffic was a bummer, but I had time to visit this orphanage before coming here."

"All right, thank you."

Understood. He isn't entitled to know about her day. "Like" and "wow" figure here and there, but how could he be so lucky as to find himself on a date with a twenty-six-year-old who knows a word like *pesky*? They drink and smile at each other in the bar mirror.

Even so, he again feels self-conscious. What about her friend, the club's bookkeeper? Or some bridge player who may call Natalie and ask about "that woman." No, Brady thinks. You want to make a statement. To yourself, and everyone here.

"You said you drove your family to the airport."

"At two," he says. "They're back in Kalamazoo now. Ashley wanted asylum as a political refugee, but we got her on the plane."

"I don't understand." Sunshine's smile slips away. Is it something about politics? Refugees? She's Polish, is she related to Polish refugees? *Are* there Polish refugees?

"Ashley is Jane's youngest," he says. "Jane is my younger stepdaughter. Ashley needs to control every situation. When you're four, you do it by being a good actress. Ashley is going places, let me tell you. She has brains and will. I don't think she'll let conscience get in the way."

Sunshine's smile returns. "You mean she's a *bad* girl?"

Good, he thinks. Back on track. "No," he says, "she's not bad. But I don't see Ashley over-thinking questions of right and wrong."

"What's with the parents? Don't they like teach her discipline?"

"Yes, but Jane and Dan are more like tutors. Or nannies. They never say 'no' or 'bad' around the girls. Nothing negative. They made a decision before Ashley's older sister was born. Madison. They decided never to use baby talk. To always stick with grown-up, rational explanations. Except Ashley's already gaming the system. She knows how to use her parents' own words to get what she wants."

"Huh." Something he just said has again caused Sunshine to stop smiling. She gets back to her drink. Was it talk of doting parents? Children? Does *she* have children?

He takes the moment to turn on his barstool and face the lounge. A couple looks away. The Wrights, from Carnarvon Court. As many Donegal couples do, they have coordinated their clothes. Red his-and-her striped shirts. They look to Ritz like a vaudeville act, or half a barbershop quartet. Natalie says such couples make her think of Russian nesting dolls. Seated at the table next to them are three golfers. Two are talking, but the third, Scott Thompson, is gazing wistfully at Sunshine. When he sees Ritz, Thompson stares at him a moment before turning to the others.

Ritz swings back. Such men are part of the reason he asked Sunshine to meet him here. He wants to send them a signal. A week of Jane's silent treatment has confirmed his status as a victim. He hates the idea. The self-pitying, bleeding heart at the center of the American compost mound. But that's what he is, a victim of pettiness. Small-mindedness. Besides, the people here won't see Sunshine for what she is. No teased hair or stiletto heels. She told him she's never *dated* anyone from Donegal. The point is, an attractive woman is with him. He's not alone, and everyone here can go to hell.

"So, are you on Jane's shit list, too?" Sunshine asks.

"For now."

"Is she like one of these tiger moms?"

"Not really. I'd say she's more a hovercraft mom. She's an artist, I'll show you her paintings. She's very maternal, very loyal to her husband. Generous."

"When are you going to tell me what you did to piss everyone off?"

Ritz finishes his Rob Roy and knocks the bar with the glass. Tommy is washing dishes, and nods without looking up.

"That bad, huh? Actually, I'm not talking about these people. Or your daughter. I mean your wife."

Ritz isn't ready for this. He hasn't talked about Natalie. We're estranged, he said at dinner, that's all. Sunshine asked what the word meant and he explained, nothing more. But he needs to say something. Tommy sets down the fresh Rob Roy, and Ritz nods.

"Natalie is too good for me," he says. "It doesn't always make for harmony."

"I get this a lot," Sunshine says. "It's weird."

"What's weird about it?"

"Because it's good for you," she says. "Being with someone better than yourself. Someone that doesn't cheat, or max out your credit cards." When Ritz doesn't answer, Sunshine says, a little bored now, "Okay, so how is she like better than you?"

For months, Brady Ritz has grappled with such questions. He knows all the psycho-babble about good and bad being relative, but some people are *less bad*. Even now he is sure his wife is one of them. But for months he has asked himself why a good person would leave him down here alone. Someone who knows what really happened. And Alex Brubaker, there's another *good person*.

He glances up at the TV. Lefty Mickelson and his caddy are walking now, squinting in bright sun. "Natalie is conventional," Brady says. "A team player. She worries about others."

"Give me a break." Sunshine turns to face him. "That's what makes her better? She like says 'please' and 'thank you' and worries?"

"You asked," he says. "The worry is real. It's not the kind people talk about to sound good to themselves. She suffers."

With odd certainty, Brady knows this is true. And knew it all those nights he woke next his wife, seeing her staring at the ceiling after another failed attempt to reach Anne. Sitting in a bar with a hooker, he believes he has thought his way to something worth remembering.

"That's how she's better," he says. "She suffers."

"If you say so." Sunshine sips her martini and squares the glass on her napkin. "Old Brady the scumbag meets Natalie the saint."

"It's more complicated."

"Right, more complicated. You're just saying that to be more interesting to yourself."

Sunshine turns to him again. "Remember? You said that to me first thing in Vergina. When you sat next to me at the bar, you said 'Look at all these people.' You talked about all the different ways they were trying to be interesting to themselves."

"Did that interest *you*?" Ritz asks.

"Sort of. But if you mean like is that why I talked to you, no."

Sunshine fishes out the lemon peel in her martini and squeezes it between thumb and forefinger. "I was working," she says. "You didn't keep looking at the entrance." She drops the peel into her drink. "That meant you weren't meeting someone. You were dressed okay, but not like from coming from your job. Like a profession. But you cleaned up to be there. And you had good shoes, not these old-man shoes with Velcro. And a good watch."

It's an Omega, Natalie's father's watch. He did say something like that in Vergina. He thought she'd tell him to get lost, but after two calls that afternoon from people telling him how bad a man he was, Ritz wanted to say something he actually believed. When Sunshine went on looking at him, waiting for him to say more, everything after that was cause and effect.

"What would have made you tell me to get lost?" Ritz asks. He was sure she would. He never saw any of it coming. Sunshine now runs a finger around the rim of her glass, thinking about it. When she seemed interested in him, he noticed she wasn't wearing nail polish. Natalie never wears polish.

"It depends," she says. "Partly on money, of course. *Duh*. If I was short, what you said wouldn't make any difference. Even if you were sort of slobby. Except for smell," she adds. "That really bad, acid type BO? No way. Cash flow or no cash flow, that's a deal breaker."

Cash flow. Deal breaker. The business lingo helps to make what he's doing a simple cash-on-the-barrel head transaction. "Let's say cash flow happens to be good," he says. "Do you raise your standards?"

Perhaps she is looking at herself in the mirror, not the TV. He can't tell. She now seems close to beautiful. Her hair is drawn back, she has small ears close to her head. A high forehead. No, she isn't beautiful. But a very good-looking face is reflected next to his own, above the premium brands.

"Okay, dirty hands," she says. "Somebody doesn't wash their hands, that's a big negative. I mean somebody white collar. That's not enough, but things like that. They're part of what you'd call the package. Not *that* package. Like nose-picking and ear... that thing where people rattle their ear with a finger? I was with this guy. I didn't go with him, but this guy is talking, talking. Buying me drinks, talking. This wasn't Naples, this was in Fort Myers. The whole time he's using Q-tips. He had like this sliding box on the bar. If you don't believe me, fine, but he had a box of Q-tips. He takes one out, reams his ear, keeps talking. He put the used Q-tip in his pocket before he got another. So he wouldn't get the used ones mixed up with the new ones."

"A deeply troubled person," Ritz says. "An aberration. A freak," he adds, not wanting to throw things off with vocabulary.

"I know 'aberration,'" she says. "Like a shoe fetish. Or someone wants to watch you take a dump. He wasn't one of those. He just had this thing with his ears. Thinking about the used ones in his pocket—" Sunshine shakes her head "—that really put me off. Plus his hands were dirty. And he *never* stopped talking. Actually, the talking should come first on my no-fly list."

Sunshine nods to herself, remembering. "Honey, darlin', sweetheart. But that's not a deal breaker, either. The country-western thing. You wouldn't believe how many guys think it works. Getting cutesy first thing? A definite type of guy does it. Bullshit isn't the problem." Now she looks at Ritz in the mirror. "Bullshit is like universal. You can't do anything about it. Not if you know next day you have to like buy bandages for bed sores."

She smiles, seeing she has blind-sided him. Ritz laughs, and Sunshine leans against his shoulder. "I'm going to the ladies," she says. "Then let's book." She shoves off and he turns to watch her, straight-shouldered and all-business as she moves down the hall.

8
Familia Interruptus

Men cutting him in the bar is one thing. Wives and widows who know Natalie—women swathed in cruise jewelry—that's something else. Brady has no intention of eating in the dining room.

Outside, they start down the circular drive. The Bilge again falls silent. "Whatever you did really pissed people off," says Sunshine. As they near the parking lot, he hears a tennis game in progress. Hidden behind green canvas, a player grunts, feet scuff. After college, he and Alex Brubaker played every other Thursday. He sees Brubaker dropping back for a lob, dropping back... missing.

"That one's mine—" Sunshine points to the silver Sebring convertible parked next to his Ford Explorer. This is the first time he's seen her car. Ritz opens his passenger door, and as she slides in, he sneaks a peek inside the Sebring. Neat and tidy. He slams her door, comes around and gets in. "How does Alice Sweetwater's sound?"

"Good."

He backs out and heads for the gate. Natalie's car is a Buick. She leases one every three years, always white to reflect the Florida sun. She is careful to keep it washed, but some speed bump in her orderly self is revealed inside. As she drives, Natalie drinks Diet Coke and drops the empty cans on the floor. The carpet is stained, littered with mint wrappers and gas receipts. She says Coke and mints help her to concentrate. Noticing such things says more about you than me, she tells him.

He drives to Alice Sweetwater's on Airport-Pulling Road. Alice's is nothing fancy, but reliable in a loud, Friday-night way. As they follow the hostess, Ritz scans the room for familiar faces. He sees none and relaxes. Once seated, they order gin and tonics, and the stuffed grouper special.

They agree the grouper is good. He likes beer with fish, but leaving home always makes Ritz mindful of his enlarged prostate. It means no beer unless he has guaranteed, unimpeded access to toilets. After roaming around in his rectum and peeling off the rubber glove, his boy-man urologist always reassures him. Don't worry, he says. Benign prostatic hyperplasia is standard operating procedure for men your age. Then he always adds his little joke: Besides, he says, men either die with prostate cancer, or from it.

As they eat, Sunshine talks about her apartment complex in San Carlos north of Naples. The price is right, she says, but management has discovered a mold problem in the walls. Ritz excuses himself and goes to the Men's. As he pees, he fishes out the small blue pill from his breast pocket and swallows it. He got the pill and more cash from the cigar box he keeps on his side of the walk-in closet.

Once he's back and seated, Sunshine continues with the mold issue. Ritz nods and shakes his head, trying to remember something he heard or read about alcohol and the blue pill. If you drink too much, the two together can torpedo your blood pressure. He always knows when it starts to work. His face feels flushed, and there's pressure behind his eyes. It also seems to affect his sinuses. Experience with Natalie has taught him that before they get down to it, he will need to blow his nose.

* * *

By the time they're ready to leave, he is conscious of more sensation. The pills *do* work. He started using them four years ago, when his libido dialed back to next to nothing. By then, sex had become something done mostly to confirm that he and Natalie could still cut the mustard. He had come to think of ejaculation as something like the compressed air used to clear the lines in his lawn-sprinkler system.

He signs the receipt, and they make their way to the exit. Brady holds the door for her. Out in the warm Naples evening, Sunshine takes his arm as they move along the deck. In the first draft of his *Grumble* column on ED, he trashed a popular commercial: a couple spooning in side-by-side bathtubs, people too young to need anything but elbow room. Using actors in their thirties and forties was meant to flatter geezers like himself. See? the ad said. Young guys need help getting it up just like you older sports. Instead of sleek actors, he had flatulent senior citizens farting bubbles in the bathtubs and playing with rubber ducks. Two burly attendants stood at the ready with defibrillator paddles. Eventually, Ritz decided against the farts and paddles.

He opens the car door for her, closes it. Then there's a drug that claims to keep your pecker at the ready for days. Brady gets in, and guides his Explorer out onto Airport-Pulling Road.

Right, he thinks. Take a pecker stiffener, then wander around waiting for that special turn of phrase or raised eyebrow from the one holding your hand and looking fondly at you from her own claw-footed Kohler bathtub.

"What's bothering you?" Sunshine clicks on her seatbelt. "If this isn't a good time—"

"It's an excellent time," Ritz says.

"Sometimes, guys start worrying about money, the doctor. Real estate."

"None of the above," he tells her. "The money is fine. I mean nothing big, but secure." No reason to encourage price gouging. "In terms of health, I'm doing reasonably well for my age."

True. His doctors all say he's in good shape. Brady now remembers being scheduled next month for a colonoscopy. Until you're eighty, you're supposed to have one every five years. At that point, the risk-reward ratio nosedives. Otherwise, visits to see sick people are the only times Ritz goes to a hospital.

"The real estate is safe, too," he tells her, "Assuming we don't have another bubble. I mean safe for whoever's still around after I pass."

"Good, but don't pass yet," Sunshine says.

* * *

He pushes the button and pulls into his drive. The garage door slides up, and he parks next to Natalie's Buick. The car of someone better than you, he thinks. Someone who worries, who drinks Diet Coke and eats mints to stay focused. He comes around and opens Sunshine's door.

"Thank you, sir."

Is she being ironic about all this door-opening for her? At the entrance he pushes the button to close the garage, and follows her in. "I thought we might use the spa," he says.

"Sounds good. Want to smoke some weed?" Sunshine leads the way toward the back.

"Is that part of the package?"

"Right, weed isn't an add-on. Weed is comped."

"I smoked a few times in college," he says. "Pot always made me suspicious."

Sunshine laughs. "Like I'm surprised."

"They're legalizing it now for medical use," he says. "Rows of giggling patients hooked up to dialysis machines."

Sunshine laughs again. It's not Jane's laugh, but he's grateful for it. Natalie's jokes are usually better than his. You've corrupted me, she used to say. He remembers Jane and Dan that morning, coming from the guest bedroom. He sees them slung with sacks and bags, shuffling past Jane's paintings. He prayed she wouldn't ask for them back. Madison is trailing after, and now Ashley, lecturing the fuzzy snake he bought her at the Naples Zoo.

The family room is dark blue, the pool outside placid under moonlight. Sunshine drops her handbag on the kitchen island, and crosses her arms. She plucks her loose-fitting blouse straight up. Airborne a second, it floats down at her feet. She picks it up and straightens. Her shoulders taper to a narrow waist. The gesture works with the pill as she steps before the glass door wall.

But first Brady turns away and moves into the kitchen to check for messages. No number is flashing on the machine. Jane promised to call, but never did. Resolved, he turns away and steps behind Sunshine. Such moments can be tricky, but he avoids fumbling with the hook on her bra. It's been years since he took off Natalie's bra. By unspoken, mutual agreement, they always have sex in the morning, after coffee and separate bathroom preps.

He pulls his camp shirt over his head, then embraces Sunshine from behind. Smells her hair. If he's right, kissing is probably comped like weed. Not technically an add-on, but something to factor into the tip. He kisses Sunshine's neck, and turns her slowly. Before marriage, the women he had affairs with told him he was a good kisser. Natalie thinks so too. He risks it now, and Sunshine answers the kiss convincingly. She holds him close, and presses into him with practiced force. In the moment, holding the kiss, he wonders whether losing interest in sex has mostly to do with protecting happy memories.

"I bet you like it in the dark," she says.

"I do." He kisses her again.

"It's nice out."

Ritz pulls open the door wall, and takes her hand.

The floodlamp in his neighbor's pool cage casts a static triangle between the two houses. As they cross the deck, a recorded voice drones from Grunwald's open door wall. The sound, and the wedge of light join with the young woman's hand in his to restore Brady's sense of vindication. Sunshine sits on the spa and pulls off her sandals. He kicks off his loafers, and sits beside her. Loosens his belt.

"You don't care about the neighbor?" She peels off her slacks. "He's another asshole?"

"Grunwald's fine. He's legally blind."

It sounds callous to him. *Don't worry, Grunwald's blind.* He unzips and shoves down his pants and briefs, tosses them toward a chaise, and sits again. The pleasantly cool tile under his butt is reassuring. He's been regular all month, with no hemorrhoid flare-up. *There's* a deal-breaker in the old pecker department. His now-liberated penis is almost at full attention. Chemically enhanced, true, but the original Buzz, no question.

Sunshine looks down. She smiles and slips off her bikini briefs. How civilized, Brady thinks. How decorous, even reserved. As though agreeing with him, Sunshine stands and walks with her briefs to the chaise. She picks up Ritz's pants, drapes them over the chair's backrest, and comes back. Perky breasts and girlish figure—really, the only hooker thing about her is the total absence of pubic hair. Based on his limited range of anecdotal guy chat, a shaved beaver is strictly professional. Or was before bikini waxes.

"Shall we?"

He gestures for her to go first. When virtually everyone including your wife has followed Tony Minetta in flipping you the bird, what can be wrong with paying for company? With contributing to a junior college student's income stream? Really, Ritz thinks, you could argue it's close to philanthropy. Sunshine steps daintily over the edge and slips down. Some drinks, some dinner—Brady climbs over. Two or three *stolen hours of bliss* shared by a well-behaved gentleman who doesn't bore wax out of his ears, and a charming young sex worker earning the cost of tuition and books. He slides down to the subsurface bench.

Sunshine nestles close and takes him in her hand. "I think you're having a good time," she says, working him slowly.

Water jets trained on his lower back gurgle up in a frothy mix of chlorine and something he can't identify. Brady smooths the surface with his free hand. He doesn't really like spas. After a few minutes, his heart rate increases dramatically. Once in a hotel sauna, he became convinced he was going into atrial fibrillation. But the spa came with the pool, so he uses it.

"Who's that talking?" Still working him, Sunshine has turned to listen.

"Next door," he says. "My neighbor listens to books."

"The blind guy? Good for him."

"I get them for him at the library. He's listening to everything he skipped in college."

"You said he plays golf."

"In the afternoon. After three, you have the course to yourself. Murray's pretty good, considering."

"His wife takes him around?"

"She's in assisted living," he says. "In the early stages of Alzheimer's." Brady wonders: is Sunshine conducting market research? Maybe a blind golfer would like a girl caddy. Then, after, they could take a shower and listen to a book.

"So, who takes him around?" Before he can answer, she squeezes him. "Never mind, I'm hot. Both ways. Let's go inside."

Brady gets out and slaps over to the towel closet. He's pleased to see the Ritz member bouncing stoutly. Usually, there are stacks of towels here, but Dolores didn't wash this week. He gets the last two and comes back. Sunshine stands, and he hands her a towel. They pat themselves dry, wrap themselves. Arm-in-arm, they move toward the open door wall.

"Something about alphas and epsilons," she says. "What's he listening to?"

"I'll tell you later."

They enter the house. Chilled by air conditioning on wet skin, Brady closes the slider. He keeps his arm around Sunshine as they move toward the foyer. "You have quite a tent there," she says of his towel. "Alphas, betas. Is it about fraternities?"

"*Brave New World.*" To stay in step, Ritz holds her close. "About genetic engineering." This is an odd time for book chat. No career hooker would be so off message, but that's Sunshine. From the first, he thought she was new to the business, that she had probably learned her craft from an experienced boyfriend or two. No doubt a business major.

"I heard the title someplace," she says as they reach the stairs. "Young guys talk about fraternities in McCabe's and Murphy's."

"It's science fiction, not fraternities," he says. "People being manufactured in laboratories."

"In vitro." They start upstairs. That's to let you know she understands the word, he thinks. Night lights on the two landings cast a blue glow.

"Are these your stepdaughter's paintings?"

"Yes."

"Cool. Can I see them?" She slows, but Ritz gently urges her on. "I don't know art, just what I like," she says.

"Neither do I," he says. "Beauty lies in the eye of the beholder." That's one of Natalie's catch phrases. She uses it when he makes fun of PBS's *The Antiques Road Show*.

The towel is sanding his tent pole, but Ritz isn't getting carried away. He was too nervous before to bring her here. Too guilty. But after a week of silent treatment from Jane, Ritz mounts the stairs with confidence. I'm not *hurting* anyone's *feelings*, he thinks. I have nothing to apologize for.

At the top, more baseboard night lights make a cave of the hall. They pass the closed guest bedroom. Bugs Bunny, *The Cartoon Network*. He didn't hear it earlier, but in her haste to be gone, Jane left the TV on. Brady squeezes Sunshine's hand as she kneads his tent. Whisking her children away from the degenerate grandfather, he thinks. The one who made fun of current fashions in parenting, and brings home sex workers. There's something gratifying about it. Jaded and worldly.

He eases open the door, and follows her into the master bedroom. Nice and dark. Shiny bedside tables and dressers glint with moonlight. "Cool," she says again.

Sunshine drops her towel and falls backwards on the bed. She scuttles up using elbows and feet. Ritz drops his towel, and crawls above her. But when he looks down, her face is too

Someone Better Than You: A Comedy of Manners

small. *Cool.* Young people no longer say *cool.* How old is she? She doesn't look twenty-six. In the moment, she looks to him like someone in high school. If she was held back, maybe even the last year of middle school.

"What's wrong?" She reaches down and squeezes him. "Are you nervous? You seem nervous." She squeezes more vigorously, looking earnest.

Calm down, Ritz thinks. Ask if she's under the age of consent and she'll just lie. But he has to ask. "How old are you? Really?"

Sunshine stops squeezing. "I told you, twenty-six. You don't believe me?"

"You look so young."

She shakes her head and resumes the hand job. "It's like optical," she says. "Because of the bed. I got this once before, a guy worried about statutory rape. The king-size bed freaked him out. I can show you my driver's license." Even before she finishes the sentence, Sunshine must know the positive effect of her words. She smiles at him. In the dark, her teeth are definitely those of an adult. Even so, Ritz is reassured by the driver's license.

"Scootch up, I'll give you some head."

Scootch up—he does as asked. Scootch up is an adult idiom, not a child's figure of speech. There is some lingering uncertainty—a driver's license can be easily forged—but *scootch up* is good.

"Id dat dou, gwampa? Gwamma?"

Backlit by the hall nightlights, a small gowned figure stands in the open entry. Ritz vaults off the bed and snatches a pillow to cover himself.

"Mom!" The cape or sheet drags after the figure. "Hey Mom!"

Brady rounds the bed and slams the door. He runs back, snatches two more pillows and dumps them on Sunshine as the door clicks open.

"Buzz? You okay?"

"Don't turn on the light. Close the door and go away."

"We just got here. I got the key—"

"Close the door."

"Jeeze, fine." The door clicks shut.

Sunshine is up and pressing the pillows to her chest and crotch. "Your family came back, their flight got cancelled." She drops the cushions, snatches up her towel and wraps it around herself. The shock has given Brady better night vision—he can see she's twenty-six. And she's not upset, this has happened to her before.

"One minute."

He quicksteps with the pillow into the walk-in closet, snaps on the light and snatches a pair of khakis out of the laundry hamper. Then a polo. He pulls on the clothes before reaching up to the shoe box where he keeps the pills and cash. Under recessed lights, he flips off the lid, fishes around, and takes out three one hundred-dollar bills. The kissing—he takes out another fifty before fitting on the lid. Ritz puts the box back, snaps off the light and comes out.

"My clothes."

"I'll get them." He hands her the money. "Just wait, don't let anyone in."

Brady cracks open the door. Listens. Then quicksteps along the hall and pads downstairs. Quickly he passes to the back of the house and grabs Sunshine's blouse and his shirt before moving out to the deck. His older stepdaughter and her children—their sudden nighttime appearance has happened before. What he smelled earlier in the spa was Anne's patchouli or sandalwood. The Jacuzzi is frothy now, bubbling pointlessly. He gets Sunshine's briefs, his own clothes, the two pairs of shoes.

Pressing everything to his chest, Brady reaches the foot of the stairs. Be calm, he thinks. Could Natalie have left her Valium in the bathroom? Breathing deeply, he goes back up, speeds past *The Cartoon Network*, reenters the master bedroom and closes the door. The bathroom light is on at the back of the walk-in. He steps to the half-open door. "I'm back," he says.

She puts out her hand. Ritz gives her the blouse and slacks. "Shoes?"

"I have them."

"What's the deal?"

"Get dressed, I'll explain."

In no time Sunshine steps out. She watches him pull on his shoes. She isn't upset, this isn't new. The sudden return of significant others, police at the door, repo people. But as they now hustle down the hall, her first-responder speed and lack of drama fill Brady with gratitude. They enter the garage. The door is still going up and twangs the Explorer's antenna. He backs into the street, and sees a Jeep parked in front of

Grunwald's. The back bumper and tailgate are plastered with stickers. How could he have missed it?

"A houseguest," Sunshine says. "Someone who like showed up after you left. Someone with kids. There's two. When you went downstairs, the other one came to look in. Don't worry, I was in the walk-in, she couldn't see me. She was tall, she said her name's Iris. Her mom remembered you keep the house key in the flower pot under the bushes."

Brady glances at her. Sunshine looks exactly as she did when they left Alice Sweetwater's. Except her hair is back, held in place by one of his wife's elastic bands. From the medicine chest, he thinks. Please, Natalie, I was wrong. They pass a white-haired couple walking a Dalmatian.

Ritz faces the road. "They aren't guests," he says. "It's my older stepdaughter Anne and her children."

"I get it, you have more kids." Sunshine folds her hands in her lap. "Like from a different marriage from… the word you used."

"Estranged."

"Right. Like separated, but without legal mumbo jumbo." After a moment, she says, "You know, sixty-five isn't really old anymore."

"I'm sixty-six."

"Whatever. It's more like the new fifty." Hands in her lap, Sunshine is now waiting for it to be over, but being courteous. Trying to cheer him up about the new fifty.

"I had a good time," she says.

This sounds like the school girl he feared she might be. "So did I," he says. "I'm sorry. Next time, things will be different."

"Okay. You have my number. I have to ask something."

"Of course. Anything."

Brady already knows there won't be a next time. What was he thinking? He regrets all of it, he can't believe what he risked. But right now, Sunshine can ask him whatever she wants.

"Are you actually married?"

"Of course, yes," he says. "Just once. What you saw was Anne, my older stepdaughter, and her two children. They're part of the same establishment."

"I don't understand. What establishment?"

"It's an expression. It means the same family. The same household."

"Okay."

Anne. When Sunshine asks no follow-up, Ritz is disappointed. Please, he thinks, ask me something else. Tell me another story about guys washing their cars. It's all business with her, but given what's waiting for him back at the house, he longs to go with her. No one has more reason to resent what he wrote than Anne. Please—he glances at Sunshine and back—just for the next few hours. Wherever and whatever it is, Brady thinks, I want to be part of it. A slack-jawed boyfriend playing video games, a girl roommate watching *Sleepless in Seattle.* I don't care, just so you let me in.

9
Grumble

For eight years married life went remarkably well for everyone in the Ritz establishment.

Brady had turned out to be a good husband and stepfather. He went to PTA meetings, helped Anne with Spanish, Jane with math homework. He felt what it was like to be treated with affection, to be accepted into his new package-deal family. Intimacy, and domestic routine made him less sarcastic and critical, more tolerant. Compounding it all was an editorial job he was respected for. Knowing how to make other people's writing *right* was very gratifying. His only regret was that his gentle, doting parents had not lived to meet Natalie and the girls. Even so, it made him proud to know that Walker and Irene would be happy for their son.

Then the puberty tidal wave.

Shortly after her thirteenth birthday, Anne was swept into a storm-tossed sea of hormones. Arguments and slamming doors, dope smoking in the garage, sleeping until noon. Curfews ignored, calls from school counselors. Very quickly, Ritz came to see that adolescence was nothing he could fix with words. Being right didn't matter, and the only thing in his puberty-parenting toolbox was sarcasm. It failed miserably. Her younger sister had always been prematurely grown-up, and now the contrast served to amplify Anne's rebellion.

That same year, the tidal wave was joined by a typhoon: a looming strike threatened to shut down all three Detroit daily newspapers.

Alex Brubaker was the friend who had gotten Ritz hired at the *Post*. Alex was now the assistant city editor, and one afternoon he waved for Ritz to come into his office. "Have a seat," he said and closed the door. "Bad news, the shit's finally going to hit the fan. I can't go into detail, but you now have a family to think of. Trust me, Buzz, this strike is going to be take-no-prisoners. It will probably last a year or more, so before you hit the picket line, you need to think about making a change."

The change Alex had in mind was for his friend to remain at the *Post,* but as a member of the non-union advertising sales staff. "It's easy work," he said. "Frankly, anyone can do it."

The monthly mortgage nut and car leases, private-school tuition for the girls, saving for the exploding costs of college—Ritz didn't need to think about it. "Yes," he said. "I'll do it."

He felt like a scab, a turncoat. But everything Alex predicted came to pass. The strike lasted a year and a half, until the unions were finally broken. Guild members who had walked the picket line or refused to cross it—columnists and reporters Buzz Ritz knew and liked—weren't brought back. Nor did they forgive Ritz: they too had car payments and mortgages.

And as an ironic form of justice for Ritz having left the union, the strike's costly aftermath led to his editorial job being one of many cost-cutting casualties. So, instead of returning to the work he was good at, work that had served as a refuge from his failure with Anne, Brady Ritz went on taking ad customers to lunch.

He trained himself to chuckle at the lame jokes of replacement-window sales managers and the owners of luxury-car dealerships. He nodded and pretended to take notes when ambulance-chasing lawyers and overdressed realtors told him their ads must feature photos of themselves with their wives, children, dogs, girlfriends. Alex had been right: selling ads was easy work. But it was demeaning. It didn't matter that he was no better at selling than he had been as a teacher at Michigan. People bought ads anyway. And the bonus money was good. Both factors made him more cynical. His age, and the shrinking world of print journalism argued against Buzz Ritz bothering to look for another editing job.

In his monthly lunches with Alex at the Anchor Bar, he often complained about losing both his old job, and his newspaper friends. "Why not write?" Alex said finally. "You know you can do it, you've edited thousands of stories. There's something called *Grumble, A Magazine for the Dyspeptic Skeptic*. That's definitely you."

He had never heard of it, but Ritz found *Grumble* in the little-magazines section at the main library. He studied back issues, and liked the publication's grumpy, anti-technology bias. Because of his problems with Anne, what Ritz liked even more was *Grumble's* skeptical take on youth culture. He quickly picked up on the magazine's tone and flavor, wrote three sample pieces, and submitted them. In all three, his theme was taken from Ecclesiastes: "Vanity, vanity, all is vanity."

Within six months, *Grumble* was publishing his bimonthly column, "Vanitas—Bitter Pills for a Saccharine Nation, by Zeno Kowalski."

That was the pseudonym he dreamed up for himself. Zeno of Citium had founded Greek Stoicism, a philosophy that advocated indifference to emotion. To feelings. "Kowalski" was the name of a Detroit bologna maker. Ritz chose it to show—if only to himself—that he wasn't taking himself or what he wrote seriously. Once again, Brady Ritz was able to enjoy the satisfactions of being *right*. The fake name freed him to use details taken from family and suburban life.

But he didn't tell his wife about *Grumble*.

He loved her. Against real odds, they had come together as a couple. With each New Years anniversary, Ritz felt more grateful that Natalie had rolled the dice and taken a chance on him. But along with being smart and funny, she was also conventional. A good neighbor, a bridge-playing team member. Since his columns were abrasive and critical, he knew what her reaction would be: *What will people think?* And something else: being divorced had led Natalie to blame herself for Anne's teenage rebellion. It pained him to wake at night and see her lying on her back, staring at the ceiling. "She's a lot like her father," Natalie would say. "She told me she wants to use his name."

Natalie had done the old-fashioned thing by taking Ritz's name. He had written about Anne, and her mother would know it. What would be gained by adding to his wife's burden?

With Natalie's inheritance, they were both able to retire. But Ritz went on writing: a Naples golf community offered endless possibilities for satire. And since Zeno Kowalski was doing the writing, he had no reason to worry about offending his new neighbors. Besides, what most people at Donegal read were Tom Clancy thrillers and bodice-ripper romance novels. Certainly not obscure little magazines.

But publications like *Grumble* don't usually last for long. Before the final issue went to press, the editor called. "I really enjoyed publishing your work," he said. "I still have quite a few contacts, and I want you to think about putting together a *Best of* collection. It would be *Grumble's* legacy."

A *book*. The idea had never occurred to him. The nest was now empty, he had plenty of time. When Anne went to Michigan State, the hormonal tsunami subsided long enough for her to finish a degree in anthropology. Two years later, Jane finished hers in Fine Arts at Michigan. Ritz was now playing golf all winter with men he had little in common with. Putting together an essay collection would be a welcome distraction.

He had trouble choosing which columns to include. Reading them all chronologically convinced him they were better than he'd realized. By the spring he was ready to shop around *Vanitas: An Essay Collection by Xeno Kowalski.* "Nah, we're not shopping it," the *Grumble* editor said. "No agent would take something like this from an unknown. But it doesn't matter. Half the publishing business is cronyism and nepotism. My old girlfriend is an editor at SUNY Buffalo. It's a university press, but they publish essay collections."

Because the manuscript had already been carefully groomed and proofed by a professional editor, the SUNY editor said yes. She had a slot open, and there was nothing much left for her to do. As the cover design was being completed, she called. "I just sent you the galley proofs," she said. "This is last call for making any final changes."

Ritz hung up, flushed with a strong sense of pride and validation. Reading his columns multiple times had convinced him they were more than just cranky blasts of opinion. What started as a hobby had morphed into his *work*. He no longer needed to think of himself as a peddler of newspaper advertising. He was a writer. Someone his wife could be proud of.

For the same reason, Ritz began seeing his own name on the cover.

Diagnosed with prostate cancer the previous year, Alex Brubaker was now also retired from the *Post*. When he had his prostate removed, Ritz visited him in the hospital. Aside from the humiliating gown, Alex looked like himself. But he was uncharacteristically distant. Uncommunicative. Ritz tried to stay in touch, but each time he called, Betty Brubaker told him Alex was sleeping, or at the hospital for chemo.

The day the proofs for the book arrived, the two men finally spoke. "I owe you a lot," Ritz said. "You've been my best friend for fifty years, and I need your advice. My *Grumble* editor found a publisher for a collection of my columns. I'm thinking of using my own name."

Alex agreed to meet him at The Anchor Bar, Detroit's newspaper hangout. When he came through the door, it was apparent why Betty Brubaker had been evasive about her husband's diagnosis. Alex was dying. His sport coat was the one thing Brady fully recognized.

"Never mind, I know." Alex gingerly, slowly took the bar stool next to him. "One drink and I have to go, but I thought about it, and my answer is this. Definitely you should use your own name. Life is short, I should know. Publish *your* book with *your* name on it."

"It's pretty rough in places," Ritz said. "You know, snarky. Critical. Don't you think people might complain?"

"What if they do?" Alex said. "You're a writer now, not an ad salesman. Take the credit, and whatever fallout comes with it. Good for you—" He raised his Scotch. "Go get 'em."

Looking down from The Anchor Bar walls were photos of Detroit journalists. Until the strike, Brady had known and worked with some of them. He had edited their work and made it better, but it was their by-lines that always appeared in the *Post*. His column's main theme had been vanity. Would using his own name be vain? No, he decided. It's something you've earned, your just desserts. The idea of having his photo up on The Anchor Bar wall with such men and women appealed strongly to him. Somehow, it would also be a kind of redemption for his scab's decision to leave the union.

But the fallout. Even though he wrote under a fake name, Brady had taken pains to conceal his source material, the people and incidents he had made use of. Being published by a university press would all but guarantee that the guy-fiction/bodice-ripper readers at Donegal would never see his book. But what if he was wrong? The idea had an immediate, chilling effect.

"No," he said, "No, Alex. I want to do it, but I don't think so. It's too risky."

"Goddammit, don't be a pussy."

Ritz turned on his barstool, inches away from the ravaged eyes and un-shaved, concave cheeks of his friend. "Yes, look at me," Alex said. "Do it for me if not yourself. Who put you on to *Grumble* eight years ago? Frankly, I think you should write me a little tribute. No Brubaker, no *Grumble*, no *Grumble*, no book."

Brady drove home in a state of conflicted defiance. Alex had spoken almost in anger. As though Ritz not using his own name would represent a kind of betrayal. He would obviously avoid risking trouble by not doing it. But that would make him a coward. A pussy. And what Brubaker had said was true: no heads-up from him, no column or book. For that matter, if you went back much further, no career at the *Post*. And no Natalie.

As he pulled up in front of his house, Ritz was already composing a heartfelt tribute to his lifelong friend. Someone who had run interference for him for almost forty years. In the last week of November, the tribute appeared as the forward to *Vanitas, A Collection by Brady Ritz, AKA Zeno Kowalski*. By the end of December, the book was enjoying a modest success. SUNY Press ran some ads, and a few copies found their way to Naples.

10
Woodstock Nation

On the drive back to Donegal, he tries to strategize, but nothing comes to him. He has no cards to play. Jamal and Iris both know it wasn't Grandma that Grandpa was hovering over. One after another, every explanation is more laughable than the last. *Who? Oh that was our cleaning lady Dolores, she was helping me make up the bed.*

He comes in from the garage and finds them waiting in the family room. *Lying* in wait. Brady prepares to be dressed down, lectured, hectored. If anyone has a right to go after him, it's Anne.

"Hi, Buzz." She waves from his recliner. Only Anne and her mother still use his *Post* nickname. She points the remote and freeze-frames *SpongeBob SquarePants*.

"Hi Grandpa." Iris also waves, and Ritz waves back. Lying face down on the leather sectional, she lets her arm drop to the floor.

"Hi Gwampa."

"Hello Jamal."

The boy raises a hand, and lets it drop. Jamal always repeats what his sister says or does. He is seated in front of the TV, doing something with something. The boy rarely watches what's on, always busy assembling, stacking, dismembering.

All this transpires as Anne is now on her languid, flipflop way toward him. It's confusing. In the car he steeled himself, not for another helping of Jane's silent treatment, but something much more punitive. He readies his argument. I'm no aging libertine, he will say. No Gray Panther on the make. I've been abandoned, I need human contact.

But Anne doesn't look punitive. As she nears, his older stepdaughter is giving him her universally-open-to-all-possibilities smile. It's the smile that serves for greetings or leave-takings, moments of happiness or contentment. The smile has been Anne's dominant facial effect since she replaced dope with yoga and vegetables. Anne has other facial expressions—gravity for stories of grief or misfortune, earnestness during philosophical speculations, patient waiting when being given advice, taking criticism or receiving threats. All this is at work in Brady as she reaches him and slips into the embrace he is obliged to offer. She holds him close, and kisses him on the ear above the mole.

"How *are* you? Having a little company, are we?"

"Much more than I expected."

"Hey, listen, ain't none o' my bidness." Anne squeezes him and pats his back. "I'm not judgy about what I don't know."

Normally, Ritz breaks off Anne's greeting as soon as possible, but *ain't none o' my bidness* leads him to hold the hug. Even so, it's frustrating. The Lady of Misrule has arrived with perfect timing. Anne of all people is now in possession of high-value information about him. Drugs haven't impaired her memory, and she definitely knows how to use intel.

"We're sort of in transit," she says and lets him go. "We were in Key West when their dad pulled another typical Jeff move."

She turns and ambles back to his recliner. Denied his usual seat, Brady is unsure what to do. He goes over, sits on the couch's armrest and looks down at Iris. Something has happened. Iris is alarmingly long. The hand still resting on the carpet looks huge to him. When he glances up along her body, Ritz takes a breath. Her naked feet are long and bony, not those of a child. Almost a year ago, he started boycotting Anne for an offense, a last straw. In that time, he hasn't seen Iris or her brother.

"Yeah, they both had a growth spurt you wouldn't believe," Anne says. "Just after Labor Day. I buy food by the skid."

"What Jeff move are you talking about?" he asks.

"He's screwing with the schedule."

"How's he screwing with it?"

"He knows I have court permission to travel with them," she says. "But like the small-minded man he is, he makes up this big threat he'll go back to court if they aren't in Michigan by next week. He knows the tickets are paid for, but you know old Jeff. He wouldn't cut me any slack. Ever."

Perched on the couch's armrest, Brady leans back. Cutting slack is good, he thinks. Please cut some for me. Jamal is playing with magnetized sticks and ball bearings. He, too, is longer. And for this reason he looks even more like his germplasm donor. That's how Ritz and Natalie refer to Jeff, the father. He and Anne never married, but since they split up, Jeff has re-invented himself. Natalie says he has given up dope and joined a megachurch, the kind with stage lighting and pyrotechnical special effects. He is now married, and has donated more germ plasm to produce another child.

Jamal's blond hair is cut short, like a refugee's. Or a child with ringworm. Jane had ringworm twice in junior high. Natalie said it was impossible, but Brady believed Anne's wide-ranging movements explained the problem. She herself never had ringworm, but he thought of her as a carrier.

"I hope there won't be another custody battle," he says.

"Not a problem."

Anne gets her drink and mouths *We'll talk later.* After Jeff's bible-thumper transformation, his deep-pocket parents rewarded him by financing a joint-custody battle with Anne. During the infighting, they sent Natalie a cassette tape of phone calls wiretapped by a private investigator. The enclosed note was full of spiritual homilies, spliced into dire predictions. At the end, Jeff's mother admonished Natalie to "think of the little ones!" This from people who had, wisely in Brady's view, bought off their remittance-man son with cars and houses, always at a safe remove from their own orderly life in Delaware. Whatever was on the tape hadn't impressed the court. Natalie burned her copy, and refused to tell Ritz what was on it.

He focuses on Anne's steaming beverage. What is it these days? Last time she was here, it was something in a shell or gourd full of twigs and leaves. She brewed batches every day, and the dregs left a silt deposit in the sink.

"You look well," he says.

If he can keep Anne focused on herself, maybe she won't ask about what Iris and Jamal saw. Besides, her children have seen so much that Brady is hopeful they won't ask about it. But he is wary when his stepdaughter puts down her drink and shoves up from his recliner. She extends her arms and turns.

"They have this whole boutique in Key West devoted to hemp," she says, still turning. "You like?" She completes a final dervish move, and now performs a sclerotic shimmy or hula. Ritz is sure this move was inspired by a YouTube video of senior citizens vacationing in Hawaii. It's Anne's way of commenting on retirement. I'll never retire, she told Natalie. I'll go down swinging.

"I like," he says.

Since she was thirteen, he hasn't liked Anne's fashion sense. That's when puberty and pot led her to replace the L.L. Bean crewneck sweaters he gave her at Christmas with tie-dyed shirts illustrating the brain during acid trips. Her costume tonight is saffron and brown, the top allowing for glimpses of Anne's flat stomach. Something metallic blinks from her navel. The pants take their inspiration from the Punjab or Bali.

She winks, returns to his recliner and plops down. Brady is beginning to relax. Whatever Anne is thinking, it doesn't appear to involve retribution. And however skeptical he is of her, he must admit she's in great shape. These days she is wearing her hair in a style he associates with his own youth. Back when girls ironed it.

But it wasn't Anne half an hour ago who saw him hovering above Sunshine. It was Jamal. He is sure it was too dark for the boy to see much. Besides, both children have seen things that would set the friend-of-the-court twirling like a spinning jenny. Jamal and his sister would be hustled out of the courtroom and sent to live somewhere at state expense. For years, Natalie lay awake, exhausted by worry over another failed effort to reach Anne. She says Ritz long ago gave up on her older daughter. That says more about you than her, she tells him.

"Okay, kids. We got to stay up late and say hello to Grandpa. Time for beddy-bye."

"It's urwy," Jamal says. "You ded we could day up."

"And so you did, little man, it's way past your bedtime."

"No, id idn't."

"Oh yes, little man. Come on, now, give Mom some cooperation here. You, too, Miss Iris."

Ritz glances at his watch. Ten after one. Staying up late for Iris and Jamal would actually mean watching the last pre-dawn set played by a band in the harvest stubble of a wheat field. The lanky girl doesn't move.

"Come on, Iris, don't make me come over there."

"I'm fine," Iris mumbles. "Leave me alone."

"No can do. Come on. Now."

Ritz remembers this, too, the nagging needed to get Iris to move. Groaning and groggy, at last she shoves herself into sitting position. As he watches her brother gathering together the components of his engineering project, Brady is close to siding with Iris about sleeping down here on the couch. That way, he won't have to talk to Anne.

"Good job. That's it, honey, you don't want to lose any of it."

"I deed more mangads."

"We'll get more magnets, just give Mom a hug and take it upstairs."

Jamal clatters the last of the ball bearings into a cylindrical container. That Brady remembers this toy or game means it dates back over a year. The boy comes to his mother, and Ritz stands. "Good night, kids," he says. On her feet now, Iris turns to him, half asleep, and puts her arms around him.

"Goodnight, Grandpa."

For a moment he is at a loss, being held by this girl who is now only a head shorter than himself. Ritz puts his arms awkwardly around her sharply angular shoulders. What did Anne say to them about his boycott? It makes him self-conscious, his granddaughter's willingness to hug him after all this time. "Good night, Iris." Her father is six feet five inches and Iris and her brother will be tall. No doubt Jeff's own parents are tall, the ones who cautioned Natalie to think of the little ones.

But the weight just now of the girl's days in the joint custody of two people he does his best to not think about shapes itself warmly and damply against Brady's stomach and chest. She's ten or eleven, he's not sure. Still she holds him, with how much need or purpose he can't tell. Maybe she's just falling asleep, he can't tell.

At last Iris lets go. Bare-footed, she shuffles toward the front of the house as Jamal finishes hugging his mother. Now the boy comes to his grandfather. He hugs Ritz around the waist. "Thank you, Jamal." Ritz places his hands on the boy's head, a buzz-cut mini version of his father. Holding the canister of ball bearings, Jamal lets go and follows his sister.

"Don't forget to go potty," Anne calls. "And wash your hands, brush your teeth. And no more, that's no as in N period O period TV."

A door closes upstairs. She gets the remote next to her still-smoking mug and clicks off the TV. "I can understand him much better," Brady says. Natalie has told him Jamal is seeing a speech therapist.

"Yeah." Anne sips. "He still has issues with wetting the bed, but we're making progress. Mom told me people here are giving you a really hard time."

"They'll get over it." He can't remember anything about bed-wetting.

"When you were out you got two calls. Some woman said she's suing you for using her mother's name in 'Christmas Carol.'"

He steps behind the kitchen island. "Did you tell her you have no idea who Carol is? Or her mother?"

"Of course, but come on. You changed some things, but I knew who you meant. Like you know this woman's family," Anne says. "And how her mother treats people at Christmas. Like you were there for the dinner. It just means there are lots of Grandma Normas."

Exactly, he thinks. But the truth of this again makes Brady uncomfortable. "I suppose you think I was unfair," he says. "You think it's wrong to be critical of someone in a wheelchair. Especially your grandmother."

"Hell no," Anne says. "Who says being handicapped keeps you from being mean? Like being handicapped makes you a good person. Besides, you left out the wheelchair. Grandma Norma was a witch. Grandma Abnorma you used to call her."

More grownup good sense. The granite counters look shiny. He glances at the sink and sees it's clean. "Did Dolores come after you got here?"

"No, I cleaned up." Brady moves to the refrigerator. "She treated mom like a servant," Anne says of her grandmother. "When I read it, I laughed my ass off. I didn't blame you a bit, you just knew the woman, that's all. She was bad to the bone."

He opens the door. Stuffed above jars of condiments and pickles are collard greens, carrots. Some tuber he can't identify is jammed between milk and orange juice cartons. He lifts a limp thatch of leaves, finds a beer and closes the door. Now that he's home and has access to three bathrooms, Ritz can pee at will.

"'This is good, Carol, I can't believe you made it,'" Anne says, quoting him. "I almost busted a gut. I remember the Christmas she said that, after all the work Mom put in. Like who can believe you made anything this good? And all the stuff you said about Grandpa Max being her native bearer. That was dead on."

He pops the top, and drinks at the island dividing kitchen from family room. Anne is facing away, and has the chair reclined. She sips from her mug. In the moment, Brady is frustrated by the contrast between Jane's silent treatment, and solid common sense coming from her older sister. Not to mention flattering quotations.

"The second call I didn't follow," she says. "Something about a house."

"A green house," he says. "Green as in environmental. Did he say anything about suing?"

"He just said he wanted you to know how totally out of touch you are on environmental issues."

A woman who shares the fake name he gave to his mother-in-law is no problem. Green House is different. He's rich, and proud of his new thirteen thousand five hundred square foot mansion. Large enough to house the average rural village in Bangladesh, Ritz said of it.

"Does 'Christmas Carol' come near the end?" Anne asks.

"They're chronological."

"'A magazine for the dyspeptic skeptic.'" Anne snorts. "That's perfect for you."

11
Flight Plan

She tips the recliner forward and stands. "I'm about two thirds of the way through." She stretches, and gets her drink. "Want to go outside? It's so great down here now."

Two thirds. That means Anne has read about her grandmother, her sister, and herself. The rest of the book is mostly devoted to politics, and life at Donegal. Anne pulls open the door wall and steps outside. Balancing her drink, she stretches again. "We all went in first thing," she says. "Iris and Jamal are total water babies."

That explains what he smelled earlier in the spa. Anne uses scented oils sold in the health-food co-op she manages. He follows her out. She's been a sun seeker all her life, a lover of hot springs, mountains, beaches. And she's right, it's a very nice evening. Beyond the screen cage, the moonlit golf course appears touched here and there with silver.

Iris five, Jamal three. That's the visit he most remembers. Ritz and his wife had still been stumped by the boy's name, this blond-headed, blue-eyed water baby leaping and pounding in the pool in early January. Given the New Age names Anne had considered for her first child—Bluebird/Wonder/Glory—Iris's solidly old-fashioned name had given Natalie hope. Then Jamal. It's the name of a highly respected healer, Anne said in a call from her latest address, this one in Oregon. He works wonders with crystals and deep massage. By then, Jeff and

Anne had called it quits, so Ritz and Natalie assumed the father was black. That proved they were one or two decades off the pace. Jamal was now a name for all seasons and people. Before loser Jeff left, he had made a final germ-plasm donation. He was Jamal's dad.

As Anne stretches out on a chaise, Ritz looks to his blind neighbor's deck. The floodlight is still on, but the audiobook has been silenced. He looks to the house on his right, the Jungers. Their deck is stripped of furniture, but two eyeless classical statues still stand guard. Berthe and Hans Junger live most of the year north of Cologne, Germany. With luck next fall, their phrasebook English will keep them from joining the Donegal posse.

"I hope you won't tell your mother," Ritz says. "I know you have every—"

"Tell her what? Ain't none o' my bidness," Anne says again. "What happens in Naples stays in Naples."

"No doubt you resent what I wrote. Your sister does."

"I know Jane's pissed. Personally, I don't get it. We know you. We know how you are. So you write some funny shit about us, so what?"

More solid reasoning from Anne. It makes him wary. But she's been right more than once tonight, and she's right again. What *is* the big deal? Ritz looks down at her, from her glossy head to her carefully manicured feet. Her Balinese dancer's pants have hiked up. The wedge of light from Grunwald's house is shining on smooth, glossy calves. For as long as he can recall, Anne hasn't shaved her legs, but taking a principled stand on woman-as-object in Michigan has given way in Florida.

He stretches out on the chaise next to her. Please don't tell Natalie, he thinks and sips his beer. It was a mistake. Absolutely there won't be more *dates*. I'm not the type. I never was.

But suspicion returns. Even if Anne were angry about what he wrote, she wouldn't hesitate to come here. Not if it suited some purpose. He made a few comic observations about her sister's pedicab approach to carting around her children. He gently mocked Jane's overly protective approach to what he called "carpet-bomb parenting," plus her habit of spritzing disinfectant on table tops in restaurants ("the immune system's equivalent of ethnic cleansing"). But Ritz went into far more detail about Anne.

"Well?" he says finally. "Why don't you want to join the class-action suit?"

"I'm not like her," Anne says. "You always said you hated the hippy thing, so I get what you wrote about me. Jane's middle-of-the-road, you like that. You said I went counter-culture to punish you and Mom for something you did or didn't do."

"I never said any such thing."

"Not to me, to Mom. She told me."

"If I said that, it's because the whole hippy thing was old to me," he says. "I was there, Anne. Present at the creation. It's so *done*. It makes me crazy to see people decades later living a rerun."

"Right, Buzz. Except I don't live in a gated community where no one will play golf with me. Where only two people talk to me. One blind, the other with Alzheimer's. Mom told me all about it. I don't care what you write. To me, all writing is fiction, why should I get bent out of shape? I always cut you some slack, so please do the same for me."

Ritz balances his beer on the chair arm before shoving up in the chaise. Scooching up, as Sunshine might say. Maybe Anne's asking him to cut her some slack is a quid pro quo offer to keep quiet. But isn't that what he wants from everyone? Some slack?

You're her stepfather, he thinks. She's loony, but she could have flipped you the bird from Day One. When the Jekyll/Hyde divide developed, he began wondering about the girls' own germ plasm donor. Unlike her sister, Anne was nothing like her orderly, worrywart mother. That's why I divorced Gordon, Natalie told him. We were too different. I liked it with him, it was exciting. As you know, I'm this buttoned-up, orderly type, and Gordon was all impulse. But after Jane was born, I knew it couldn't last. A year later, Natalie had divorced Gordon. He moved to Montana, just in time for a red deer to leap in front of his pickup and cause him to crash into a jack pine. That's all Ritz knows about Natalie's first husband. And that Anne now uses his name.

All impulse. He sees himself looking down at Sunshine. *Scootch up a little.* How could impulse lead him to risk so much?

"Okay," he says. "I'll go with the flow. Me casa es tu casa.'"

Anne laughs and Ritz sips his beer. Anything you want, he thinks. Anything to keep my secret. For years he has thought of Anne in terms of arrested development. As someone who grew up to be too young for her age. As a stepfather, standing firm about the need to mature seemed important. You're right, he shouted as she stormed off after another faceoff. I'm not your father, but this is not a romper room for adolescent potheads.

She'll be thirty-four in September. What does he hope to accomplish now? Whether her father's genes had anything to do with it—whether it was nature or nurture—seven years after he and Natalie got married, every fire bell, siren, beeper and alarm clock in Anne's wiring was set to go off. And right then, with perfect negative timing at the *Post*, Ritz was forced to stop doing what he was good at.

Heat lightning slashes above Donegal's ninth hole. He remembers grad school in the seventies, living in Ann Arbor in a converted mansion full of freaks. One willowy couple had looked and acted like everyone else in the building, except they had a baby. Had one in the sense of having a minor appliance, like a microwave or George Foreman grill. With the exception of Ritz, everyone living in the shabby mansion had tripped communally on Fridays. Forty-two years later, sitting outside on a nice night in Florida, Ritz still clearly remembers watching from his second-floor window as the couple put their one-year-old in a Carrier air-conditioner carton before dropping acid. Seeing this ritual on Friday nights no doubt helped years later to flip his own switch about Anne.

"If I said something about you punishing us, your mother had no business telling you," he says. "It was said in confidence."

"Come on, Buzz. If I was really mad, I wouldn't be here with the kids. Besides, we'll be out of your hair tomorrow. We're going up to visit someone in Sarasota. We'll be back on Thursday, then I'll drive back down to Key West."

Ah. Reality restored. Anne is here because it serves some purpose. She's a networker, a schmoozer. She is schmoozing him right now. Chatting him up in his isolation. Waiting for the right moment to explain what she really wants. Money, plane tickets, letters of transit from Casa Blanca to Lisbon. Whatever it is, it will have to do with The Grid.

Like the routing map in an in-flight magazine, The Grid for my niece takes the form of a globe threaded by intersecting lines. The lines connect houses, apartments, auto mechanics and other tradesmen who respond positively to praise and flirtation. The lines also extend to venues for music, folk and arts festivals, reliable sources of temporary work, money and food, along with web sites related to homeopathic medicine, and chat rooms devoted to colorful political discussion. As my niece's Grid expands, so do life's possibilities. The quagmire of human limitation is made firm under foot. The point of The Grid is to fashion an experiential trampoline by which to bounce as far and as often as the laws of physics and networking permit.

"We're going to see Brandon's mother," Anne says. "When we get back, I hope you can look after the kids for ten days. While I'm finishing my course in Key West."

"What course is that?"

"Oh I know what you're going to say. Go ahead and write about it. I'm taking a seminar in community political structuring for development of food co-ops."

"I thought Jeff was giving you trouble," he says. "You said he'll make waves if you don't get back next week."

"Not if the kids are sick. There's plenty of documentation for sinus-related issues. He can't do anything about that. We came down here, they got a bug or something, so now they have to stay with their grandfather for a few days."

"What about the drive home to Michigan? I hope you aren't planning to drive straight through. It's dangerous."

"We're flying from Fort Myers," Anne tells him. "At a *great* summer rate. I have a friend at Delta. He also fixed us up with a commuter flight from Key West. Fortunately, Glynnis and Manuel happen to be in the Keys. They're driving my car back to Michigan."

The Grid at work. A personal Interpol. Anne laughs softly, and sips her drink. "Water." She sets her mug on the small table between them. "'Over the course of several days, I am presented with dozens of instances of adults and children twisting open bottles, one from as far away as Fiji.'"

It surprises him. Anne has memorized whole passages. She gets her drink and cradles it on her stomach. "'From Tom's All Natural Toothpaste to the procession of plant-based dishes my niece feeds herself and me, not to mention the endless hot showers necessitated by the risks posed by chemicals in my swimming pool—enough!'"

She chuckles again. "Did you really think anyone would buy the niece thing? But you could've been nicer about Brandan," she says. "He's a good guy. He said his mom needs some company."

Ritz finishes the beer and thinks to get another. No, that would mean more chitchat. The last time Anne was here, she took her mother's car up to Siesta Key. Brandan was staying with his mother in her beach house. The next day, he drove his mom's Volvo down to Naples, behind Anne in her mom's Buick. That night, the two drank wine, chopped and sautéed. Hours later, they served up a curry dish that made much of chickpeas.

The meal wasn't bad. He remembers Natalie's lavish praise, how she kept prompting him with her eyebrows to pay compliments. Brandon sat at the patio table placidly taking it all in. He was in his late thirties, and to be fair, not offensive. Like all Anne's friends, he was whippet-thin, his flowing hair secured in a ponytail. But he was well-spoken and calm as he talked about his life of travel in Mexico and the Caribbean. Three months here, two there, he said. I have this rent-controlled apartment in New York. I sublet it when I'm gone. I clear a thousand a month that way. I take temporary jobs and live modestly. Brandon's métier made use of brick-and-mortar lingo: he "built" websites, something he could do anywhere. As he talked, it became clear that he, too, put to considerable use The Grid of human resources. Parents, stepparents, uncles, cousins, brothers and sisters. Many of them must be working un-modestly to support beach houses and Volvos.

"This course you're taking," Ritz says. "Is it a credential? Negotiable?"

"Absolutely." Anne combs her fingers through her rich hair. "These people in Key West are fantastic. What they know about getting the vote out, getting people involved to support environmental issues, food, health—" She shakes her head. "They really know how to push the right buttons to get Joe Sixpack writing that check."

Ritz squirms, but keeps quiet. Joe Sixpack isn't writing the checks. People like you and Brandon's mom are writing them, he thinks. As Anne continues, he tunes out. His stepdaughter's words commingle with the steady, flat tumble of water flowing from the lip of the spa into the pool. Whatever else is true about Sunshine, he's sure her own network doesn't include a stepfather's Lake Tahoe cabin, a mother's Siesta Key beach house. Or the revenue stream from a rent-controlled New York apartment.

* * *

After twenty minutes, he decides he has held up his end with enough reallys and wows to call it a night. "We'll take this up tomorrow," he says. "I'm sure there's lots more to tell."

"There is," she says. "Sleep tight, Buzz. Oh, by the way, we have a dog."

"With you? Here in the house?"

"Upstairs with the kids. We walked her before you came back. Don't worry, she's a very nice dog, you'll like her. I remember you had a dog growing up. Once I became a vegetarian, my allergy problem with pets totally disappeared."

Dog-sitting. More Grid-related activity.

Ritz says goodnight. He climbs the stairs, wishing it weren't too late to call his wife. He wants to hear her voice. Wants to tell her that Anne's sudden appearance means her feelings aren't too *hurt* to visit him with her kids and a dog.

But as he passes Jane's dimly lit paintings, Ritz slows at the guest bedroom. The TV isn't on. Iris and Jamal have obeyed their mother, and this is new. Just a behavioral hiccup caused by strange surroundings? No. Strange surroundings can't be it. On a regular basis, Anne drags Iris and Jamal along with her to Deadhead concerts. To folk festivals in muddy farmlands blasted by speaker systems guaranteed to alter the lactation cycle of dairy herds in surrounding counties.

But Ritz is now sure Anne will keep his secret. For some reason he's certain of it. He feels lighter. Free of a burden. Anne and her kids are welcome here.

12
The Golfer Teiresias

"Are you grateful for some company?"

"I don't get it for long. They're driving up to Siesta Key after breakfast, to see Brandon's mother."

"That's generous," Natalie says. "Anne really is generous, you know. When they get back, be generous yourself, okay? Please, Buzz, do something with those kids. They haven't seen you in ten months."

"And we know why."

"You can't keep doing this," she says. "You didn't used to be like this. You used to be like other men."

"I was never like other men. Haven't you been listening? I'm a spy. I just pretended to be like other men."

"Have you ever thought about that?" Natalie's voice has again dropped into the register reserved for grave matters. "Really, I'm serious. In all this time, have you ever stopped to ask why you wrote a column for almost nine years, and never told me?"

"I knew what you'd say. And by the way, back in the last century you told me that's why we were good together. Because we were both different in the right way."

"Yes, you knew," Natalie says, still using the portentous voice. "You always know, don't you? But that's not all of it. You had doubts. I see now that's why you kept what you were writing to yourself. You had misgivings. You knew what you wrote was unfair."

"Satire is never fair," he says. "That's the whole point."

"Know what *I* wish?" Having been told many times in the last four months, Ritz does know. "Really," she says, "I wish you'd go back to faking your 'regular guy' thing. If you did that, things could be better."

"She brought a dog."

Today, he loves hearing his wife's voice. But Ritz is also glad to have the dog ready. Natalie says nothing. Driving back this morning loaded with fruit, Ritz passed them. They were walking on Donegal Boulevard, and looked surprisingly presentable. Anne was again in her hemp outfit. Iris's hair was brushed, Jamal had on a Detroit Tigers baseball cap. Plodding next to them was a black dog.

"She sent me a picture," Natalie says. "It's precious, don't you think? Soulful and sweet. She said it was mostly border collie."

Precious, sweet, darling, adorable, cute as a button. When talking about animals, Natalie likes to re-purpose words used for small children. "What difference does it make what kind of dog?" he says. "The doomed kind."

"Please don't."

"Oh, sure, let's not go there. Let's move on. That was then, this is now. Let's just forget about Tushy and the three weeks in Puerto Vallarta."

"Anne was wrong," Natalie says. "She still feels awful. She just forgot. She had to do all the planning, she had Iris and Jamal to keep track of. Tickets, packing."

Ritz is out on the bedroom balcony with the cordless. Below, Iris and Jamal are in the pool, throwing and diving for sea shells. The dog is nowhere in sight. Something else is always conveniently at hand to explain why bad things happen. Tushy is what led to his boycott.

"Maybe that's why Iris and Jamal remembered the cat but their mother didn't," he says. "They didn't have to print out e-tickets."

"She called immediately. She can't be held responsible for the person she called forgetting."

True, he thinks. Just held responsible for relying on a Grid moron. Two days into a trip to Mexico, Iris had asked who was feeding the new kitten in their rented Michigan house. Anne called one of her contacts and told him where she hid her spare house key. Whoever it was wrote it all down, but somehow (Ritz remembers "somehow" figuring in the aftermath), he believed the writing part completed his Grid duty. Via con Dios, Tushy.

But Ritz stays silent. Anne is careless, not punitive. She will keep his secret. His wife actually *is* generous, and her tone of voice is telling him: I will be grateful if you let Tushy go.

"Anne said the dog had to be treated for heart worm," she says. "Does it look healthy?"

What you should ask is whether it looks hardy, Ritz thinks. Able to endure lots of neglect. "It's black," he says. "With white on the chest and paws. It looks depressed. Morose."

"You had a dog growing up," she says. "A dachshund. You said you loved him."

"Tunnel was my first attachment outside blood kin," he says. "We played ball. I threw, he retrieved. I used to shovel a path in the snow so he could pee and poop. He wore sweaters in the winter. Very festive at Christmas."

"Border collies are supposed to be super smart. Please put Anne on."

Ritz covers the mouthpiece, and calls down. When Anne comes on, he pushes the button. It surprised him earlier, seeing the dog. It had been in his house all night. As he drove past, it pained Ritz to think of it in the care of his stepdaughter. It would be dragged around for a month or a year, then taken to the nearest shelter. Natalie's own sentimental view extends even to the raccoons in Michigan that tip over the trash barrels. She says they're just trying to put food on the table.

Below, Anne is talking under the balcony. He listens to the cheery pitch and lilt of her voice, and now she steps clear of the roof. As she strolls with the phone, Iris and Jamal are still diving, coming up with shells, shouting. He can't understand Jamal from up here. Natalie says he will eventually grow out of his speech impediment, that it's common. The boy does seem more intelligible.

He now listens to Iris's high-pitched voice. She's already well on her way to being beautiful. And often says things worth hearing. When Ritz last saw her, she had a solid body of information on the Stone Age. No, grandpa, she told him. It's called the Neolithic Period.

The big innovation with Anne—shaved legs—now presents itself as she talks and moves around the deck. Her white bikini is striking against her tan. It suits her, even though much of her back and upper arms are tattooed. Seen from above, what looks like a bird of prey is soaring skyward between her shoulder blades. Strolling with the cordless, she looks to Ritz like a fully assimilated Maori mom.

* * *

An hour later, he waves as they pass in Anne's Jeep. She blows him a kiss. Iris and Jamal wave from the backseat.

Back inside, he collects Grunwald's audiobooks. His neighbor's pool cage is entered like his own, through a screen door. He crosses the lawn, steps inside. The pool water looks clear, the deck has been rinsed. That means Dolores' nephew Coco is doing something besides driving Murray around the golf course. And stealing the Grunwalds' furniture.

He pulls open the door wall and steps inside. When Esther Grunwald went to assisted living last November, Murray had his house modified to live here alone. Matching easy chairs and two floor lamps are all that's left in the big family room. Murray had the carpet taken up and the cement floor varnished. He says his macular degeneration reminds him of a solar eclipse rimmed with milky light.

The recorded voice is again droning up the hall. A tiller-operated Amigo scooter rests next to the door to the garage. Murray used to steer himself up to the club and around the cart paths, but that came to an end last year. Dolores cleans here as well. She says the changes make it possible to do the Grunwald house in under two hours. Her nephew Coco drives Murray around the golf course. Ritz thinks Coco will soon sell the Amigo.

As he moves up the hall, the recording grows louder. He passes the empty room where Esther used to do her sewing and needlepoint. *'It makes me feel as though...'* He hesitated, searching for words with which to express himself, *'as though I were more me, if you see what I mean. More on my own, not so completely a part of something else. Not just a cell in the social body. Doesn't it make you feel like that, Lenina?'*

"Coco? Is that you?"

"It's Brady." He reaches the study's open entry. *" 'But Lenina was crying, 'It's horrible, it's horrible—' "*

Grunwald feels for the CD player. He pushes a button as Ritz comes in and sits in the club chair opposite. He sets down the audiobooks. His neighbor is in his leather swivel chair, behind the big mahogany desk brought here from his office in Cleveland.

"I suppose you read it," Murray says.

"In high school. The teacher was almost fired."

"Do you remember the scene?"

"All I remember is Lenina being very 'pneumatic.'"

Grunwald smiles. He isn't wearing the big wraparound sunglasses that discourage others from asking about his eyes. "Pneumatic as hell," he says. "Screwing everyone in sight. That's the point, isn't it?"

It's been fifty years since Brady read *Brave New World* in Mr. Squires' eleventh-grade English class. "People are manufactured," he says. "Engineered for certain slots in the economy. They're conditioned to like things the way they are, to not think. They pray to Our Ford, not Our Lord."

"Because he invented the assembly line." Still smiling, Grunwald rocks back in his chair. The room is darkly paneled, and holds the pleasantly sour smell of leather. "What about Lenina?"

"Lenin, Lenina. Everyone belongs to everyone else,'" Ritz says. "It's like the Sixties. In the brave new world, it's politically incorrect to not have sex with lots of partners. That's how you avoid forming attachments. Attachments make you depressed."

"Which is bad."

"De-stabilizing." Ritz remembers something else. "'A gram is better than a damn.' They have a drug called Soma. A form of Prozac. Take Soma, and you can perform sexually like an eighteen-year-old. Right up to the day your timer goes off."

Grunwald nods. "You remember it well," he says. "Go to the head of the class. Still got your family down? I hear kids over there, but different ones."

"This is the second shift," Ritz says. "Iris and Jamal, Anne's kids."

"They're the lively ones, I remember. How's this one treating you?"

During his unhappy week with Jane and her family, Ritz made up reasons to escape next door. He brought Murray his mail, bought him a new golf glove at the pro shop. "Anne's okay," he says. "Very laid back, very southern Cal."

"Tolerant, you mean. That's good."

"The last I heard, she claimed to be a Taoist," Ritz says. "She told me Taoists view everything good or bad as part of The Way."

"Please educate me," Grunwald says. "I'm just a retired GP."

"You can think of The Way as a cosmological superhighway. Yin and yang, up and down. Everything is part of The Way. Evil is just the result of ignorance. Stepping on insects, putting millions of people in ovens, baking brownies. All part of The Way."

Smiling again, shirtless, Grunwald rocks forward. He raises a hand to the desktop, and leans to open a desk drawer. Unlike the rest of him, his hands are still beautiful. They're artist's hands, suited to delicate palpations and probings. His gold wedding band glints under a recessed light.

"I still had all the books from college," he says opening the drawer. "From sophomore English at Ohio State."

"That's your project."

Grunwald nods. "They were in a box out in the garage, mostly falling apart. I had Coco bring them in and make a list of titles. He reads me the ones you can't get recordings for."

"I didn't know his English was that good."

"Pretty good." Grunwald closes the drawer.

"I see he's still selling things."

"Oh yeah." Grunwald straightens. "I know you don't believe me, but he's not stealing. It's what I want. By the time I go, Coco will have this place ready for the kids to put on the market. It'll save them a lot of hand-wringing over what to keep."

In his own hand is a copy of *Vanitas*.

Ritz's heart does a little kip. Blood rushes through pipes and valves in his chest. It's inevitable that Grunwald would eventually get a copy, but Ritz has feared this moment. He believes his neighbor won't become part of the cold snap. But isn't sure. People he never imagined would turn against him have joined the posse.

Grunwald rolls his chair forward, until the empty dugs of his naked chest are flush with the desk. He places his elegant hand on *Vanitas*, and slides it forward.

"Coco read me the greenhouse one," Grunwald says. "Can the guy sue?"

"He might, out of spite. But it's all true."

"Ain't life grand?" Grunwald shakes his head. "Write a book and get dumped on. Like your high school teacher and Huxley's novel. I'm sorry, Brady. Tony Minetta was here Tuesday, asking did I want to play a scramble tournament. He knows I just play solo now. He really came to find out my position. I told him I was on your side, I asked him did he read it. He said no, why bother, what he heard was enough."

Grunwald gives the book a tap before folding his arms on the desk. "Read the one about karaoke," he says. "That one punched everyone's buttons."

Ritz looks down at the book. It's so innocent, a small, harmless object on a huge mahogany desk. "I'd rather not," he says. "It's embarrassing to read your own stuff."

"Come on, indulge me. Writers do readings all the time. I want to hear it from the horse's mouth."

"Let Coco read it."

"I don't want it with an accent, I want the genuine article. Ritz does Ritz."

He really doesn't want to. The study's mahogany-paneled walls and huge desk make him feel on trial. But more protests will sound coy and vain, so he takes up the trade paperback and flips pages. He finds the essay, and spreads the book.

"After I took the early buyout from Blodgett & Cram, my wife and I retired to a Florida golf community. I am beginning to think it was a mistake.

"You may know the lifestyle in such places. Not just in Florida, but other warm, joint-friendly locales. The beach and shops, luxury cars, lunch under an umbrella, dinner with patio heaters in January. Don't get me wrong, it's very nice."

He glances up. Arms still folded, Grunwald is listening. His eyes look fine, not like those of a blind man. Maybe he's *not* blind. "Go on," he says. "It's good. You're setting me up, something's coming." Ritz looks down and finds his place.

"It's because of karaoke.

"That's what people do here every Wednesday. When Happy Hour starts at four, men and women begin taking turns in front of the crowd in the club dining room. They sing, so to speak, under the guidance of a young woman who operates the karaoke machine. When someone needs a duet partner, she joins in.

"She can't sing, either, and this helps to explain why she is Naples' most successful karaoke leader. You don't want the jarring effect of someone who can actually sing causing people in the bar to hear something strange, and stop talking.

"An inclination to specialize figures at our club.

"For example, there's the epicene, white-haired fellow who only takes the stage for Sinatra tunes. The sole Sinatra aspect in his performance are his attempts to produce the higher register moments for which Sinatra is famous. The man clearly lives for these moments. But only his head thrown back and his arms jerking down for emphasis reveal that's where we are in the song. This is because his voice is dominated by a vibrato so extreme as to de-couple from the melody. An oscilloscope would short out. But the gentleman has a level of self-acceptance that frees him every Wednesday. At least until his engagement here on earth is cancelled."

"Talent night in the brave new world," Grunwald says. "Go on."

Hearing himself is making Ritz self-conscious. He wants to get it over with.

"Two other specialists figure on Wednesdays. The first concentrates on the work of Barbara Streisand. This woman is plump and tall, with lots of blusher. She can be counted on to take the mic for 'People' or 'The Way We Were.' She also does 'Feelings,' which wasn't a signature Streisand tune, but should have been. Along with blusher, the lady favors a broad range of cruise jewelry to accessorize her Lilly Pulitzer outfits.

"In one respect, she is the best of the lot on Wednesdays: she has some self-consciousness. This keeps her mindful of the yawning gap separating her voice from the one she emulates. The result is a modest volume level that never intrudes on dining-room conversations about golf and football, the degenerate, native-born Kenyan occupying the White House, or recent surgeries and deaths."

"Dee Wiggins. She's thin, not plump, but you're right about volume control. When Esther and I went, I remember being grateful."
Ritz looks at Grunwald and wants to protest. The piece is almost entirely invented. He went to karaoke just twice, and if some of the details suggest this Dee person, he wasn't writing about her. Or anyone else. But it's futile, and he looks back down.
"*The third specialist has no such restraint. Like the white-haired gentleman, he has unstuck himself from inhibition, but without the vibrato. His voice is as flat as Iowa, and this somehow fits with his commitment to the tunes we all learned as children. By 'all' I mean all of us living here on the golf course, not 'all' in places like Harlem, or Little Italy. Children there probably grew up with Billy Holiday and Renata Tibaldi. With us, it was 'Red River Valley,' 'I've been Working on the Railroad,' etcetera.*
"*The man I'm talking about has a brush cut. He's stocky, with a solid jaw. He always wears short-sleeved white shirts, which leads me to think he may have been an engineer. Anyway, the songs of childhood still live for him. When the young woman operating the karaoke machine gives him the signal, he marches up the single step to the riser, takes the hand-held mic and straightens his broad shoulders.*"

"Uh oh." Ritz looks up again. Grunwald's eyebrows are raised.

"At least the first time, it's something to see: an engineer who replaced calculus and physics with singing. But he doesn't stretch his neck or jerk down with his hands. He keeps time by oscillating from the waist up. Since he is both tone deaf and free of rhythm, this is what anyone watching will focus on. The lyrics are there—Oh Clementine, my Clementine, and so forth—but the singer is taking the words on aimless flights. With his body metronoming to one tempo, and the synthesizer offering something altogether different—

"But to the man's credit, a time always comes when awareness dawns. If you're a regular, you can see it coming. Maybe it's his engineering background, but all at once he understands: his singing is progressing at radical odds with whatever is playing on the machine. But he doesn't stop and run away as I would. He races tonelessly through the verse, quickly steps down, goes to his chair and sits as the recording wends its leisurely way to conclusion. Or the kindly, quick-thinking young woman starts clapping, and appeals to the crowd to 'give it up!' or 'put your hands together!'

"My problem on Wednesdays is that I am more and more feeling a sense of urgency. I can't sing and never wanted to, but more and more I am sensing an impulse. What if I've been wrong? What if all these years I should have been letting my child out? What if I went through with it now, and died on stage? Those few minutes would be my whole story.

"That's why I'm no longer sure about the buyout from Blodgett & Cram."

13
Chekhov's Gun in Act One

He closes the book. The cover presents the Statue of Liberty with a golf bag slung over her shoulder. The torch is raised in her right hand, a martini in her left. At Ritz's suggestion, both the title and his name are printed in the font used at The Detroit *Post*.

"It's pretty good," Grunwald says. "But I know why you're having trouble."

"I'm glad," Ritz says. "That means you know humorless, vain people have talked themselves into thinking I wrote about them. I didn't. I don't name anyone, I don't vilify anyone."

"No, but you mock them."

"Not personally, Murray. I changed the details. I mostly made things up."

"Brady, please. That doesn't matter. You make your singers sound and act foolish. The real singers feel it's aimed at them. And here's something else. Do you know any of these people?"

"Of course I know them, Murray. I made them up. They aren't people, they're *inventions*. When we first moved in, I went to karaoke twice. That's all I could take."

"Jerry Greiner is the third singer. You made the hair and shoulders different, but I recognize him from how you describe his singing. He's been here as long as I have. And you're right, he was an engineer. I think with GM. When did you write that one?"

"2006. A year after we moved in."

"Yeah." When Murray lifts his arms off the desk, the sound is that of masking tape peeled from a wall. He leans back and rests his elbows on the chair arms.

"Yeah *what*, Murray?"

"It's because you didn't know many people," Grunwald says. "You should've been more careful."

Ritz leans forward to defend himself, but leans back. What if the only mentally healthy Donegal resident still talking to him decided to join the posse? The thought again sets his chest in motion—duh *duh,* duh *duh.*

"I think it must've been soon after that time," Grunwald says. "I know I was no longer driving. I stopped going, but Esther still went with women from her water aerobics class. She knew him because he was always there. Doing pretty much what you say. She had her own joke about karaoke. She said the whole point was to sell more drinks, that's how you got through it. Jerry Greiner developed laryngeal cancer. He uses what's called an electrolarynx. You have grandchildren, so I'm sure you've heard it. They make a sound like a cartoon voice."

Ritz raises his shoulders and rolls them. He lets out a breath.

"See what I mean?" Grunwald says.

"I wrote a column," Ritz says. "I borrowed details from wherever and whatever, taken from my own experience. *My* experience, Murray. People and places I encountered in life.

But I changed it. Altered details, concealed identities. I invented the rest."

"You're thinking in legal terms. People know themselves."

"That's the mistake everyone's making," Ritz says. "It's vain. Egotistical."

"What is? I don't understand. What's the mistake?"

"You can't recognize yourself in what I wrote unless you want to. I never name the club or the town. How many thousands of people in retirement communities fit those same descriptions? That's my point, Murray. The descriptions are generic. How many engineers have crew cuts and wear short-sleeved white shirts? It's a type, a cliché. How many women in clubs like Donegal wear Lilly Pulitzer, to go with the junk jewelry they buy on cruise ships? If people want to think I wrote about them, what can I do about it?"

Grunwald says nothing.

"One more thing," Ritz says. "I think people are using me as a scapegoat. A lightning rod. It's like the letters to the editor in the Naples Daily News. All these people with money and gold-plated health care can't stop hating Obamacare. Why? We know why. Here, people find out I wrote Vanitas, and start looking for themselves. Why, Murray? Vanity, that's why. And they 'find' what they're looking for, even though I didn't write about them. They find a generic detail here and there, and grab the chance to be offended."

"You're mad about what I said."

"No, Murray, not mad. Just disappointed."

"You thought I'd be sympathetic."

"I don't want sympathy, I want understanding. I want thought."

"Ah." Grunwald taps the desk with his thumbs. "Wait, though. You wrote it in 2007, but you refer to the Kenyan in the White House."

"I updated some details before publication."

The front door opens and closes. "That's Coco," Grunwald says. "We're going through some old files today." He folds his hands on the desk, just the way he must have done when speaking to patients. "It'll blow over," he says. "Do charity work."

"What's that mean?"

"You know, good deeds. Do something that shows you in a better light."

"Murray, you can't be serious. You want me to do penance? Humble myself?"

The recessed light above the desk is glinting off Grunwald's bald head and wedding ring. He makes a placating gesture and refolds his hands. "That's my advice," he says. "Do something social. Visit the sick, read to children. What are they going to do, tell you you're not fit to sit with hospice patients? It'll take a while, they won't forgive you first thing. But over time they will. Just make nice and get a good report card. Women love that sort of thing, rehabilitation. When they see you doing good, you watch. They'll put the screws to their husbands to play with you during recess."

Amazing. Murray Grunwald is advocating a good act of contrition. A display of humility. "I won't do it," Ritz says. "I'm not guilty of anything. I'm not evil."

He turns to see Coco Ruiz standing in the open entry. In Ritz's view, Coco may actually *be* evil. "Com es sta?" Grunwald says.

"How you doing, dottor?"

"Good. You ready to go to work?"

"Any time. How you doing, Mr. Reetz?"

"Fine, Coco." Ritz gets up. As always, Ruiz has on a black cowboy shirt, black jeans, black cowboy hat. Either his wife or aunt washes his clothes every day, or he has multiple sets of the same outfit.

"Will you be seeing Dolores?" Ritz asks. "Any idea when she's coming to clean?"

"I see her tomorrow," Coco says. "You want me to give her a message?"

"Tell her to plan on extra time at my house. I have guests. Plus there's a dog."

"You got a dog?"

"It's my stepdaughter's. She's here for a few days."

"What kind of dog she got?"

"Black."

Coco smiles. "That's a good kind. I got two dogs. Pit bulls from the shelter. People don't like that kind, but these is nice dogs. Real friendly."

Ritz smiles back. Pit bulls fit Coco. His black cowboy boots are tipped with pointed wedges of highly polished stainless steel. Everything about Coco demands you look at him. And also makes clear that if you look too long, bad things will happen.

"I hear you're reading to Dr. Grunwald."

"Oh yeah, he got all these books. Is good for me, helping with my English."

"What are you reading now?"

"The Death...." Ruiz looks to the doctor.

"of Ivan Ilych," Grunwald says. "I suppose you read it. It's what you literary types call a novella. We're going to give that one a rest today. The Russian names are tough going for both of us."

14
Assume a virtue if you have it not

Ritz walks back to his house. He can't believe it. A secular Jew is recommending a lapsed Presbyterian make use of Catholic Best Practices. Grunwald stopped just short of recommending Confession.

Ridiculous, he thinks. At sixty-six I'm supposed to retrofit myself with a new set of values? Perform acts of contrition? But nearing his pool cage, Ritz slows. The cold snap has been going on since February. He spends half his time in the periodicals room at the library. Last week, he caught himself reading Martha Stewart on how to gild maple leaves to make a centerpiece.

Is Murray right? Was it the karaoke piece that blew things up?

He stops outside his pool cage. It's easy to dismiss someone like Tony Minetta, but not Murray. Or Jane. After two visits, he and Natalie never went back to karaoke—but some of his wife's friends may sing. What if Grunwald is right about doing penance? Natalie said she wishes he'd go back to faking it. To pretending he's a regular guy. You don't understand how words affect others, she keeps telling him. Language has been your life, that's why you don't understand.

What if you did it? Ritz thinks. What if you could hit the reset button by getting up and making a fool of yourself? When the girls were in high school, one of Natalie's catch phrases at breakfast was "Do the hard thing, not the easy thing."

He pulls open the pool-cage door. Just the idea of humbling himself before the karaoke crowd makes Ritz shake his head *No!* The door claps shut behind him. Even the thought makes him feel queasy. Much of his adult life was spent fixing others' mistakes. After marriage, the goal was to keep a low profile, to avoid conflict. To stay married to someone better than himself. Even after losing his editorial job and being forced to sell ads, that was the goal. Performing at karaoke would be running face-first into conflict with his own nature. It would be the hardest, most humiliating thing he can think of.

How would he present himself? Ritz steps inside the family room. He turns, closes the slider, and stares at the pool. Styrofoam noodles are still floating. Again he sees Ashley at Christmas in her Wise Person robe. Slowly, with perfect timing, she lowers her arm for effect. He has nothing of her inborn gift for theater. Unlike Ashley, he hates public displays. So many happy years being right, he thinks. Spent alone in an office cubicle fixing other people's mistakes. That's why you proposed to Natalie in a shopping mall—how would you fix a no? At Donegal he pretended to be a team player, he took up golf. He sat with others and banged on the bar when a wide receiver dropped a forward pass. He did his best to be One of the Guys.

Would he dress in his blue pinstripe suit and play a drunken Japanese salaryman?

As he defrosts a frozen lasagna for lunch, the phone rings. It can't be Natalie. It must be another angry reader. He shuts down the microwave and picks up the cordless. "Hello, I'm happy to report Brady Ritz has agreed to set himself adrift with nothing but a bag of organic Brussels sprouts."

"Hello?"

"Jane! That wasn't for you."

"Are you expecting a call from Anne?"

"No no." He mustn't waste the call. "You never told me about your flight home, did Ashley get through her audition for *Tosca?*"

"She was like that all the way," Jane says. "I was so embarrassed. There was no movie, something was wrong with the system. Dan tried reading to her from one of her books, but she wouldn't listen. It was a rash. I raised her shirt and her tummy was covered with little bumps."

From the microbial swill in grandpa's swimming pool. "I'm sorry," Ritz says. "I wish I could help." Lame, he thinks. What would you do, airmail a poultice?

"I said I'd call when we got home, the rash made me forget. So, we're home safe."

Ritz shakes off his confusion. What must he say to be allowed back into the fold? He sees his stepdaughter's pale, serious face framed by bangs. Yearns to hear her bubbly laugh. He remembers *old stepdad*, and decides to play the age card one more time.

"Listen, your mom tells me you think I stole what was yours." Jane doesn't answer. "It was all in jest," he says. "I thought it would give old geezers like me a laugh or two. You know, the generation gap, us seniors versus them young'uns. Really, that's it. I never meant for you or anyone to be offended. I made up names, I changed everything I could think of."

"I've thought about it a lot," Jane says. She would, Ritz tells himself. Jane would *think*. "I know you never meant for me or Anne or Mom to be hurt by what you wrote."

"Exactly, thank you, I—"

"But you did think it," she says. "And then you wrote it and published it. It says what you think in your true self about how we live and raise our children. You think it's a joke."

"That's not—"

"Yes, I know you wouldn't ever say it to us. And you didn't use our names. But I still can't see what you said as just a joke. Anne says she does, but you hurt her, too. I know it."

After a pause, she says, "So, we're home safe."

"Yes, thank you. How's Ashley now? And Madison, and Dan?" Ritz wants to keep it going.

"They're all fine. The rash is better. Bye." She hangs up.

As Ritz lowers the phone, he sees Tony Minetta trundling across the road, giving him the finger. His stepdaughter's words lead directly back twenty years or more to his wife's catch phrase at breakfast: *do the hard thing*. This is followed by *no pain, no gain,* then *face your fears*.

He restarts the microwave. Self-abasement is the most hard, humiliating thing Ritz can think of. For what reason would *anyone* freely, consciously open himself up to criticism and ridicule? Columnists and reporters at the *Post* showed him their hate mail, the letters and later the emails sent to them by angry readers. They laughed and pointed to instances of semi-literacy and misreadings of their stories. Stories Ritz had edited for concision and clarity. The reporters laughed, but their hate mail hardened Ritz's contempt for the Regular Guy.

The idea of getting up in front of the karaoke crowd is registered by the ceiling-fan breeze on his sweaty scalp. The microwave buzzer goes off, and he opens the door. How can a ceiling fan breeze and a microwave seem coordinated, like a coded message? Ritz takes out the lasagna. You, he thinks, the man of hard-nosed reason. But he will do it. He will put his Regular Guy role to the ultimate test by humbling himself in front of the Philistines. He will sing for his supper.

* * *

After lunch, rehearsal begins before the full-length mirror in his walk-in closet.

A recessed ceiling light shadows his face as he sings in the dark. First, Billy Joel's "Uptown Girl," then The Supremes' "Stop in the Name of Love." He tries out gestures—bouncing his hip and wagging a finger at the crowd. Slow sweeps with one hand, then both. No, absolutely not, no hand gestures. And no show-stopper high notes.

He shifts to tunes remembered from childhood, but has to Google the lyrics. He writes them on three-by-five cards, and goes back up to the closet. A process of elimination leads to "Red River Valley." Good, that's the one, that will be his song. It's modest and nostalgic, politically correct for senior citizens. And the lyrics even fit with his own life: a cowboy laments his lady love leaving town. Actors trained in The Method connect moments in the script with their own experience. If he can conjure up Natalie while he sings, that should make his performance more heartfelt.

At four he goes down for coffee, and now sees a note left on the kitchen island. "Hi. Truman's a vegetarian—ha ha! Give her the kale, carrots and potato I boiled this morning. It's in the fridge, the pan with the copper top. See you Thursday." The note ends with three hearts.

The dog. Anne said nothing about leaving it.

He looks behind the family-room sectional. It must be upstairs in the guest bedroom. Ritz runs up and along the hall. He pushes the half-open door and snaps on the overhead light. It isn't on the Aerobed. On the far side of the actual bed, the dog lies facing the wall. A stain forms a dark circle on the beige carpet.

"I'm sorry." The dog won't look at him. It's been in here since nine this morning. Eight hours, and not a sound. "Your name's Truman."

Nothing. The dog won't look at him. Ritz goes in the bathroom and grabs a hand towel. He runs it under the faucet, rings it out, comes back and drops to his knees. "I know all about it," he says, rubbing hard next to the dog. "I have an enlarged prostate, I couldn't last three hours."

He again wets and rings out the towel, comes back and drops to his knees. What you're doing has nothing to do with the rug, he thinks. You want the dog to look over and forgive you.

He keeps softly talking, rubbing with the towel, mixing apology and explanation. "Very confusing around here," he says. "Very distracting." A third time Ritz rings out the towel and comes back. "That's wrong, I'm making excuses," he says, rubbing. "Nothing is confusing, there are no distractions." The dog still won't look at him. Ritz finally sits next to it, and begins tentatively stroking its back. "Tell you what, we'll have dinner. Anne left something she says you eat. I'll believe it when I see it."

Finally he gives up, and stands. "I'm going now. Please come down, we'll eat." He backs away, watching for some movement. "I'll be in the kitchen." In the hall he scuffs his shoes on the carpet runner, hoping to sound like someone leaving forever. At the stairs, he looks back. "Come on, Truman—"

He gives up and starts down. As he reaches the painting of drowned peonies, the dog passes him. When Ritz reaches the foyer, it is sitting in front of the door. "Of course, I understand." He crosses and opens it. The dog steps through and waits for Ritz to open the screened entrance. Once outside, it moves to the lawn and squats.

"Right, Number 2. Sorry for the delay." Braced on its front paws, squatting, the dog is facing Grunwald's house. "Being fed vegetables might make matters worse," Ritz says. "Whenever Anne cooks, I'm in the can half the next day."

The squatting seems lady-like to him. Civilized. It had to pee but exercised bowel control. Until the booby singing in the closet went for coffee. Finished, the dog stands and turns. Still not looking at Ritz, it scratches the grass, then steps to the screen door and sits. He lets it in, watches it run upstairs. "Nothing to eat? Do you want to try my food?"

He still feels a need to make amends. "Just relax! I'll fix you a plate!"

He finds the pan in the refrigerator and takes off the copper lid. Incredible. He can't believe Anne's vegetarian religion is being imposed on a dog. He scoops what's there onto a china dinner plate. But who wants cold glop? Ritz puts it in the microwave and sets the timer for one minute. The buzzer sounds. He takes it out, tests it with his finger. Still cold. After another minute, the glop is now ready. Whatever "ready" means to a dog. He gets a soup bowl from the cupboard.

"Truman!"

When it doesn't come down, he goes back upstairs. The dog has moved into the bathroom, and is now bunkered against the bathtub. It looks at him as he lowers the plate. Ritz fills the soup bowl with water, and sets it down.

"Mostly veggies for me too," he says. "A leftover egg roll and kung pao chicken." The dog keeps looking at him. "No rush. Take your time." At last the dog gets up and begins eating. It strengthens Ritz's sense of purpose. He *will* go through with karaoke. He decides to prepare with some marketing by seeding the community with apologies. If year-round residents spread the word, that might beef up attendance.

* * *

The following morning, he uses notecards to keep names straight, and begins making calls. "Madeline this is Brady Ritz and I'm sorry I hurt your feelings I honestly would never guess you had plastic surgery but if you had some work done the results are wonderful and I again regret offending you and I hope you believe me when I say I was not in any way thinking of you when I wrote on a subject I now see was not appropriate have a good day."

Not appropriate. Ritz can't believe he said it. Not appropriate is on his cosmic Delete list. Politicians use it in place of *I lied I cheated I'm evil.*

"Hi Harry it's Brady Ritz before you hang up let me tell you I admire good golfers especially scratch golfers and that certainly includes you if I'd realized what I wrote was going to offend you I would never have been so inappropriate because God knows I've drunk my share of brewskies out on the course and peed in the bushes many a time so I never repeat never had you or anyone else at Donegal in mind besides myself when I wrote so inappropriately take care of yourself."

He hears himself using actual people's names, and at some point Ritz realizes he didn't just "make it all up."

"So Madge Brady Ritz here and really I have to say straight off it's very depressing for me to learn in your recent phone message that you took offense at my little nonsense article on karaoke but Madge you must know your worth as a singer because everyone at the club knows it and that includes me that's the God's own truth stay well."

He isn't always allowed to finish. People hang up, tell him to go to hell, call him a liar. It's the off season, so most of his messages go to voicemail. But the more calls he makes, the easier it gets. By early afternoon, the groveling is working on him if no one else. He regrets what he wrote. Last week, he resorted to watching an MTV show called *The Real World,* about young people suffering angst, lethargy, and romantic disappointments in a glamorous house. In your Real World, Ritz thinks, dialing Tony Minetta, people lose their minds and eyesight, not just their hair.

"Tony hello it's Brady Ritz please don't hang up I want to tell you my crack about hair transplants had nothing whatever to do with you and the truth is I have personally been to more than one hair-restoration clinic because looking good makes people feel good—"

"Take a flying fuck on a donut."

"I hear you Tony say hello to Denise—"

15
Show Time

Late the following afternoon, he puts on his favorite outfit: linen slacks, and the black silk camp shirt he wore on his date with Sunshine. Black will help make him look serious, more respectful. But standing before the floor-length mirror, he sees this idea is all wrong. He looks solid. Confident and healthy. The point is to humble himself.

Back in Wardrobe, Ritz scrapes through hangers, until he comes to an aloha shirt. The sales tags are still attached. He takes it out, steps to the mirror and holds it up to his chest. A shirt so ugly you never wore it, he thinks. When he showed it to Natalie, she covered her mouth and shook her head. Should he leave the sales tags on? No. People might think he was ridiculing Minnie Pearl, the Queen of Country Comedy. She wore hats with sales tags. He remembers a pair of pants dating from a time of weight gain in his fifties. Ritz finds them, puts them on with the shirt, and steps back before the mirror. The effect is that of someone diminished and rural on holiday. A sodbuster on a cruise. Perfect for the Red River Valley.

* * *

At six he trudges up the drive. The Bilge again falls silent. Has word circulated about his apologies? Those here will be just starting dinner. Golf carts are parked on the circular drive, waiting to be put in the shed. Ritz has never been more nervous. He now doubts his costume decisions. He thinks to turn back, but keeps going.

At the canopied entrance he pulls opens the door "—enchanted eev'ning, you will see a strangerrr—" The door wheezes shut behind him "—across a crowded rooooom." Ritz straightens his shoulders and walks quickly down the hall. No turning back, he thinks. Once in, all in. Ahead, Terry Condin is in place at the bar. Ritz keeps going, turns left in the cocktail lounge, and steps down to the dining room.

The host Jeremy, or *maitre d'hotel* as he prefers to be called is chatting up a table of six. As always, he is overdressed to encourage appreciation of his power over table assignments. He stops talking and looks at Ritz crossing from the stairs. His change of expression confirms Ritz's wardrobe decisions. A stickler when it comes to haberdashery—matching tie and breast pocket square, aggressively cufflinked—Jeremy straightens. "Mister Ritz, I...."

"Hello, Jeremy, don't let me interrupt. I don't need a table, I'm here to sing."

"What a surprise. You of all people, a *chanteuse*."

Ritz smiles back before crossing the dance floor. Chan*teuse* applies to no one more than to Jeremy, but the word serves to dial down Ritz's fear. Ahead, dressed in a chartreuse running costume, the young *maître de karaoke* is just now stepping to the mic. Tall speakers and pieces of sound technology are stacked behind her, next to a white baby grand piano.

"Okay, it's time now for another line dance. Let's see some action out here!"

Something country-western starts thumping. When Ritz looks, people are getting up and moving to the dance floor. Mostly they are women his wife's age, and their daughters. Many are doing eye rolls, feigning resignation. Some are herding grandchildren in front of them. When Ritz turns to the karaoke woman, she smiles and motions to the straight chair next to hers.

He sits facing the crowd. Good, the men seated at tables are hidden behind the dancers. The women take no notice of him as they form two rows. Like a close-order drill team, they extend their arms to measure space, and work into position as the music thumps its way to some launch point.

Once it arrives, the women begin a more or less coordinated series of arm motions used by football referees. Sweeps left or right (out of bounds), straight up (field goal or extra point), scissor-like dusting motion (incomplete forward pass).

Most of the dancers have it down, but there are some good-natured collisions. The overall impression is one of lunging or cross-stepping in unison, something like the Lippenzaner horses he and Natalie saw on their trip to Vienna. The memory makes Ritz less nervous. He even watches the women with qualified admiration. They stay in step, and manage to body-block the less adept back into line. In two instances, one of the not-knowing is on her way to toppling, but is caught and brought upright.

He remembers Carl, and glances down at the three-by-five card in the palm of his hand. The karaoke person sits next to him and leans close. "You're new," she says.

"Yes and no. New to karaoke, not to Donegal."

"Yeah, well, there has to be a first time. What's your poison?"

"Red River Valley."

"Good choice."

He had thought to sing "You are My Sunshine," but Carl might be here. Since dropping her off at her car, Ritz has hardly thought about her.

His momentary confidence vanishes. All at once he wishes Truman was on the floor next to him, wearing a service-dog vest. It would humanize you, he thinks. Show how you too are a victim of something. He's made a mistake. Why can't the line dance to go on indefinitely? The country-western song is heading for home. You shouldn't have listened to Grunwald, he thinks. Ritz takes deep breaths as the dancers reach a shuffling, hand-jive finale. All of them are now pretty much synchronized.

"What's your name?"

"Brady."

"Brady what?"

"Just Brady."

"I get it." The karaoke girl nudges him. "Like Little Richard or Cher." She turns to a console, pushes buttons, and turns back. "Okay, Brady. 'Red River Valley's all set to go. Just stand up when I do. When I move away, take the mic. I have some announcements first. Got it?"

"Yes."

"Nervous?"

"Yes, very."

"Don't be. Between you and me, unless you have family here, nobody listens."

When the music shuts down, the women clap and cheer for themselves. Some pump fists on their way to the tables. Ritz again looks at the notecard, song lyrics on one side, remarks on the other.

"Okay great!" The young woman is on her feet and clapping. Ritz stands. "Let's give it up for the line dancers!" As they sit, some are still applauding themselves.

"Okay, great. Before our next singer, a few announcements. Mark down next Wednesday. For karaoke, naturally, but also for the seafood buffet. You don't want to miss this one, so sign up early. It's all you can eat, guys, yum yum. Next Thursday is the Men's Scramble Tournament. The pro shop says they have some serious prize money in the works, as well as trophies, so make a note. And thirdly we have a speaker a week from Friday from the Paradise Dream Cruise people. They have news you won't want to miss about next February's booze cruise, excuse me, the Donegal annual cultural visit to the Caribbean." This gets a laugh. "Seriously, those who have been on this trip know what I mean. A good time is had by all, including the last man *or* woman standing." More laughs.

"Any questions, just catch up with me later, but now we have a new singer. A first-timer he tells me—right?" She looks at him and Ritz nods. Duh *duh* duh *duh.* "Sure you're not a ringer?" She pauses for must be another proven laugh line, but except for the whine and crunch of the bar's blender, the room is quiet. As she turns to activate the song machine, Ritz tugs her sleeve.

"I want to say a few words first."

"A speech? No politics, sir... Brady, right? Absolutely nothing about anyone elected to anything. And nothing about assessments, we had some punching once, that's really not—"

"No, I promise, nothing political. Just a few words I want to say before I sing."

Assessing Ritz for the first time, the woman looks into his eyes as though gauging the size of his pupils. She frowns at his shirt, looks up at him and nods. "Really," she says. "I mean it. Anything political, anything about the proposed mosquito spraying, I cut the mic."

"I understand."

"People can be touchy."

"Very true. I promise, nothing political."

She steps away. Ritz takes her place and raises the notecard. "I want to express my appreciation—"

He brings his fist to his mouth and coughs. As he was working everything out in front of the mirror, Ritz remembered Ashley at the airport, the catch in her throat. He decided a bit of stage business was needed to emphasize seriousness of purpose. He clears the cough and brings up the notecard.

"I want to express my appreciation to everyone here for giving me the opportunity to express my heartfelt—"

"Who gave you anything?"

"—to say how much I regret the publication of work of mine, work I did everything possible—"

"Work he calls it. Get a job."

"—short essays I wrote for a little magazine, most of which appeared years before my wife Natalie and I joined this wonderful—"

A tray of dishes and glassware is dropped in the kitchen. Ritz keeps reading as the metal tray wowwows on the tile floor. Now more glassware and china crash from some nearby surface, a domino effect. Crockery is still breaking as the tray speeds its way to silence. Muffled kitchen voices are still shouting and laughing as Ritz finishes reading.

He turns to the karaoke girl. The look she gives him says *You did this.* Taking a deep breath, she turns to the machine and pushes a button. Like an act of mercy, the folksy, familiar opening bars of Ritz's song compete with voices in the kitchen. Glass shards are being swept as the girl points to him.

"From this valley they say you are going,
We will miss your bright eyes and sweet smile,
For they say you are taking the sunshine,
That has lightened our path for a while—"

No one interrupts. Ritz realizes he was counting on being interrupted by catcalls and forced to stop. In the pause before the second verse, he glances out. Except for two men sawing at prime rib, everyone is closely watching him. He continues singing, still hoping for dinner rolls to be thrown, knives banged on glasses. None of it happens. It should be worse than this. That's why it *is* worse. As he now waits to begin the last verse, Ritz looks up to the bar above. Drinkers are turned on their barstools. Fingers of both hands fitted together on top of his head, Tommy the bartender is watching him.

As Ritz sings, a man appears in the lounge, and crosses to the stairs. He comes down the three steps, narrow-shouldered, his white hair with the defined part of a wig. He is wearing a short-sleeved white dress shirt open at the collar. It's not Carl, not anyone Ritz remembers. He comes off the last step, moves to his left and stands erect at the back of the dining room. Ritz holds the last note until the recording shuts down. Filling the void is the once-again sound of glass shards being swept. The man raises something like a pocket flashlight, and presses it to his neck.

"That was my song. You get your own song."

Anyone with grandchildren knows the voice from *The Cartoon Network*. It's the man Murray spoke of. Except this isn't Daffy Duck or Bugs Bunny. The voice is deep. Inhuman. The man lowers the instrument, and Ritz nods. He moves quickly across the parquet dance floor, up the three steps, down the hall. Once outside, he passes down the incline without looking to The Bilge.

16
Catch and Release

Someone is talking. Ritz turns off the hand vacuum and looks down. Dolores is at the foot of the stairs giving him *the look.*

"I said you don't got to do that. I going to take care of it after I finish the kitchen."

"I just thought I'd help out," he says. "My stepdaughter has a dog. It sheds." Dolores keeps staring at him. Ritz sets the hand vacuum on the landing and starts down. He woke needing to tidy or clean something. To do penance for last night.

He passes without meeting her eyes and moves along the hall. You don't say no to Dolores. You don't cross Dolores in any way, or inspect her work while she's here. He did that once, after she cleaned the oven, and got *the look.* At parties, her customers speak in near-reverential terms about Dolores's gift for Going Where No Cleaner Has Gone Before. She is not much younger than most of them, people whose golden years don't include Scrubbing Bubbles or Tidy Bowl.

He reaches the family room. Outside, Iris and Jamal are at the table eating. They got back this morning, and he was grateful to see them. Last night, after The Fiasco, he felt too exposed to be seen walking the dog. He put Truman on the leash, and took her behind the pool cage. Then he heated up what was left of some tuna and rice, shared it with her, and went to bed early.

He pulls open the door wall.

"High grandpa."

"Hi Gwampa."

"Hi Buzz." Stretched out on a chaise, Anne turns from the newspaper and smiles. She is wearing the white bikini. Along with her tattoos and sunglasses, the bikini gives her an aura of glamor and worldly competence.

"How was Siesta Key?" he asks.

"Incredible. I forgot how great the beach is there. The sand is the exact color and texture of powdered sugar, it's that white. Brandon's mom says that's why it's cool all the time. It reflects the sun and never gets hot."

"Good. How's Brandon?"

"I thought I told you, he wasn't there. He ran into a glitch in Grand Cayman."

"Ah."

"But we had fun, his mom's really cool. We all went to this little nearby town called Nokomis. They have this incredible drumming on the beach."

"But it was cold at night," Iris says. "Brandon's mom had the air conditioning way down. She gave us blankets."

"Mom ded it will make your doint bad." Jamal takes a handful of carrot strips from a platter and drops them on his paper plate. "Can we ged dum new poo doy?"

Ritz looks to Iris. "Mom said your joints go bad from air conditioning. We think you should buy new pool toys. The noodles are crumbling, the Styrofoam is getting in the water."

"New noodles it is," he says.

Anne is back to reading the *Naples Daily News*. Beginning in junior high, she read the morning *Post*. It meant he had to wait for it until she left for school, but reading the paper was Anne's one habit that Ritz approved of.

He sits at the table, and takes a carrot strip. There are also slices of soy cheese, a bowl of grapes, oranges. The two are drinking a purplish liquid. After driving home last night, he went upstairs, changed out of his costume and lay on the bed. The man kept lowering the device as sweeping sounds came from the kitchen. Ritz had the impulse to call Natalie. I did the hard thing, he'd say, but changed his mind. She would learn all about it from one of her bridge partners.

Lying in the dark, along with *do the hard thing,* he also remembered *do something with those kids*. The boat, he thought. You haven't been out on it since March.

When golf got old last year, he began looking at ads. Ritz knew nothing about boats, but there were dozens for sale. Most of them offered by family members after the owners had died. As he read the descriptions, he began seeing himself out on the water. People said it was always changing. Weather conditions, what fish were running, what bait they were hitting. He looked at several, and finally bought a nice twenty-foot Sea Ray. It was fun at first, going out with other club members and learning from them how to fish. But once the cold snap set in, going out alone made him lose interest. Especially after the second Tuesday in March. He can still see himself sitting on the engine housing as his boat silently lolled out into the Gulf of Mexico. The Naples Harbor Patrol gave him a tow, and he hasn't been out since.

Someone Better Than You: A Comedy of Manners

"I have a great idea," he says. "How'd you like to go fishing with your old grandpa?"

Steady mastication. Iris swallows first. "Cool," she says.

"Would dey die?"

"Catch and release," Ritz says. "Any fish we catch, we'll let them go."

"Won' d' ook urd dem?"

"They're different," he says. "They don't feel pain like we do. And they're used to it."

"Only the ones someone caught before, grandpa." Iris is prying skin off her orange. "The rest couldn't be used to it if it never happened to them." Someone committed to the empirical method at ten, Ritz thinks. This kind of granular detail figures often with Iris, and he admires her for it. He believes it's her way of trying to impose order on the chaotic life she is forced to lead.

"'Ow do you d'ow?"

"How do you know," Iris says. "We talked about it in school. People say animals don't feel like people. How do they know? People who eat meat are called carnivores. They kill cows with this thing called a stunbolt gun. Like hitting them on the head with a sledge hammer. How'd *you* like it?"

"Dey dit d'neck on pigs."

Anne laughs at something in the paper, or what's being said. Ritz has been down this ASPCA road before. "We won't slit the necks of the fish," he says. "We'll take the hooks out with needle-nosed pliers and return the fish to their natural habitat. We'll take our own food, and a cooler with soda."

"Water," Iris corrects.

"Water."

Anne looks from the paper. "Didn't you have some problem? Mom said you ran out of gas or something."

"The tank was defective," he lies. "Don't worry, I got it fixed. We wouldn't go out in the Gulf, we'd stay in close. Want to come?"

Anne shakes her head and silently mouths *motion sickness.* Ritz nods, and she turns back to the paper. Good, he thinks. I want them to myself.

He watches them. Iris looks remarkably grown up in the way she's eating her orange. She cuts it from end to end, then removes the peel in sections. That's how Ritz does it. Did she learn that from you? he wonders. The idea is very appealing to him. Her brother is carving a piece of soy cheese into tiny cubes.

"We'll go out," he says. "We'll cruise the flats west of the Gordon River. Probably we'll see some dolphins, maybe even a manatee."

"*Dolphins.*" Iris drops her orange. "Let's go now." Chairs scrape, knees bang the table.

"Not so fast, young lady." Anne again peers over her sunglasses. "Clear the table, please. And wash your hands. And make sure you go potty before leaving. Jammy, that goes for you, too."

Iris pulls open the slider and runs inside. Jamal follows, and Anne resumes her reading. She just sounded exactly like her mother twenty-some years ago. This side of saying no to handling nuclear waste, it's hard to think of Anne giving instructions. But he remembers that first night, passing the guestroom and not hearing the TV.

"Do they help at home?" he asks.

"Damn right they do. They clean their rooms, they help me in the garden." All last fall, Natalie kept giving him sanitized reports about Anne, to make him give up his boycott. He stayed firm, and now regrets it.

"What do you grow?" he asks. "Vegetables, of course."

"And lots of herbs. I have basil you wouldn't believe, I make a pesto to die for. I'll put some together before we leave. Super cabbage. We would've had some nice Brussels sprouts last year, but the bugs did a number. Organic gardening isn't easy."

"I'm sure it isn't."

"I'm putting in more hours at the co-op, and organic's pretty labor-intensive. And lots of flowers this year. You should come see."

"I will."

Anne smiles and returns to the paper. He remembers always finding her retainer on the bathroom sink. In middle school she had a paper route. And played hockey. He hasn't thought of that for years. He sees her smiling at him in her new braces, kneeling with Jane to have their picture taken in front of the fireplace. Both girls are wearing the L.L.Bean crewnecks he got them for Christmas. The photo is upstairs in Natalie's study. Then the hormone tidal wave broke, bringing with it new friends with things to smoke, and later to drop or snort. Things that stirred his anger, and fueled several of his columns.

When he steps through the open slider, the dog is trotting from the family room. Black and wolf-like, she lopes down the hall. As she starts up the stairs, the phone rings. Ritz steps in the kitchen and takes up the receiver.

"Is this Mister Brady Ritz?"

"Speaking."

"Mister two-faced bottom-feeder—"

He hangs up, and follows the dog. As Ritz heads upstairs, he sniffs for something doggy. Nothing. No flea powder, or damp dog hair. As a boy, he loved his dog. Yes, *loved* the little guy, he thinks, climbing. A feisty, up-for-anything black dachshund. That Christmas day, Brady went out to the garage for his sled. He would get his father to pull him and the puppy, but Brady left the door ajar, and his new dog scampered off in the snow.

He reaches the top step and moves along the hall. The guestroom door is open. "Getting ready?" Iris yells something from the bathroom. The dog is on the Aerobed facing him.

That Christmas day, he searched in the new-fallen snow. Crying, looking. Ritz remembers being terrified. Your first crime, he thinks. Losing a helpless dog. But in seconds he found him under snow-covered bushes next to the back porch. You dropped on your knees and scooped him up, he thinks, again feeling snow clinging to the puppy as he cradles him and gets up. Remembers the door being held open by his father and coming inside, crying and saying I'm sorry, your name's Tunnel, I promise to take care of you.

The dog stops panting to regard him. Is she scared? Frightened of men? He read somewhere that many dogs fear men. This one is much bigger than Tunnel, but looks small on a mattress strewn with children's clothes.

He turns away and moves toward the master bedroom. Natalie got Aerobeds when they first moved in, before they bought furniture. He remembers Anne and Iris curled together in slack-jawed sleep, like camera-shy natives in a yurt or teepee.

17
Old Salts

He has maneuvered the Sea Ray out of the marina. Now they are moving up the channel leading to the Gordon River. As the kids helped with the tarp, Brady saw they knew something about boats. Iris asked about life vests. He pointed to float cushions on the seats.

Now he feels chipper. Renewed. It's been over two months since he last went out. He forgot how good it is to stand at the controls and work the wheel. It's a hot, humid day, but the runabout's slow, no-wake progress is producing a breeze. Out here with your grandchildren, Brady thinks. A grandfather teaching them to fish. He wishes the karaoke crowd could see him. And Natalie. And Grunwald. He's following his neighbor's advice by doing good. By helping children on life's journey.

"Tell me about your dog," he says.

"Her name's Truman," Iris says, "but we mostly call her Tru, or Trumie. The way people call Mom Annie and Aunt Jane Janey. Or Jamal Jammy. We got her in Key West, she's a border collie. Or border collie mix. They didn't know."

"Who didn't?" he asks.

"The shelter lady. She's a volunteer. She said this woman dumped her when she got a puppy. I mean the mom in the family got the puppy, not Trumie."

On both shores, houses and foliage hang limp in midday torpor. To the south, bulbous white thunderheads float above bowed palm trees.

"Why the name Truman?" he asks. "What's the story?"

"D' pwesiden," Jamal says.

"The first person who dumped her, the shelter woman said that's where they did it," Iris says. "Where President Truman lived in the winter. Not the president now, the president way back. He always went on his vacation to Key West." Iris pushes back her hair in just the way her mother does. "That's why mom thought we should call her Truman. If you change a dog's name, you're supposed to make it sound like the old one."

He is mildly curious what the often-dumped dog's first name was, but asking would lead to more granular detail. He glances once more at his granddaughter, back to the canal. Her hair is dark red in the sunlight, her skin very pale. She and Jamal will need more protection. Anne rubbed in sunscreen before they left. She steadied each child with a hand, her movements identical to Jane's fussing over Madison in the airport.

"The shelter lady said, when the second dumper person brought her in, Trumie had heart worm. And she was covered with mats, where the fur gets to be like in knots. When dogs are sick with heart worm, Mom says they have to be put to sleep. Because the medicine costs too much. But the shelter lady said the volunteers felt sorry for Trumie, so they gave money. Mom calls it passing the hat."

"I see."

"She's blind in one eye, and her tail's crooked."

Ritz steers right to make way for a massive, grumbling cigarette boat. He is having trouble putting the story together. Out of what must have been lots of dogs to choose from, Anne picked a one-eyed collie with a defective tail. No, he thinks, I get it. *We'll give her a good home, kids. We'll give her a nice home where she can feel safe with just one eye.* Right, Ritz thinks. With just one eye, Trumie won't be as likely to see what's coming her way.

"I'm hod," Jamal tells him. "When do we fiss?"

"This canal leads into a bay," Ritz says. "That's where the fish are. So are the dolphins."

"Mom said to use lots of sunscreen." Iris lifts the canvas sack with towels and snacks, and starts rummaging.

He found the boat advertised in the Naples *Daily News*. Ritz called, and learned the owner had broken his hip. A visit to the Sea Ray website convinced him the boat was underpriced for quick sale. He drove to the address, and walked down to the owner's dock. The boat looked new and spotless. He made his decision, and walked back up the ramp. The owner's house loomed above a broad marble terrace overlooking the bay. Ritz sat at the outdoor tiki bar next to an infinity swimming pool, and wrote out his check. Without looking at it, the owner put it in his pocket. I want to say goodbye, he said. Ritz followed the attendant as he pushed the wheelchair back down the ramp. Take good care of her, the owner said. Eyes moist, he leaned out and patted the hull.

Iris raises her leg to the gunwale, and squeezes out a blob of sunscreen. "Don't forget behind your knees," he says.

Someone Better Than You: A Comedy of Manners

He regrets not having seen them in almost a year. But Ritz was acting on principle. He hasn't seen the father in—he can't remember. The last time, Jeff had shaved his head, this to go with the requisite tattoos, and the heavy crystal bolts that sagged from his earlobes. If Ritz remembers, that was shortly before Jeff and Anne split up. In the years since, Natalie says that along with joining an evangelical mega-church and getting married, Jeff has done well selling replacement windows. Like Anne, he has also sworn off "chemicals." Natalie says Iris and Jamal adore their new half-sister.

Iris finishes smearing on lotion, and hands the bottle to her brother. The Gordon River is just ahead. When he looks again, Jamal is duplicating his sister's movements. He worships Iris, she is his organizational principle. He relies on her to tell him what to do, to serve as his channel or medium, his translator. They have always been locked in a childhood master-slave relationship. Once, though, Jamal was being his passive self in the backseat. Ritz and Natalie were driving them to some point of rendezvous with their nomad mother. Pinched, noogled, bumped and elbowed for an hour by his bored sister, Jamal grabbed Iris's hand and bit it. *"He bit me! He bit me!"* Ritz smiles as he steers the boat. *"Grandpa! He bit me!"* Seeing Jamal in the rearview, he knew the little guy was both shocked and delighted by what he'd done. *Yed, and I'll do id again.* A handsome, tow-headed boy named for a Jamaican healer, a Rastafarian priest.

"Ooh, pretty!"

The canal's last undeveloped tangle of mangrove widens into the Gordon River. Ritz looks both ways before turning to port and bumping the throttle. The breeze strengthens. When Iris and Jamal look to him for permission, he nods. They creep forward to the bow, and kneel side by side on flotation seat cushions. Jeff's parents have a summer house on Chesapeake Bay, which is why Iris and Jamal know something about boats. But Captain Ritz is at the helm today. He feels expansive. Masterful.

And confident. Before casting off, he called to a marina employee painting the bow of a cabin cruiser. The young worker jumped onshore and came over. Ritz gave him a ten to listen to the motor. Jamal and Iris watched as the kid raised the engine housing. He listened, gave a thumbs up. Then he unscrewed the gas cap and checked the fuel level. A second thumbs-up, this one with a wink. That meant he knew why Ritz had come close to floating off into the sunset.

Not today, he thinks. A minute later, he guides the boat under the bridge traffic on 41. The water turns to dark aqua. Mourning doves are perched on the bridge's supports under the rumble of midday traffic. The cooing is audible above the low grumble of the boat's engine.

They emerge into bright sun, and Ritz again bumps the throttle. He's brought three rods with spinning reels, his tackle box. At the marina, be bought a pail of bait shrimp. They work well in the mangrove flats. There are three kinds of mangrove, black, white, red. Knowing these details contributes to his sense of mastery. His former friends taught him to use shrimp. Every fish he's caught has been on shrimp—snapper, sheep head, the rare prized snook or pompano.

For the next mile, architectural excess crowds the shore. A condo complex lifted off the Grand Canal slips behind them. Now come houses inspired by biblical epics, French chateaux, Rome under the Caesars.

Iris looks back at him. "Do people live there?"

"Only in the winter. Most of the houses are empty now. "

"Where are the people?"

"Where's it's cool," Ritz says. "Somewhere less humid."

"Like Michigan. Mom says you'd be in Michigan, except you and Grandma had a fight."

When Ritz says nothing, Iris faces forward. Too much talk, he thinks. Too many empty communications. People at the beach yammering on cell phones, shoving carts down the aisle in supermarkets. His favorite took place in the men's room on Naples Pier. The kid peeing next to him was on the phone with his girlfriend. When he stopped talking to listen, a turd plopped in a toilet stall, delivered by a man talking to his broker. No to pork bellies, yes to orange juice.

People are waving from the large pontoon boat coming toward them. Iris and Jamal wave back. Ritz nods as they pass, a skipper with grandchildren keeping both hands on the wheel. He wishes Murray Grunwald could see him, and the karaoke line dancers.

Being responsible and knowledgeable, he thinks. Being right. A purveyor of grandparent *lore*. He feels liberated from angst and critics. After the episode with Tushy, he lost track of how much he missed Iris and Jamal. Natalie said the boycott meant he was a short-ball hitter as a grandfather. As he steers the boat, Ritz knows she was right. He was always glad to see them arrive, tumbling out of the car, racing into the house to reclaim it. But also grateful when they left. Early on, Ritz had instituted the Rule of Seventy-two. He held up well for three days, but then the half-life of his tolerance began to degrade.

"Gwampa! Dobbins!"

Both children are craning to see, holding to the chrome guardrail. "Right," he says. "What kind?"

"Bottlenose!" Iris says.

"Very good!"

"Look, a baby!"

After several seconds, the three dolphins rise together, and coil beneath the surface. "Get cloder, gwampa, cloder!"

"Okay, hold on." Where the dolphins will come up next is anybody's guess, but Ritz changes direction to please the boy. It's a metaphor. Where does anything come up next? At the point where they disappeared, he puts the engine in neutral. The boat lolls in a light chop. The air grows warm.

"We'll see others," he says. "This is good dolphin weather."

"Why?" Iris asks. "What makes it good?"

Both children are gripping the handrail, peering over the side. Iris looks back at him for an answer. Ritz meant *all* weather is good for dolphins, but that's not enough. He's at the helm, the skipper, full of sea wisdom. Yesterday's karaoke experience has made him needy of success. He hopes dolphins weren't in last year's curriculum. "They mate in the winter," he says. "December, January. That's why these two have a baby. They're the parents."

Someone Better Than You: A Comedy of Manners

Iris frowns before turning back to the water. "It takes nine months for a human baby to be born," she says. "Dad says dolphins are a lot like people. He says they have bigger brains than we do. Why do they have a baby so soon? Is it a preemie?"

"Mother Nature works in mysterious ways," he says.

Iris again looks back at him. Standing at the controls, Ritz smiles the benign smile of an old tar. But he needs to steer things away from dolphin reproduction. "Tell me about school," he says. "What was your favorite subject last semester?"

When Iris turns back to study the water, Jamal does the same. "I hade mudic," he says. "I hade d'deeder."

"His music teacher is a nerd," Iris explains. "She makes them sing the same songs over and over, they never get new ones from now. Just 'You Are My Sunshine' and 'I've Been Working on the Railroad.'"

Too close to home. "How about you?" Ritz asks. "What's your favorite class?"

"FACS. Family and Consumer Science."

Idling much longer will make his boat a nuisance in the channel. Ritz shifts from neutral, and bumps the throttle. "What do they teach? How to shop as a family?"

"No, grandpa. We cook in FACS."

"Okay. What have you cooked lately?"

"Cookies."

"Were they good?"

"They were okay. You want me to make some?"

"We could do that," he says. With luck, Iris will forget about Family and Consumer Science before they get home. Did

Sunshine Urbanski take FACS in school? On off days, does she bake? He hasn't thought of her all week.

"Do you cook alone, or as part of a group?" he asks.

"In teams." Both children are still looking over the bow. "There are five or six in each team," Iris tells him. "Depending on how many are in school that day. How many are sick or something. There are five jobs. One is head cook, one is dish washer, one is dish drier. There's another person does the actual cooking with the head cook. That's the secondary cook we call him or her. And the last person in the team is the cleanup person. To clean everything that needs cleaning besides dishes. The counter, the sink. We made no-bake cookies last time. Oatmeal and chocolate chip. The recipe says you can put in peanut butter, but we didn't because of allergies. And the teacher said also because of lawyers. You mix the cookie dough with plastic gloves, and make it into cookies on a cookie sheet."

A fully articulated organizational flow chart. "I came in second as team leader," Iris says. "I was so mad, just because Janine didn't rinse out the skimmer thing in the sink. Otherwise, I would've been first. They give awards for it."

"Did you get one?"

"For second place."

"I god one."

"That's good."

Jamal is leaning over too far, holding on but angled precariously. Watch him like a hawk, Anne said as they left. He has limited impulse control. "Please don't, Jamal," Ritz says. "Never take chances out on the water. We don't want an accident."

Jamal leans back, and Ritz focuses ahead. Buoys mark the widening channel. Soon, the palatial houses will be replaced by inlets and passages into the tangled mangrove. The western sky is cloudless; he would like to go south to Marco Island, but what happened in the gulf is still fresh. He must be responsible.

"So, young man, you got an award too," he says. "Was it for cookies?"

"It wad bor being a deerbul berdon who may briend eadly."

"A cheerful person who makes friends easily."

No child left behind. Last spring, it seemed every third house in Ritz's Michigan community had posted signs congratulating someone for graduating from middle school or high school. One read "Congratulations to Lindsey for passing third grade!" Ritz wanted to post a sign commending the unborn for reaching the second trimester, but knew how far that would get. By the time his four grandchildren reach high school, the walls of their rooms will be covered with framed plaques and citations. He sees Jamal and Iris on the stage of a high school auditorium, festooned with diplomatic sashes and medals. Their peers go mad as brother and sister thrust Lucite trophies above their heads.

Iris screams and Jamal grabs for the dolphins. In the second it takes them to surface and vanish, Jamal tumbles. Ritz reaches fast and grabs the boy's forearm.

Against the boat's forward motion, he hauls Jamal back over the gunwale. The boat is turning sharply—he is still gripping the steering wheel for leverage. Jamal could have been caught by the motor's prop. You should have thrown float cushions, Ritz thinks. Then just circled back and picked him up. He corrects the steering before letting go of the boy and throttling back. Jamal is dripping, bowed over on the floor, crying and coughing. Iris works her way from the bow and kneels in front of him. "It's okay," she says. "Grandpa told you not to lean out—"

He isn't crying from fear or embarrassment. Or to cover up for doing something wrong. "What is it?" Ritz now has the boat trimmed and moving at medium speed. "Come on, Jamal, you're all right. You got a little wet, that's all. We'll be fishing in five minutes."

"I think he's hurt." Iris is still kneeling in front of her brother, patting his knee. "Come on, Jammy, he didn't mean it. Don't you want to fish?" The boy is sobbing. Face contorted, he cradles his arm and looks up. You didn't need to grab him, Brady thinks. All you had to do was throw the cushions.

"It's all right, son." He turns the boat in a slow curve. "Be brave. We'll go back, you'll be fine. We'll go fishing some other time."

"I'm dod your dun," Jamal says. He coughs, and yells in pain.

18
E.R.

Framed by the divide in the muslin curtain, Iris looks even taller to him. She is stretched out thirty feet away, on a sectional sofa in the waiting room. She is by herself, watching a wall-mounted TV. It's a soap opera, a young couple sharing a tense moment. Flashing eyes, lashing hair. A slap is followed by a crushing embrace.

Iris is too big for her skimpy denim shorts. She looks forlorn, a lanky waif he would like to cheer up. Take to Barnes & Noble to get her a book, do anything for that might restore her lively, child-on-the-cusp-of-adolescence self.

"Okay, I guess that's all."

The nurse seated in front of Ritz is still typing on her laptop. She wears a smock and white slacks, no nurse's cap. Traditional uniforms must now be viewed as emblems of servitude. These days, the only way to see a nurse in a white uniform is to watch soap operas or *Turner Classic Movies.*

The smock is floral, the nurse Hispanic. Small and serious, she has her black hair held in place by a barrette like Madison's. Still clicking away, perhaps she finished her report and is now working on an email to her cousin in Guadalajara. But the typing is intimidating. Three times she asked Ritz how it happened. Two times how often it happened before. That he regularly abuses children by dislocating their arms was taken for granted.

She stops typing and gives him a wintry smile before she stands and steps through the curtain. When he looks again, Iris is gone. He remembers the still-wet boy seated in the back of the police car that came to the dock. Ritz is seated up front, so the Collier County deputy can keep an eye on him. Jamal is cradling his arm as Iris talks to him. Finger prints and dried matter obscure the Plexiglass between front and back seats. It's a reality TV show, the kind Ace Foley watches between ESPN sports and *Bang News*.

The image should not be sordid or shaming, but to Ritz it feels like fate. The man who has angered so many people is the same one responsible for Jamal's suffering. The one who didn't think to throw float cushions.

Voices sound above the TV. An old man is moaning, and now Ritz hears his stepdaughter. He thinks she sounds matter-of-fact. Feet approach, the curtain is swept aside.

"Hi there, I'm Doctor Rouse." Ritz stands. A tall man in a lab coat steps in, followed by Anne. "You're —" he looks at his clipboard "—Mister Ritz?"

"Yes."

"Captain Ritz?" The rangy, boyish black doctor smiles. "Sorry," he says. "My little joke. What happened is called Nursemaid's Elbow. If you're into medical jargon, the term is radial head subluxation. It's very common, and not just among yachtsmen grandparents." The smile broadens. "It can happen very easily. The bones of someone Jamal's age slip easily in and out of alignment. There's usually no real injury, it's just painful."

"He took Jamal's arm and popped it *once*," Anne says. "It was amazing. The pain stopped like *right that second*."

"I'm glad," Ritz says. "I'm sorry."

"Okay, you're good to go," the doctor says. "Take him home and fix him up with some ice cream." He shakes Ritz's hand, and leaves. Ritz and Anne follow. "Where are they?" he asks.

"Waiting in the lobby."

He has trouble keeping up with her. Did she dress for the hospital? Replacing her bikini are a white linen shirt and slacks. The old man is still gasping behind one of the curtains. When they pass the nurse's station, his interrogator is studying a chart, and doesn't look up. They pass through double doors and move down the hall.

"I can't believe you wouldn't put life vests on them," she says, marching. A patient using a walker angles out of the way. "I really can't."

"Nobody goes fishing in a vest," he says. "Vests are for jet skis. The boat's full of floatation cushions."

"Why didn't you use them?"

Why didn't he? This is not the breezy, cue sera sera Anne he knows. Marching down the waxy hall, she offers no cheerful "Hi" as they pass a patient pushing an I.V. pole. That's what she always does in public places, greets people. Strangers, security guards. Somehow, Anne's Birkenstocks and tan make her look much older.

"Even Jeff's crazy parents have enough sense to use vests out on Chesapeake Bay," she says. "Why didn't you throw some cushions? I talked to Iris. She says you yanked him like a sack of corn. What were you thinking, pulling him that way?"

She's right. He didn't think. "Anne, please—" He waits until they pass a custodian using a mop. "It happened very fast."

"I told you to keep an eye on him."

"I kept both eyes on him," Ritz says. "I wore corrective lenses. I drove slowly and carefully. I made sure they drank lots of water, I made sure —"

"Yeah, look what happened."

Ritz doesn't answer. Nothing he might say is going to matter. What happened took place when he was supposed to be in charge. But as they near the main lobby, another thought comes to him. Anne has picked her moment. Three nights ago, she was easygoing. A one-woman booster club for *Vanitas* full of memorized quotes. Now, she's taking full advantage of his mistake. She, too, resents what he wrote. All along she was lying in the tall grass, waiting to pounce.

* * *

During the drive, Iris and her brother keep quiet in the backseat. Anne has replaced the sheriff's deputy at the wheel, but Ritz is still under surveillance in the molester's seat. The boy's injury hasn't required a sling, but when Ritz turns to check on him, Jamal uses his good hand to hold up the injured arm. Ritz faces forward.

Back at the house, Anne lets both children put on their swimming suits and go in the pool. "But do *not* use your arm," she tells Jamal. "And you, Iris, no fighting. No beating with noodles." She goes inside.

He watches them. Jamal shows no sign of favoring his arm. After a minute, Ritz goes inside. The family room is empty. When he looks in his study, Anne isn't there conducting grid business on her laptop. He goes upstairs to give her more details, to put himself in a better light. At the open guest bedroom he sees her on her knees next to the Aerobed.

"What's this?"

"I don't blame you." She stuffs Jamal's canister of ball bearings into an open duffle bag.

"You're leaving? You're taking them back with you to Key West?"

"I'll just feel better."

"So they can study cooperative small-business promotion? They seem a little young."

"We'll manage." Anne keeps stuffing things into the bag—shorts, books, dirty socks. "We always do," she adds. "They have daycare and supervision at the hotel. Someone will be looking after them when I'm in meetings."

"Someone more responsible than their grandfather," he says. "This is payback plain and simple, you see this as an opportunity—"

"No, I don't. Even though you haven't liked me for twenty years, I don't."

"How do you think Iris and Jamal will understand this? As a reaction to what happened, how else? As being protected from dangerous contact with Grandpa Brady."

"What do you care? You're boycotting us, remember? Besides, it gives you more proof I'm a shitty mom. It should make you happy, you can write about it."

She goes on jamming in dirty laundry. Toys, DVDs, books and shoes go into a second canvas duffle. Truman is lying before the brightly lighted bathroom, watching. She seems mildly interested. No, Ritz thinks. The dog looks resigned. Stoical.

"That's why I let them have a last swim." Anne gets up. "Look out, Trumie—" She steps over the dog, into the bathroom. Things made of plastic clatter into a cosmetics bag. "I don't want them to dislike you. I'll just feel better having them with me."

Ritz shoves his hands in his pockets. "Take the boat," he says. "It'll be faster."

This stops her. Anne turns from the sink holding a tube of toothpaste. "Not *my* boat," he says. "The shuttle to Key West from Marco Island. It takes just three hours. You can catch it tomorrow morning on Marco, I'll drive you. You can leave your car here and rent one in Key West. It'll save you the drive. I'll pay for it."

This is a simple bribe to keep Anne and her children with him overnight. His stepdaughter loves novelty, never turns down such opportunities. He's sure she's never taken the shuttle to Key West.

"No." Anne reaches to the sink for a bottle of shampoo. "No more boats," she says. "I don't want Jamal to hate being on the water."

*   *   *

Down in the kitchen, he opens the freezer compartment and shoves through rock-hard tubs of lasagna and chicken. Sacks of frozen peas and green beans. One of Natalie's few guilty pleasures is sweets. Concealed at the back are chocolate eclairs, and a quart of butter pecan. Death Row delicious—that's what she calls her favorite desserts.

He peels off the ice cream lid. I am not on Neighborhood Watch lists, he thinks, and brings down bowls from the cupboard. I don't *do* abuse. He gouges out generous helpings of ice cream, then pulls open the refrigerator and begins a second search. But he must act quickly. If Anne catches him, there will be a lecture on empty calories.

He finds chocolate syrup, and squeezes a generous glob over each mound of butter pecan. Then Ashley's fire-retardant whipped cream. With a spoon stuck in each bowl, he hustles outside. "Guess what, Jammy? Remember doctor's orders? He said to give you ice cream. It's medicine."

Shouts of approval. The children start slogging their way across the pool. Good, they will eat fast, knowing to collude with Grandpa. It's a relief to see them smiling again, working their way toward him. Jamal doesn't seem to be favoring his injured arm. Ritz kneels down and hands each of them a bowl.

"I hope you're not mad at me, Jammy."

"D'o."

"I just wanted to get you out of that water."

"Ogay. Did id good."

"I'm glad, young man. I guess your mom's decided to take you two back with her to Key West."

Iris loads up her spoon. "Because of what happened? It wasn't your fault."

She puts the spoon in her mouth. As Natalie always does, she closes her eyes. "It's not that," Ritz says. "Mom just thinks she'll feel better if you're with her. She says there's lots of fun things to do at the hotel."

Like video poker in the bar, he thinks. Or shopping with husbands in the hotel gift shop, looking for something at the last minute to give the wife after a week of fishing and boozing. The two children are now in a semi-trance. He wishes they weren't leaving. They aren't even halfway through the Rule of Seventy-two.

19
Sturm und Drang

An hour later, he checks to be sure they're safely strapped in the backseat of Anne's Jeep Liberty. The interior is littered with CDs and empty water bottles, fliers from concerts, books on homeopathic medicine. He slams the door and comes around. Anne buzzes down her window. "Call me when you get there," Ritz says. "It's a long drive. I wish you'd wait and take the shuttle."

She shifts her eyes to the back, to remind him why this won't work. While the children were rinsing off, Ritz got two hundred-dollar bills from his shoe box. Conscience money, he thought. Now he tucks them in Anne's breast pocket. "For the hemp boutique," he tells her. She pats the pocket and nods, then backs down the drive. As the car moves toward Donegal Boulevard, Iris and Jamal may be waving. He can't tell but waves back. Plastered on the Jeep's tailgate are stickers for bands and causes.

The late-afternoon sky is bright, the driveway's brick pavers warm under his boat shoes. To the south, cumulonimbus thunderheads have formed. With the coming of hot weather, the clouds roll up from the Caribbean, evolving and hypnotic, like the aftermath of nuclear explosions. So much color brings Jane to him. She hoists Madison on her hip, then places her hand flat on his chest.

"Hey Meester Brady—"

Coco Ruiz is standing in his black getup on Grunwald's driveway. He starts across the lawn. "Dottor G get a call. Some lady name Daisy."

"Daisy Pruitt."

"That one." Coco reaches the drive, and points to the end of the cul-de-sac. "The guy across the street? Ace? Dottor G say he down there an' you should go get him."

"It might be better if you went. Mrs. Pruitt and I aren't on the best of terms."

"Dottor G say I make her scared if she see me." Coco smiles. "He say she lock herself in a closet and you should go. She call him from in there."

Ritz starts down the street. Foley lost track while running, and let himself into the wrong house. Before February, Daisy would have called Ritz, but now she prefers a blind man to come to the rescue. She has had lots of "work" done, along with blazingly white porcelain caps installed on her teeth. Last year, she went in for a second liposuction procedure on her stomach. That was well after Ritz had written about cosmetic surgery, but it doesn't matter. Now she hates him.

The rumble of thunder rolls from the south. The sky is still bright, but Anne will soon be tunneling her way through sheets of rain. If it's still pouring when she reaches the Seven Mile Bridge to the Keys, they may close it. Good. Anne will have to pull over and wait. If he hadn't hurt Jamal, they'd all still be here.

He nears Daisy's house. It's a ranch, with heavy emphasis on yard art. Two life-size greenish bronze alligators peer out from under ferns. On the right, cranes stand sentinel under two

Christmas palms. The palms form a canopy above a rock waterfall cascading into a pool. Two ceramic lions flank the entry.

He steps between them, and cups the screen. The heavy front door hangs open. "Daisy?" He opens the screen, enters the foyer. All Ritz hears is the steady luff of air conditioning. "Ace!"

He listens a moment. Daisy has nothing to fear. Ace Foley's conquests are sports-related, like senior marathons and ski ropes held in his teeth. Of course another possibility is that the widow Pruitt would *like* Ace to conquer her extensively restored body. Ritz moves into the house and opens the door to the study. The TV room. A laundry room. When he pushes open the fourth door, Ace is seated on the edge of the bathtub. Eyes closed, he is furiously masturbating. Ritz shuts the door.

"Is he still in there?" Daisy is at the far end of her living room, with something on her head.

"Hi, Daisy. Yes, he is."

"Oh, it's you."

"Murray asked me to come."

"Why didn't he come himself?"

"He's not seeing very well these days."

"I don't like you in my house. I heard what you did at the club. What's wrong with you?"

"Ace will be out soon." Foley looked to be near climax. "We'll leave when he's done."

"What made you think you had a right to go writing about people the way you did?"

Standing next to her glass door wall, Daisy forms a black cutout. "Who said you could do that? I feel sorry for Natalie. I really do, being married to someone like you. Everyone despises you, you know that, don't you? Everyone, I'm not exaggerating. Come in here, move down here. People are nice to you, have you over for drinks. Play golf and bridge with you, go out to dinner. What do you do? You insult them. Attack them like it's funny. For your information, mister, I got porcelain caps on doctor's orders. They don't 'blaze brighter than Ronald Reagan's,' they retard decay. I tried everything this side of bariatric surgery to lose weight. Weight my doctor said I *had* to lose. 'Lose weight or die,' those were his exact words. That's the sole reason for the liposuction."

Ritz looks to the closed bathroom. "Ace! Finish up in there!"

Looking back at Daisy, all at once he feels exhausted. Small-boat handling, dolphins, child abuse, interrogations, bribery, hasty leave-taking. Daisy Pruitt is not wrong, and just now he has no answer for her.

A sigh issues from behind the door. "Clean up, okay!" A toilet-paper roll rattles in the dispenser. Ritz turns back to Daisy. "I wasn't talking about you or anyone else," he says. "That's all I can tell you. If I hurt your feelings, I'm sorry."

The toilet flushes. For several seconds, Daisy Pruitt doesn't answer. "I'm old." She comes toward him. "I'm alone." As she may intend, her words are underscored by her pink mules scuffing the rug in a defeated way. "My children live in Seattle and Maine. Their children *hate* coming here."

Still scuffing, she reaches to the wall. Recessed lights come on with garish effect. The plastic bag on her head is similar to the one Natalie wears when she tints her hair. The effect on Daisy is to isolate her face under the unforgiving ceiling light. She stops in front of him, round-shouldered, diminished. Her shorty housecoat is aqua. Above each knee are eyebrow-like creases. When Ritz looks back at her, he sees Daisy's eyebrows are tattoos.

The bathroom door opens, but she doesn't shift her gaze. "It hasn't happened to you yet," she says. "That's why you think you can do anything and say anything. But it's going to happen, mister. Mark my words, it's going to happen to you sooner than you know."

As he steps out, Foley is adjusting his golf shorts. "How you doing, Daisy?"

She doesn't look at him. She nods at Ritz and raises jet black eyebrows. "You'll see." She turns and walks away without scuffing.

"Buzz, what's the problem?"

"Let's go."

He waits for Foley to step out and open the screen. "Why the hell did we come here?" Ritz follows and closes the door. "Her toilet paper smells like avocados. What's *that* about?"

20
Heavy Weather

"I don't know what's come over you," Natalie says again. "I really don't. I meant what I said before. I honestly wish you'd go back to faking it."

Once Ritz got Foley back home and returned to his own house, the answering machine was blinking. "'What's come over you?'" he says. "Nothing's come over or under me. How would my faking it keep Jamal from jumping out of a boat?"

"I hate when you're sarcastic," she says. "You weren't before."

"I was always sarcastic."

"Not like this. And before, you would never let a child of yours get in a boat without a life vest."

"Keep things straight, don't mix sarcasm with what actually happened. 'Child of yours—' Jesus, Natalie, one cliché after another."

"There it is again, repeating what I say. You know what I mean. Any child you're responsible for."

"Please answer me this. This is not sarcasm, just answer this. Describe all the times you've seen me strapping someone into a life vest."

A safe question. The Sea Ray is the first and certainly the last boat Ritz will ever own. To do her wifely duty, Natalie went out twice with her "yachtsman husband." Both times she clutched the gunwale, waiting for it to be over. Back on shore after her second "brush with death" (Natalie knows a thing or two about sarcasm), she watched as he tied up. Okay, she said. I sort of see the appeal, but no more Moby Dick for me. By the look on her face, Ritz saw she had actually been frightened.

"Yes, it's sarcasm," she says again. "It's sidestepping the whole thing. We could have had a family tragedy. We could have proved true every awful thing their other grandparents think about us. You've had it in for Anne since she was thirteen. Do you *ever* think what the effect was? An editor stepfather full of words and sarcasm arguing with a teenager? Winning every time, like you were having a pissing match with yourself?"

The image is confusing, but somehow true. It shuts him down. When Anne started rebelling, he bullied her.

"By 'other grandparents,' you mean the people in Baltimore with the surveillance recordings," he says.

"See? You're doing it again," she says. "Sidestepping. You know I don't really care what they think. What I care about is Iris and Jamal and Anne."

"So do I, Natalie." *Anne* is the one risking a family tragedy—that's what Ritz wants to say. Risking herself and her children by trashing him on her cell phone as she drives one-handed to Key West in a downpour. But there is truth in what his wife is saying. He's been suspicious and critical of Anne for a long time.

"I know you care," she says, relenting. "Even with your boycott. Why I don't' know, but I do. Did they take plenty of water and food?"

This side of loading her car with cases of military Meals Ready to Eat, yes. But no more sarcasm. "They left with a case of water, and a large cooler of snacks and fruit," he says. "All the fruit was from Green Thumb."

"She said it looked like rain."

"It's summer—" *No more sarcasm* "—that means lots of big clouds. The kind you like."

"If it gets bad, she promised to pull off the road. I don't want them on the Seven Mile Bridge in a downpour."

"No."

"You say Foley walked into Daisy Pruitt's?"

"He was in her powder room. 'Pleasuring himself,' I think is the euphemism."

After a beat, his wife says, "Daisy is a decent person. How can I come back down there? How do I face anyone? How can I walk down the street and just say hello? It's terrible."

"Natalie—"

"No, Buzz. Really, you just don't get it. You still think everyone else is wrong, not you. You always have. You're fine with all this. You have your friends, golf. The boat. It's different for you. You don't care what people think. I can't be seen down there, not this way. Maybe not ever."

"I don't have friends," Ritz says. "A blind retired internist and a dead-at-the-top priapic jogger. That's it."

He is upstairs in their bedroom, and moves to the French doors. "That's it," he says. "Murray and Foley are the only ones here who give me the time of day. I haven't played golf or tennis in four months." He opens the doors and steps outside. Grunwald isn't on his deck. Ritz will *not* tell Natalie about the karaoke fiasco. "And what does that mean, you won't come back *this way*?"

She doesn't answer. "Murray thinks I just need to wait it out," he says. "If I 'do good deeds,' he thinks it'll blow over. Please stop being so dramatic. Does *this way* mean having to be seen with me? Is that it?"

Again Natalie doesn't answer. His karaoke mistake has almost certainly made matters worse. Deepened his pariah status. Confirmed him as a blinder of puppies, a man who steals songs from karaoke singers with no larynx. In the lengthening silence, Ritz now very clearly sees his wife walking up the street—and here comes Daisy Pruitt. Will Daisy stop to commiserate? Will she comfort the woman married not just to a man *like* Ritz, but to The Thing Itself? First comes a look of surprised recognition, followed by a raised chin free of turkey wattles. Now a nod and minimal greeting. Or, Natalie stops, reaches out to Daisy and makes some humbling apology. Or does Natalie keep moving? Does she tough it out and keep walking? Those are her choices. It pains him, seeing Natalie by herself, walking away. All on her lonesome.

"Listen," he says. "If you fly down, we could take the shuttle to Key West. We could see Anne and the kids. Come on, say yes. This time of year, you can get a flight any time."

His wife sighs. It's *her* sigh. *That* sigh. More than at any time these past months, Ritz wants his wife to say yes. For almost thirty years they've developed a domestic set of signals, a private language. Sighs, clucks of the tongue. It shocks him a little. At this point—before *it happens to you*—most of what matters is all about language. Gesture.

"'Lo?"

He says it in the faded falsetto voice they both use. 'Lo is short for Hello. They picked it up at a bed & breakfast in Stratford, Ontario. They were there to see plays, and the B&B inn keeper had trained his cockatoo to say "hello" to guests. Since then, hearing "'Lo" called from upstairs signals whoever got up first that the late sleeper is awake and ready for coffee.

"Poor Daisy," Natalie says, ignoring their private code. "I read over what you wrote about cosmetic surgery. Can't you understand how *exposed* she must feel? How vulnerable? I don't mean with you, I mean with everyone who reads what you wrote. Before, she was Daisy Pruitt. Now she's the liposuction lady."

She was the liposuction lady *after* he wrote about it, but this time Ritz holds his tongue.

"Are you visiting Murray?" she asks. "What does he say?" Ritz repeats Grunwald's advice about doing good deeds, acts contrition and penance. "He's a very good man," Natalie says. "Please say hello for me. Ask him to give my love to Esther."

"I will." Natalie says nothing more. As seconds pass, the silence becomes threatening. An LP waiting for someone to pick up the needle. "Natalie?"

"Murray's a very good man, and he likes you. That means something. Buzz, I think you used your own name on purpose."

"Please, Natalie—"

"Let me finish. You used your own name because deep down you knew you hurt people. You felt bad about what you wrote and wanted to be punished. That's why you said nothing to Jane."

"Is this from *The Doctor Phil Show*? Did Doctor Phil do a follow-up to his series on repressed memory?"

"I didn't get it from anywhere, I just believe it. Goodbye, Buzz, take care of yourself."

She hangs up, but Ritz keeps the phone to his ear. If he puts it down, her goodbye will be real in some final way. Ridiculous, more histrionics. Natalie says goodbye that way all the time. *Goodbye, take care of yourself.* It's generic, like Jane's *I suppose you'll be all right.* An air-conditioned breeze passes over his sweaty scalp.

Much like a slow-rolling bowling ball, thunder comes from the south. As Ritz lowers the phone, he looks out at the fairway. Two golf carts are passing on the far side, moving fast to beat the rain. Below in the pool, two green foam noodles are slowly turning. Iris and Jamal love flogging each other with them. Ritz doubts they will ever have any connection so intense. They play a pool game with sea shells, throwing them from the deck, diving to retrieve them. They keep the shells in plastic buckets, and insist *my* shells must be kept separate from *yours*.

The water undulates. After Christmas, before everything went to hell, Jane and her family came down. Right after Ashley's Wise Person performance. Ritz remembers watching her from up here, how she managed the stainless steel steps and handrail all on her own.

The pool's sheen now puckers with the first drops. Another golf cart trundles into view.

He goes in and lowers himself on the bed. Her father was toweling her off, and Ashley pointed. It's changing, she said. Dan explained how the pool pump had shut down for the night, how the water would soon turn smooth. She made her mother, sister, and Natalie come out to watch, until all motion stopped. The Jell-O hour, Ashley said. The pump was making Jell-O, and now it's done.

After a moment he rolls to his nightstand, opens the drawer and takes out his book.

Why bother? He starts to put it back, but a growl of thunder leads him to open it. He flips to the page listing the original publication dates for his columns. Yes, he wrote "Turkey Wattles No More" and the column on liposuction the year before he and Natalie moved in. Before they met Daisy Pruitt at a party for new owners.

But it doesn't matter. And Murray was right about being legalistic. That's what you're doing, Brady thinks. Justifying yourself with timing and dates. It doesn't matter what you wrote, or when. You alone chose what to include in *Vanitas*, no one else.

He returns the book to the drawer, gets up and shuts the French doors. Just as Ritz crosses the room, lightning stabs down through the two skylights in the hall. For half a second the flash reveals Jane's pictures. How good if in that eye-blink some message came to him from her paintings.

At the guest bedroom, he eases open the door. The weak light coming through half-closed drapes makes the Aerobed's rumpled sheets take on an abandoned look. A sharp crack shakes the house, followed in seconds by a heavy *thud*. It keeps going, the bowling ball dropping step-by-step down a flight of stairs. In the hall, Jane's pictures knock against the wall. Metal coat hangers cymbal in a closet.

Native peoples. He goes over and kneels down. Anne's patchouli scent lies with him as he stretches out on his stomach. He identifies other smells—sunscreen, toothpaste.

The bed is vibrating.

Ritz rolls off. After a moment, he places his hand on the heaped bedding. Her dog. She forgot it. So anxious to get away, she forgot her dog. His boyhood dachshund shook just this way during storms. He crawled under blankets just this way. Fled to the basement on his funny, short outturned paws to burrow under dirty laundry. Ritz would follow him down and sit with him, stroking his back.

"It's all right, please calm down, I'm here, take it easy—" He keeps his hand on the mounded bedding. It's awful to him, the dog's fear under his hand. He keeps repeating the words, stroking.

II

You dream that you might
keep it in your head.
But memories, where will you take them to?
Take one last look at them.
They end with you.

Clive James, "Star System"

21
Truman

Another flash is followed by heavy artillery. "Okay, almost over, good dog—" He keeps talking, stroking. Just as her shaking seems to slow, a new bomb brings it back.

Another explosion sinks away. Ritz brings up his watch. Almost nine. The storm has lasted twenty minutes, and seems to be moving east. Five minutes later, all that remains is a light pattering on the skylights. Natalie loves the sound. She says it makes her think of people applauding with gloves on.

He decides it's safe to peel back the covers. The dog is curled up and doesn't raise her head. Muzzle tucked into her belly, she is looking at him with her good eye. When he strokes her again, still she doesn't move. Her coat is soft to the touch. Anne's childhood allergies had ruled out pets.

"Maybe that's why she got Tushy." He continues stroking. "She couldn't have a pet growing up. She says vegetables cured her allergies." He feels a need to comfort. "See? Storm's over, what did I tell you? Nothing to it, piece of cake. This is nothing, believe me. By Florida standards, this is child's play. It's something you have to get used to down here, you just have wait it out."

Down here. Anne didn't bring the dog from Michigan. Truman is a Floridian. As Ritz keeps stroking, the idea is all at once painful. Heartbreaking. How many rainy seasons has she lived through? How many terrifying storms? How old is she?

Truman remains motionless but alert, listening for more thunder. When he again checks his watch, she unfolds her left paw and places it on his knee.

"I can do that, that I can do—" He resumes stroking. The dog retracts the paw and once more settles her muzzle into her belly. Ritz is at a loss. He has to pee. Lightning strikes mean he will need to re-set the microwave clock. Truman keeps her good eye on him.

"I had a dog," he says. "Tunnel, a dachshund. They were bred to hunt badgers and moles. Scrappy little dogs. We used to play ball. I tossed it, he went tearing across the neighbor's lawn and brought it back. In the house I got down on the floor, in the living room. I rolled the ball under the sofa. This sofa had fringe along the bottom, like a stage curtain. Tunnel was that short, he could pull himself under. When I rolled the ball through the fringe, he flipped it back with his nose. Right through the fringe, *exactly* to where I was on the floor. He did that as long as I wanted. He was a great little dog."

The rain has stopped. Ritz is crying, and needs to pee. He gets up quickly, goes in the bathroom and closes the door. But swings it back open, so the dog can see him.

"When were you out last?" he calls over his stream. "Did she walk you before coming to save her children from Doctor Mengele? That's been about four hours. I'm sorry, Truman." He shakes himself and zips up before tearing off toilet paper and blowing his nose. He drops the paper, flushes, and steps out. "We'll take a walk, then get something to eat. What do you think?"

We'll get something to eat, what do you think?

Someone Better Than You: A Comedy of Manners

Jesus. Except: the way she unfolded her paw and placed it on his knee. Ritz moves into the hall and looks over his shoulder. Truman is now standing, looking at him. Several seconds pass before she again settles herself on the inflatable bed. "Come on—" he beckons "—let's go." As she again starts to uncurl herself, Ritz moves to the stairs. He is halfway down when she slips past.

Just the way she did on Tuesday. It elates him. How good it was as a boy to be trusted. To be thought of as someone worth following. An expansive satisfaction accompanies his own leisurely steps as Truman's rump bounces down in front of him. She reaches the foyer, and again faces the entry. Once Ritz opens the door, she'll see the storm is over, further proof he is a good, trustworthy person.

"They usually last fifteen or twenty minutes," he says. "We'll get some air, then have Happy Hour and eat something." He forgot the leash. "Stay here."

Ritz turns on lights and moves down the hall. Did Anne leave more vegetable glop for her dog? In the kitchen he checks the refrigerator. The counters. Cupboards. What is he looking for, cans? A sack of kibble? Finding nothing, he opens the freezer. The butter pecan ice cream rests next to packages of frozen mixed vegetables. He hasn't touched anything in here since Natalie left. Why? he wonders. Do you think of it the way Jamal and Iris think of sea shells? Her food, not yours? He moves rock-hard plastic tubs of spaghetti and beef Stroganoff before prying loose a package of tuna steaks. Wrong, he thinks. Natalie made it for you before she left.

Ritz closes the freezer and drops the steaks on the island. He grabs the leash off the counter stool and walks back. Truman is now lying in front of the door, under the foyer's chandelier. When he comes around, she doesn't meet his eyes. She is handsome. The blaze on her chest extends up her neck to her muzzle. It runs in a line between her eyes, into the soft furrow down the middle of her head. You *know* what's going on, Ritz thinks. Anthropomorphizing, personifying. It doesn't matter. Her extended, Sphinx-like white front paws make her a striking presence on the marble floor. Her good brown right eye seems more lustrous for being matched with the sightless milky left.

"What do you think? Should we go?"

He opens the door, and she stands. When Ritz steps into the screened enclosure, only then does Truman venture forward. He opens the screen door, and she moves quickly to the lawn and starts smelling. He knows border collies are smart overachievers. With the exception of golden retrievers, they figure most often in the magazine ads he has flipped through for months at the library.

He steps out and closes the screen. The focused intensity of Truman's movements makes her look as though she's been here all her life. You just want to see her that way, Ritz thinks. Any sophomore psych major could see you want the dog to feel she belongs here. That this is home.

She reaches the street. "Truman—"

A second or two passes before she looks at him. He raises the leash. When she begins walking back, his heart skips. Unlike everyone here, the dog accepts him. He bends, she steps between his knees and lowers her head for him to clip on the leash. Together they start down the path.

At Donegal Boulevard they turn north, away from the clubhouse. Dinner is over, and those who stayed for coffee and liqueurs will be heading home. Ritz wants them to see him with a nice dog, but not now. Not so close to the karaoke fiasco. He used to be up at the bar watching sports, in his just-one-of-the-guys persona. That's what it was, Ritz thinks. You were never one of the guys.

But he didn't hate anyone. Or view others with contempt. Well, okay, a certain irony. And resentment over cheap shots taken at the first Black President. Down here, he and Natalie have always seen themselves as outsiders among country club Republicans. We're liberal co-conspirators, she'd say as they walked home. A two-person sleeper cell. But they thought in comic terms, not with contempt. Nice enough people, they'd say, but not really our kind. Now, contempt is what everyone thinks was in their heads all along.

Truman brings him up short, and squats. The storm's only trace is fresher evening air. The sky has already cleared. They move on, and Ritz looks at his watch. Nine-twenty. He hears his wife say *applause*. Sees them seated on the deck, protected under the balcony. Rain dapples the pool. Natalie's graceful, unadorned hands are steepled on her stomach.

The dog squats again. The cleared western sky is backlighting a U-shaped block of condos. On the third level, two adjacent door frames are blinking with Christmas lights. Forgotten by someone with Ace Foley's problem? Probably not. Life at Donegal is for those in good health, what realtors call Active Senior Living. The fitness center is always crowded with people plodding on treadmills, watching *Bang News* as they rise and fall on step-climbers.

Once more Truman pulls him to a stop. Another car approaches as she braces herself and starts to defecate. Ritz reaches in his pocket—No! He forgot to bring a plastic Publix shopping bag. The dog at last finishes, and as she stands and starts scratching with her hind legs, the turd is glossy in the oncoming headlights. He always carries a packet of Kleenex and pulls it out. It's important to be seen cleaning up after his dog. He stoops with a wad of tissue and the car slows. Ritz doesn't look over, but once it passes, the color and model tell him it's the Kraliks.

He uses more tissue to wrap the turd as Truman goes on scratching. Did Dennis Kralik think to buzz down his window and say something, but saw the crapping dog and changed his mind? Truman stops scratching, and they continue their walk. She seems to think every inch of the sidewalk's coco plum hedge needs her inspection. Every palm tree. When he and Natalie ate at the club, they usually walked. They sat with others and held up their end, but he sees them walking home. Natalie shakes her head. *My small-talk battery is drained.*

* * *

Back at the house, Ritz puts the wad of Kleenex in an empty terra cotta pot out in the garage. He washes his hands, defrosts the tuna, and mixes a Rob Roy before going out to the patio to start the grill. As he cooks, Natalie is at the table drinking wine, telling him about her day.

Truman comes out to watch him cook for her. That's what this is, Ritz thinks. A boutique *al fresco* soup kitchen for one shelter dog. Smoke curls up through the screen cage. He is following Murray Grunwald's advice. Doing good by cooking for a deprived, abandoned, one-eyed animal. A poor beast, Ritz thinks, turning the tuna steak with tongs. A timid, half-blind dog terrified of thunder.

He mixes another drink, and cooks a pan of Rice-a-Roni on the side burner. Above the cage, the sky is scattered with diamonds tossed on black plush. Next to his patio chair, Ritz serves the dog on a china plate like his own. All that's missing is a Rob Roy and a second paper napkin. "We'll get up early and walk," he says. "We'll have the place to ourselves."

22
R&D

After setting his clock radio for five a.m., Ritz goes to bed at eleven. He hasn't set an alarm in years, but karaoke is still fresh in mind. He wants to avoid encounters.

"Eleanor Rigby" wakes him. He dresses, and checks his shorts pocket for the two plastic shopping sacks he stuffed in before bed. Two just in case: Ritz sometimes experiences a follow-up bowel movement, what he calls the after-burner effect. It could also be true of Truman. The dog is waiting on the Aerobed, and again passes him on the way down.

His strategy fails. Half the residents are out walking dogs before sunrise. Lint balls with jeweled collars, golden retrievers grinning like car salesmen. A tall, high-stepping piece of poodle topiary shrubbery. Lost in booze or sleeping-pill hangovers, many walkers don't recognize him until it's too late.

Some straighten in passing and stare boldly—*I know you and you can go straight to hell.* Others march past, eyes straight ahead as the dog pulls them forward. But no one says anything. A dog is interested in meeting Truman, but she pulls Ritz forward. When she squats, he looks up the dark, murky street. Two people are crossing to the opposite side to avoid him. Seconds later they float past, a half-visible mix of squeaky footwear, clicking paws, panting.

Being out so early is a novel experience. Tee times and round-robin tennis don't start for hours. Like an amniotic sac, the humid air hangs heavy on his face and arms. Out on the fairway, big swaths of water sweep in slow motion. The widely spaced street lamps shine down like desk lamps.

Back twenty minutes later, he unclips the leash and grabs up the *Naples Daily News* from the driveway. Truman trots ahead and sits in front of the screen door. Last night, he put the terra cotta flower pot next to the front door, and now adds Truman's morning deposit.

As a boy, the idea of cleaning up after his puppy depressed him. From now on, every day he would have to pick up Tunnel's turds. That's what you have to do, his parents said. If you have a dog, you must be responsible. He'll be your dog, and you're the one who walks, feeds and cleans up after him. Sixty years later, the lesson has held: he has no trouble gathering up something from a novelty shop.

He opens the outer screen. Truman enters, and when Ritz steps next to her to open the second door, she remains seated. She looks resigned to him. Sad. She looks like Jane at the airport. The good eye is trained ahead, but her face expresses something like loss. It *is* a face, not just the head of a dog. Does she associate some risk or fear with looking up at him? A slave who must never meet the eyes of the master? It pains him. She can't know what comes next. Her life comes and goes like morning dew.

He opens the door and watches her make her way down the hall. Ritz admires her walk. From this angle, *sashay* is the word for it. Her shaggy hind legs taper down and move with fashion-model precision. He closes the door, follows her, and finds Truman curled in front of the refrigerator.

"Hungry? There's some leftover tuna."

* * *

Natalie finally stops coughing. "Okay," she says. "Go on."

"That's all. She won't give me the time of day. I thought we were getting along, we—" Ritz stops himself before saying *had a nice dinner* "—took a good walk. I fed her, we walked again this morning. Nothing. A blank."

"It's all strange to her," Natalie says. "Be patient. Give her time to adjust. You don't know what she's been through. Maybe someone blinded her eye. And don't forget, she had heart worm. Anne said they told her the dog was covered with mats when she was brought in. Mats and heartworm mean neglect."

"It wasn't *me*. She must know that by now."

His wife doesn't answer. Why would she? His implied meaning, that his many kindnesses should by now make him an honorary pack member requires no comment.

"In case you're interested, Anne made it safely back to Key West," she says. "Everything's fine."

"Of course I'm interested. She shouldn't have left. She said she'd call and didn't. Please ask her what else she knows about her dog."

"The shelter people didn't know much. Only that Truman was adopted to serve as the companion for another dog. The family claimed that after the other dog died, your dog quit having anything to do with them."

It stops him. "You're telling me Truman is grieving? She's been through denial and anger, now she's grieving?"

"I'm telling you what Anne told me. You don't think animals grieve?"

The idea never occurred to him. Why would it? He now knows that a dolphin's brain is bigger than his own, so Ritz can see how grief might figure with them. But dogs? After lunch, Truman retreated to the second floor. Ritz has been up twice. She was back on the air mattress, facing away as he spoke softly from the open entry.

"What should I do?" he asks. "What does canine grief counseling consist of?"

Natalie laughs. For the first time in months she laughs. How much he has missed it. Her sinus condition has made her voice husky, but the laugh is all hers.

"That's something for you to figure out," she says.

"Come down and help me," Ritz says. "Not for me, of course, for the dog."

This one she doesn't laugh at. He hears her take a breath and let it out. Hears a car horn in the background. "I'll come down soon," she says. "When the time is right."

This, too, surprises him. It's the first time Natalie has actually said she *will* come back. But now the idea angers him. *I'll come when the time is right.* It's leverage, he thinks. A quid pro quo to extract something from you.

"What do you want?" he asks. "I don't mean anything major, like 'What do women want?' I'm just asking what I have to do." Natalie doesn't answer. "I have no idea what you or anyone else wants from me," he says. "I can't make the book disappear. I can't convince people I'm innocent. Not when they choose to believe I was writing about them."

"You just have to say you're sorry," Natalie says. "Not to me, to everyone you hurt. You need to forget whatever it is you thought you were writing about."

"And how do I do that?"

"Find out," she says. "'I'm smaht, I can do t'ings.'" This is said in her Brooklyn accent, another quote from their private stash of coded signals. It's 'Fredo, Michael Corleone's dummy older brother in *The Godfather*. "Find out how to do it," she says in her own voice.

"I get it," Ritz says. "You want to take me over the jumps before you'll come back. You like the power, the control."

For several seconds, nothing. "Soon, Buzz. I'll know when it's time. Did you write or call Betty Brubaker? I sent you Alex's obituary. Also one for the high school teacher you used to talk about."

"Mr. Squires?"

"He died two days before Alex, I cut out the death notice. I also sent the reminder about your colonoscopy. Be sure to follow the prep directions. Last time, you ate a Danish and had to re-schedule."

Ritz hates the trotting back and forth to the bathroom. He started calling Natalie The Nanny Wife a year or two back. Except he did forget last time, and needs nanny reminders more and more often. She has always had the better memory.

"Buzz?"

"I heard you."

"The prep's no fun, but don't forget."

"I could post a notice in the pro shop and invite people to watch. That would be a form of 'sorry.'"

"I don't mean you should feel sorry for yourself. So many—"

"If I don't, who will?"

Natalie clucks her tongue. More code. Clucking is something Natalie does before delivering one of her schoolmarm homilies. "Believe it or not, there are people with real problems," she says. "Not the first-world kind. People really sick, or starving. How would you like to be somewhere without decent medical treatment? We have it so easy, Buzz. When I think of our well-off problems—"

She stops as though censoring herself. "What is it, Natalie?"

"Goodbye, Buzz. Please take care of yourself."

23
R&D, con.

Truman has curled herself in front of the glass door wall, next to the new dog bed. She is motionless, looking out at the pool. Ritz bends down and pats the brown faux-velvet mattress. "This is yours, Tru, I mean it. Forget the cold floor, go with the bed, it's top-of-the-line."

He keeps patting. She raises her head to look at it, and again faces the glass. A courtesy look, he thinks. A pro-forma gesture, like airport hugs. "What's the problem? You like the Aerobed upstairs, this is the same thing. Even better. Nice and soft—" He presses with his fingers.

Next to the state-of-the-art bed are matched stainless-steel food and water bowls. One is filled with top-of-the-line all-natural food pellets, the other with water. Side by side, they look purposeful. Industrial. His boyhood dog slept on an army blanket at the foot of his bed. Tunnel's habitual diet was canned Alpo. Ritz brought some home—Prime Cuts—and set down the bowl. Nothing. Tunnel had a great appetite and excellent metabolism. He *inhaled* food. Ritz can't believe any sane dog would freely choose a plant-based diet.

"There's still some tuna."

* * *

That morning, he had driven to Pets Rock!, a store in the strip mall adjacent to Home Depot. He freed a cart, and moved down an aisle with tanks of fish. This was followed by one with scratching posts for cats. Then a dizzying array of kitty litter brands. He would need more leashes, and chose two in conservative black. At the pooper scooper display, Ritz studied the different models. Some were small and pincer-like for plucking up individual turds. Others worked like the jaws of a steam shovel, suited to mastiffs and Great Danes. Ritz decided to hold off until he had more knowledge of Truman's elimination style.

But poop bags were certainly in order. People were always mooning the golf course, bent over on the sidewalk. All of them seemed to use plastic Publix shopping sacks. This had to do with Publix's approach to their geriatric clientele, people so arthritic that nothing weighing more than an orange went into any one bag.

On the drive to the store, Ritz rejected that approach. Truman deserved proper, task-specific bags, not hand-me-downs from a supermarket. But like kitty litter, he discovered poop bags were offered in many styles and colors. Scented and unscented, biodegradable, some with built-in tie handles. Liking the handles idea, he passed on the sale item—a Variety Pac in plaids and stripes—again in favor of basic black.

Then came a disorienting aisle devoted to dog treats. The same marketing strategy used to peddle laundry detergent and toothpaste figured here: many brands, each one divided into subsets with distinguishing attributes. Not fabric softener *plus* detergent *plus* bleach *plus* aroma therapy, but chewy, soft, crunchy, soft-crunchy, animal, vegetable, mineral. Some actually looked good enough to eat. He bought half a dozen kinds: bacon-and liver, Sirloin Yummy, one that resembled Chicken McNuggets. Remembering Iris and Family And Consumer Science, Ritz wondered whether nut allergies or anaphylactic shock could apply to dogs. He was getting mired in too much detail, and added something called Peanut Buddy.

Tunnel had loved balls, especially balls with a bell inside. He bought a pink one made of knobby rubber, along with a squeeze toy called "your best friend's friend." Described as a hedgehog, it wheezed when he pressed it, and re-inflated with a sigh.

He turned down an aisle being re-stocked. Hello, he called to the girl standing on a rolling set of stairs. What food should I buy for a border collie? This one's good—she raised the sack in her hand. She had green hair, and wore a maroon smock the same color as Jane's. But was the girl a no-nothing new hire, or a seasoned employee who knew her dog food? What makes it good? Ritz asked. The girl had resumed restocking, but again looked down. I dunno, people buy it, she said. You mean customers are dedicated to the product? The girl frowned. You know, Ritz said. Dedicated, in the sense of an electrical outlet used for just one purpose, like an air conditioner. Only now did he hear himself. I mean, he said, once customers try this brand, that's what they keep buying? Right, she said. And it's nutritious, he said before he could stop himself. You know, good for you, not just popular like Red Bull. Maybe I should get my manager—she started down. No no, my mistake. Of course it's good, why else would people keep buying it?

At checkout, he discovered dog beds, bowls, treats and chew toys didn't come cheap. Did he want to open a Preferred

Customer Club membership? Why would you? he thought. Truman is Anne's dog. The checkout clerk was in her fifties and tired-looking. He thought to ask for more details on dogfood, but didn't want her running for the manager. Ritz filled out the membership form, and left.

* * *

None of it matters. Faced with dog food boasting a big fan base, Truman has again retreated to the second floor. She must be hungry. All she's had today is part of his breakfast sticky bun. When he pulled off a piece and held it out, she looked dubious, but finally took it gently, as though fearing a trick.

24
Good Deeds

Noon the following day, he is on Donegal Boulevard, taking Truman for her midday walk. Someone is coming toward him. Ritz adjusts his sunglasses and keeps walking. A man wearing a tam-o'-shanter is steering an Amigo. Trotting alongside is a small fox-faced dog.

"Hello there!" Surprised to be greeted, Ritz nods. "Hot enough for you?"

"Yes, it is."

"We don't stay out long, it's too hot." The man stops the Amigo. "I'm on my way to thank my benefactor for this." He slaps the Amigo's tiller." "Doctor Grunwald. Know him?"

"He lives next door."

The man smiles as Ritz stops in front of the scooter. Truman sits and faces away. "Don't mind her," Ritz says. "She's standoffish."

"This is Pilot." The little dog is rasping, straining at the leash to reach Truman. The driver is wearing shorts, and below his knees, the legs are pale blue. "He's a Papillon."

"I don't know much about dogs," Ritz says.

"Papillon means butterfly in French. You pronounce the Ls like a Y. They all have big ears. They're good dogs for condos."

"He's a handsome little guy," Ritz says. "Truman is a rescue."

Someone Better Than You: A Comedy of Manners

The man nods, and looks down fondly at Pilot gasping at the end of the leash. But the dog reverses, moves onto the grass and squats. Perhaps the excitement is too much for him. He looks at Ritz and begins defecating. The man fishes into his shorts pocket, then the other. "Uh oh."

"I know all about it." Ritz reaches in his hip pocket. The little dog finishes with Truman's one-two sphincter pump.

"That's real good of you. I have this thing—" He points to a short pole wedged in front of the scooter's basket. "You put your bag on the end, if you remember to bring one."

Still looking at Ritz, Pilot begins scratching the grass. Ritz brings out a wad of the new plastic bags *with handles*. He separates one and feels a burst of competence. Still scratching, Pilot watches him slip the bag over his hand, reach down and collect the diminutive turd.

"Really nice of you," the man says.

Ritz stands and ties the ends. "I'll take it," he says.

"No, I'll take it with me." Pilot's owner reaches out. He forgot bags but wants to do his part. It's a matter of self-respect, Ritz thinks. Of dog-owner etiquette. He hands it over, and the man sets it on the Amigo's foot stand, next to his heavy orthopedic shoe.

"Thanks again. I'm new here," he says. "We moved from Minneapolis last month. I have to say we picked a bad month."

"It's not the best," Ritz tells him. "A lot of people leave for the summer."

"My son and daughter-in-law both got jobs in Naples. They're stockbrokers. Moving here is the only way we can see them and the grandkids."

"My stepdaughters fly down for visits with their kids." Ritz hears himself wanting to come off as a doting grandparent. No doubt because of Nurse's Elbow.

"Okay, then, thanks a lot. See you again. Let's go, boy—" The man claps. Pilot comes from the lawn and jumps nimbly onto his knees. The Amigo passes and moves along the sidewalk. A hand waves above the tam-o'-shanter.

* * *

Later that afternoon, Ritz is in his study. He bought a copy of *A Dog's Life* at the pet store, and is reading when Truman barks.

It startles him. At some point, she wandered in and lay down. Her first bark in your house, he thinks. The doorbell rings, and Truman stands. Ears at twelve o'clock, she barks again. Has she come to think of this as home? Is she defending her cave, her den?

He gets up from the desk. Solicitors aren't allowed on the property. Other than Ace Foley, Murray and Daisy Pruitt, the street is deserted. It's Anne, he thinks. She finished her course in Key West and wants her dog back. As he steps into the foyer, Ritz feels panic. Hearing Truman click after him has a disabling effect. Something like despair fills him as he listens for Iris and Jamal before opening the door.

"What kind is it?" Grunwald smiles.

"Hello! Please come in. She's a border collie."

"Coco saw you walking her. He collected our mail and got yours." Murray hands it over.

Someone Better Than You: A Comedy of Manners

"Thanks. She's not mine. Anne left her here and went to the Keys. Come in."

"How's Foley?"

"Foley is Foley." Ritz swings the door wide. The cane waves back and forth as his neighbor steps in. Ritz closes the door.

"I thought Coco might spook Daisy." Murray starts down the hall. "That's why I asked him to ask you. Hester told me Daisy is afraid of Mexicans, except for Dolores." Ritz follows. Once they reach the back, Murray taps for the sectional couch. He's been here often and knows the way. He finds the couch and turns. Feels with the back of his calves, and sits with a sigh.

"Coffee?" Ritz asks. "Mineral water?"

"*Mineral* water." Grunwald's eyebrows appear above his dark glasses. "You wrote about people paying more for water than motor oil."

"We're heavily stocked. Bottled water is important to Anne's religion."

"So I learned, Coco read it to me. Okay, mineral water."

"Still or carbonated? As I say, we're fully stocked."

"Bubbles."

Murray, not Anne. Ritz steps into the kitchen and drops his mail on the island. He would like to give Murray Grunwald something more than water. A new set of golf clubs, 20/20 vision. His sense of relief and gratitude is crazy, out of all proportion. Truman is once more lying in front of the refrigerator. Ritz reaches down and strokes her head before opening the door. But as he looks in, Ritz now remembers: gossip is the mother's milk of golf communities. That means

Murray must know by now about the karaoke fiasco. Ritz takes out a bottle of Pellegrino and gets a glass from the dish rack. Please, he thinks. Please let's talk about anything else.

"What is it with Coco's getup?" He uncaps the bottle and pours. "I assume you know he's always in costume."

"Oh, sure." Ritz walks back. He steadies Grunwald's hand, and gives him the glass. "Thank you. He told me he saw someone on TV dressed all in black. A comedian named Friedman, in Texas. He always dresses in black, with the cowboy hat. Coco liked the look."

He takes a drink. "So, Foley was in Daisy's garage?"

"In her powder room. Jerking off."

Grunwald shakes his head. "The family needs to know, I'll call. They don't come often. I don't think Ace kept up much, even before Deirdre died." Ace Foley's older son is an economist in the Washington office of the Teamsters Union. He and his *Bang*-watching father aren't likely to be on close terms. The younger son owns a profitable Go-Cart track near Disneyworld.

"It's weird," Ritz says. "The man can bench press over two hundred pounds. He must buy new running shoes every month, but as you say, the dementia thing is a lottery. How's Esther?"

Ritz closes his eyes. Stumblebum stupid, he thinks. Bringing up Foley's dementia, and in the next breath asking after Esther Grunwald.

"She still likes her fruit," Murray says. "Melon and pineapple. Delores cuts it into cubes, ready to eat. She still watches Oprah, but usually falls asleep. Her spirits are good."

Someone Better Than You: A Comedy of Manners

Late each afternoon, Murray takes a cab to Villa Bellissima to have dinner with his wife. Villa Bellissima is an upscale assisted-living complex on Davis Boulevard. Enough money means Esther lives in safe, pleasant surroundings, and Murray says the food is excellent. Once or twice a week he stays with her. When his wife can no longer manage her one-bedroom apartment, Murray will arrange for her to go to a single room with supervision. After that comes Villa Bellissima's "memory-care unit," the euphemism applied to the next-to-final address for all those losing their minds.

"We had dogs in Cleveland," he says. "West Highland terriers. Feisty little characters, full of vitality. Esther was crazy about them. Gus and Gretta, our little married couple. You should get one, Brady. They're great company."

Another dog? A different dog to take Truman's place? The idea is crazy to him. But why? Why do you think it's crazy? he wonders. "She's mostly border collie," Ritz says. "When we walk, people ignore me, but smile at Truman. I think she must make me less evil. 'Look at that, The Butcher of Donegal with a *dog*.'"

Murray smiles. "'Truman.' What's the story there?" Ritz explains about the winter White House. "A good enough reason," his neighbor says. "Why Esther named ours Gus and Gretta I have no idea. For all I know, Gus was an old high school boyfriend. Gretta might have been the name of a rival she made into a dog."

Murray sips his water. He isn't here to ask about Truman. He came to check on you, Ritz thinks. To be kind, to be a friend. Seated on the black sectional, his neighbor presents a settled confidence. Not just stoical acceptance at being old and blind, but a man at peace with himself.

"I don't know," he says. "You have to wonder these days, how you'd manage raising a family."

Here comes more advice, Ritz thinks. Has Natalie called him?

"Whatever Esther and I did, we had good intentions. I remember trying to explain those take-shelter ads on TV without scaring the kids. During Howdy Doody, and the old Flash Gordon serial with Buster Crabb. People stopping their cars and lying in a ditch. Children getting under their desks at school, as though it could make a difference in a nuclear war."

Grunwald shakes his head. "How would we be managing these days? Unless you're a religious fundamentalist, there's no free pass. Everything is in your hands, isn't it? What do you do when the latest study comes out about heavy metals in drinking water? Or how peanut butter can kill? How the wrong helmet might put your kid at risk of permanent brain damage. Every day, more of the same."

This is largely in reply to "Helmets R Us," one of several columns Ritz wrote about what he considers paranoid parenting. His neighbor drinks again, and cups the glass in both hands. Ritz still sees the Donegal response to his book as petty and humorless. But what about a standard bearer of common sense? Someone who's blind but at peace with himself?

"Go on, Murray. I value your opinion."

"Okay. Coco finished reading me *Vanitas*. I have to tell you, what you wrote is very one-sided and critical."

"Yes, it is," Ritz says. "By design. There may be some good to building a thirteen thousand six hundred square foot house with nine bathrooms equipped with low-flush toilets. And three energy-efficient ovens, not including the one outdoors for the poolside kitchen. So what? The person who builds that house shouldn't be allowed to think of himself as a visionary. What he is, is vain. Focused on drawing attention to himself. He wants the Earth Day Medal, he even hires a PR company to help him get it. He's a plutocrat who builds a mansion, and insists on calling it 'a virtual laboratory of cutting-edge green technology.'"

Grunwald holds up a hand. "Vanitas, vanity, I get it," he says. "But I think you should let a little air in. And don't forget, that house was built by Mexican laborers. People in need."

"Please, Murray, save me the trickle-down economics. Let him hire Hispanics and Haitians to work for pocket change. But a publicist? Hired to put together a supplement for the paper to advertise his client as a humanitarian? A conservationist? No, Murray, that won't fly."

Ritz hears himself being defensive. The only fully competent person still talking to him is siding with the enemy.

"I agree with you on that one," Grunwald says. "I'm talking about the columns where you make fun of people's insecurities. Like the one on karaoke. What else do I remember? The one about eating lots of fiber. 'Pretty soon, you'll be laying so much cable you'll have to put a TV in the crapper. That is, if you want to keep watching people throw chairs on Jerry Springer.'"

Grunwald chuckles. "'Laying cable.' I never heard the expression. But all the research now. The diets, the environment." Forehead lines converge, then relax above Grunwald's dark glasses. "I'm just saying, are you sure you wouldn't be confused? I'd buy all the helmets. I'd be on my cell phone making sure they were okay at recess. You have to act as though you know what you're doing."

He nods, and holds out the empty glass. "Gotta go." Ritz takes it and Grunwald shoves up with a sigh. He taps his way back down the hall and Ritz follows. "You and Natalie still talk?"

"Yes."

"Give her my best."

"I will. Natalie sends her love, please tell Esther."

"I will. She remembers you, Brady."

Is it true? Does Esther Grunwald still remember her neighbor, or is that another courtesy? Ritz moves in front of the cane to open the door. "I saw the man you sold your Amigo to," he says. "He was coming to thank you."

"He's new." Grunwald steps into the screened enclosure. "He bought a condo on the west side. He put an ad in the newsletter, did anyone have a scooter for sale. I gave it to him. Talk about problems. Diabetes, congestive heart failure. Something else I can't remember, I think related to kidney function."

Murray finds the outer door and opens it. "Hang in there," he says. "Natalie's a good one. And take care of that dog."

Ritz closes the door. Yes, Natalie is a good one. Someone better than you, he thinks. Someone who took a chance, who stayed with you. Except now, after what's happened, why *would* she come back? All at once he can't see how or why Natalie Ritz would come back.

Truman has clicked her way from the kitchen. She sits and looks up at him. Ritz walks back to the family room and taps the Michigan number. The invitation to leave a message is still the one he recorded two years ago. At a loss what to say, he puts down the phone. He can't think of any good reason for Natalie to say yes to him a second time.

25
Adaptation

The following morning, he gets up and walks Truman in the pre-dawn fog. He remembers Grunwald seated in the family room. Coco must have told him about the karaoke fiasco, but tactful Murray said nothing. *Can you be sure you wouldn't be confused? I'd buy all the helmets.*

He needs a boost. A lift. Moving up the drive, Ritz again sees Jane at the airport holding Madison. He grabs up the *Daily News,* and decides to risk calling her.

In one of those coincidences that encourage belief in divine intervention, Jane left a message during his walk. "Hi, it's me. I'm up early. Mom says someone called from Naples. Something about karaoke. And you have a dog. Just calling to say hello. Bye."

It's not yet sunup, but Jane called. And invited him to call her back. Something must be wrong. He sits on the sectional. As he taps out the number, Wise Person Ashley is on stage, peering out from under an oversized helmet.

"I'm sorry," he says. "It's not yet six, I should have waited."

"That's okay. Ashley got me up, that's why I left a message so early."

"Is she sick?"

"Yes—well, no. Or maybe. Dan thinks she's just bored because of summer vacation."

Just bored—*good.* "In your message, you said someone called your mother."

"She said not to say who it was. Mom said, not the person who called."

"I understand," he says. "It doesn't matter, but if you can, please tell me what the woman said to your mother."

Jane's account suggests the caller was sympathetic. As he was making his bogus apology, someone dropped dishes in the kitchen. "That's what happened," he says. "You could say I got what was coming to me. It wasn't an honest apology. I offended people here. I offended you as well, and I'm sorry."

"She told Mom someone got mad. A man with one of those things to help him talk."

"Someone who can't sing at karaoke. I was singing his song."

"I went back and read the essay," Jane says. "It's funny, but not if you're one of the singers."

"I wasn't—" No more *I never wrote about anyone* "—thinking," Ritz says. "I chose to believe people wouldn't take what I wrote personally or seriously. I was wrong."

Jane says nothing. In the silence, Ritz goes on stroking Truman. Once he sat down, she spread herself at his feet. She is still warm from their walk. What he's doing and saying are connected. Ritz is certain this is true. Being right is not most important, he thinks. Being called by Jane is most important.

"And that's also true for you and your sister," Ritz says. "What I wrote about you and Anne is all too revealing. Of me. That's what you said, and I've thought about it. What do I know about parenting? I show up when you and your sister are three and five. You both accept me. Years later, I get around to realizing how amazing that was. But not before I reward your acceptance by using details in your lives to get cheap laughs."

"Well, you didn't mean to hurt us."

Ritz closes his eyes, stroking Truman. *Thank you.* "But as you correctly said, I did think it, and I wrote it. I hid behind the notion that writing gave me some kind of free pass to be mean. That's really it, I'm afraid. I chose to believe I was just amusing myself. Except I was bitter and angry. Tell me about the girls."

Jane quickly offers details of summer activities. Three afternoons a week, Madison is at a local nature center studying plants and insects. Ashley is running everyone ragged in a summer pre-school program.

"It's so nervous-making," Jane says. "I go there with her, it's a requirement. Parents have to participate. The other parents and the supervisors keep looking at me. I know they want me to do something, but what? Ashley is just being Ashley. She's off in her own little world. She gets the other kids revved up, which makes everything harder. Dan and I even talked about arranging for someone to see her."

No!

Ritz stops petting the dog and covers the mouthpiece. He doesn't trust himself. Nothing could be worse than *calling someone* to shrink Ashley Vanghent's beautiful, unruly imagination. Don't say a word, he thinks. What do you know? You love a small Wise Person for blowing the whistle on the Nativity, *but what do you know?*

Someone Better Than You: A Comedy of Manners

"I suppose you don't like the idea," Jane says. "I know you don't trust therapy."

"If I said something about that, please disregard it," he says. "The truth is, I have opinions. Some are good, some are dumb. I'm trying to cut down on talking about things I know next to nothing about."

He resumes stroking Truman. "I will fail, but I will try."

Jane laughs. It's *her* laugh, no one else's. He starts to ask about her sister, but stops himself. He is basking in the laugh, and doesn't want to talk about life jackets.

26
Class Warfare

The idea of *calling someone* depresses him. But they haven't done it. Not yet. Dan says Ashley is just summertime-bored, an idea full of wisdom and level-headedness. Another good person, Ritz thinks. Why has it taken you so long to *get* Dan? Mutton-chop whiskers and tee shirts? That's it? He cradles the phone.

The ball with the bell. What makes him think of it now? Because you want to *keep the ball rolling*, he thinks. The boost you feel from Jane's call. In TV commercials, border collies hurl themselves in the air to catch Frisbees, tear back and forth in some kind of competition. Snatch balls at one end, race back, and stick them to a panel covered with Velcro. He will put Truman's border collie skills to the test.

He goes to his study and gets the new pink rubber ball with a bell. Jane phoned. It's a new day, a new beginning. "Let's go, Trumie," he calls. "What do you say? We'll play some catch." She doesn't come. He walks back to the kitchen, and again finds her spread out in front of the refrigerator. "Are you hungry?" He opens the door and looks down at her for a sign. Without raising her head, she regards him with the good eye. "There's still some rotisserie chicken, a little macaroni and cheese."

She doesn't race to food and gobble it down like the dogs in TV ads. She sits watching him eat, licking her chops. Last night, he gave her exactly what he was eating, not in the new industrial metal dogfood bowl, but on *her* plate. He arranged everything to be identical to his own, like glossy photos in a Japanese menu. This side of putting down a placemat and pouring her a glass of pinot noir, he made Truman's dinner identical to his own. She didn't eat until he finished and was washing up.

"Come on—" He motions, and she gets up. They could play catch in back, on the part of his lot just off the fairway. But Ritz's reading has taught him that herding dogs are driven by a work ethic. She might start herding golf carts, or grab someone's ball. They'd say you trained her to steal, he thinks.

He leads the way out. In the street, Ritz looks in both directions. It's still early, and the morning sun is casting shadows. This will be good. The cul-de-sac is empty of cars, leaving Trumie plenty of room to run at full tilt. It's already warm, they won't play long. As he prepares to throw, the dog sits watching from the lawn.

"Okay, girl, here we go. Do your border collie thing."

The pink ball arcs, falls, and rings on each bounce down the asphalt. Ritz looks over. "Go, girl!" Still seated, Truman is watching him, not the ball. Abruptly she gets up and trots back along the paver sidewalk. She sits with her back to him before the door. Ritz thinks to retrieve the ball—but what if Daisy is up? If so, she will have heard the bell and is now standing at her window.

He moves back up the walkway. No balls, check. He opens the door and Truman quickly enters. She trots down the hall and disappears into the kitchen. Wait, he thinks. Maybe it's not every ball, just balls with bells. Ritz closes the door, and steps into the study. His golf bag is leaning against the bookcase. He zips open the pouch and takes out a ball.

Muzzle between her paws, Truman is again lying in front of the refrigerator. Ritz squats at the far end. "Truman, look at me." The dog remains motionless. "*Truman.*" When she looks, Ritz rolls the golf ball toward her. It makes little hiccup jumps in the tile's grout. The dog watches a second before she looks at him with alarm. She gets up and moves backwards, away from the approaching ball. She circles the island and clicks back down the hall. Ritz hears her padding upstairs.

"How could I know? I'm sorry."

* * *

When he calls the shelter, the volunteer acts like someone with Protective Child Services. Ritz tells her how grateful he is for Truman, and for the humane, selfless work of shelter volunteers. She finally gives him the phone number.

"Mrs. Graham, hello, my name is Brady Ritz. I have your name from the Key West Rescue Center."

"Who?"

"Brady Ritz, you don't know me—"

"*Rescue* Center, that's a new one. Going to rescue me from my money, hah. How many times do you need to hear it? I am not in the market for storm shutters."

"No, Mrs. Graham. I'm calling about Truman, the dog you gave up recently. I got your number from the Key West Rescue Center."

"Mister…"

"Ritz."

"Okay, there, Mister Ritz, they gave you the wrong person."

"I was told you gave her up on May 20."

"Okay, I see what they did," Mrs. Graham says. "They gave you the wrong dog, not the wrong number." She laughs. "Didn't you sort of wonder why a girl dog was named Truman?"

"I'm sorry, my mistake. That's her new name."

"Uh huh, well, the dog we had was Chelsea. A border collie mix."

"That's her. With just one good eye, the right eye. Chelsea is her name?"

"Hey, you can name her what you want, she's your dog now. We called her what the first people called her. Chelsea. We got her to be a friend for our dog Coda."

"So you had two."

"Yeah. Coda was this big powerful Australian cattle dog. Really strong. That dog could *run*, you wouldn't believe it. Little Chelsea could hardly keep up, but she did her best." Ice rattles in a glass. "Where you calling from?"

"Naples."

"You're getting this heat, too. I bet I drank a gallon of iced tea since breakfast." Ritz has lost the thread. Truman was Chelsea. "Coda got sick and died from some kind of intestine thing," Mrs. Graham says. "They both lived in our pole barn. You can't protect them from everything."

"That's true."

"Which is probably why Chelsea got the heartworm. I'm happy someone took her. She was a sweetie until Coda died."

For five minutes, Mrs. Graham rattles ice and talks about the two dogs. She tells Ritz that Chelsea/Truman and Coda loved chasing cars. He can't imagine the dog snoring gently on the floor chasing anything. At last Mrs. Graham tells him something useful: the family eats on their deck, and have always fed their dogs leftovers.

"So you fed Truman and Coda table scraps."

"Hey, good enough for us, good enough for dogs, right?" He sees half-eaten plates of spaghetti, Caesar salad, the skin of a baked potato being scraped into a grimy dog dish. As she talks, Ritz stares out the door wall. He sees Truman lying on filthy straw in a barn full of sharp-edged tools. Germ-laden insects swarm around her head.

He tells her about the balls, and describes how frightened Truman is of storms. "The ball thing I remember," she says. "The thing about storms, I wouldn't know about that. She and Coda were out in the pole barn. Then, later, there was this special bush Chelsea stayed under."

He hears in her voice a wish to justify dumping the dog. "Coda liked playing catch," she says, "but not his little wifey. We decided something happened with balls in her first house. I mean trailer. They told us a trailer park was on her collar, from when they dropped her off."

Dropped, not dumped. The euphemism makes him more suspicious. "Maybe that's how she lost her eye," Ritz says. "Someone threw a ball at her. And broke her tail."

Someone Better Than You: A Comedy of Manners

For several seconds, Mrs. Graham's silence tells him she's picked up on his tone. "Could be," she says finally. "Nothing to do with us. She was okay with the one eye, but everything changed when Coda died."

"Changed how?"

"It was really fast. One day she's this nice little border collie wife we called her, for Coda. After we buried Coda, she'd be out there next to the spot where he just up and died. After that, Chelsea just lost interest. Which is why we got the puppy."

"To be friends with Chelsea."

"Well, no." Ice rattles. "My son and his wife live with us, she has two little boys. Four and five, and now the baby. Chelsea just gave up and ignored everybody, so we got the puppy for the boys. They love him, he's a purebred golden retriever. Great with the kids. You know, goldens are just the best."

More deflection. Self-justification. Ritz hears in Graham's voice everything she isn't saying. A dog with a broken spirit stopped being interesting, so the family brought home a puppy. Then dumped Truman/Chelsea at a shelter. With heartworm, covered with mats.

"See, the thing is, she just rejected that puppy everyone loved," Mrs. Graham says. "That's why we thought she'd be better off with some other family."

"So you dumped her."

"That's not a fair choice of words. Chelsea gave up on us, we didn't give up on her."

"I see."

215

"We invited her around, she just stayed out there under her bush. Later, she set up all the time out there. Even when it rained. She totally rejected the puppy. She snapped at him until we sent her to her bush."

Ritz is so angry he doesn't see Truman looking at him. "If you didn't give up on her, why did she have heartworm? What word would you like? When you delivered her to the shelter covered with mats, why was she dying of heartworm? Just say it. You didn't want to pay for the treatment. I know what condition she was in when you decided she'd be better off somewhere else. I just wanted to know more of her story. Now I do. And yours."

"Listen now, you can be all high and mighty all you like," Mrs. Graham says. "You aren't here and don't know what we have going on. We liked Chelsea, the kids liked playing with her. Until she quit. If she has a good home with you, that's good. We had bills—"

"You had money for a purebred golden retriever."

"See? You say you know me, Mister Ritzy from Naples, but I know *you*. I sure do. On some golf course up there. Lucy our golden was a gift from a friend of a friend, that's how we got her. My daughter's four-year-old has trouble with her ears, they put in tubes so they drain, we don't carry insurance—"

Chelsea/Truman is looking at him, lying on the floor next to her new bed. "Well, good, then," Mrs. Graham says. "Now you know a little what we have here, and why we decided it would be better—"

Ritz cradles the phone. A big dog is chasing a pickup, tongue lolling, powerful shoulders working. Truman is close behind, her graceful model's legs at full gallop. He sees their happiness, one-eyed Chelsea/Truman with her big male sidekick. Her companion. And hears himself assuming the worst about the Grahams. Hears the bitterness of Zeno Kowalski taking out his failures and frustrations on a stranger.

27
Plea Deal

"Her name's Truman, she's a border collie. Mostly. She has perfect house manners. I think she must have been abused, but she's not aggressive. In fact, just the opposite. Very smart, very observant. Sometimes, she seems to be taking mental notes. But then she turns off completely and settles into this Zen-like state. She barked just once, but when you get the leash she does this little dance, and yodels."

Finally, Ritz picks up on the absence of any uh huhs or isn't-that-somethings. "I guess I must sound like I'm off my meds," he says. "Off my leash."

He had no thought of ever again calling Sunshine Urbanski. After talking to Mrs. Graham, he called Natalie. Still nothing but his own voice on the recorded message. After he hung up, Ritz kept seeing Truman alone in a filthy pole barn. The image stayed with him. More and more he felt a kind of pressure, a need to share his dog with someone.

But what if Sunshine's silence means she dislikes or fears dogs? What if she went home with someone and was met at the door by a pit bull?

"*Are* you on meds?" she asks.

"Anyone my age is on meds."

"What's yodel mean?"

"Ululate. Like a wolf's howl."

"So, it howls."

"But not the way you think. Not like dogs reacting to sirens."

"Zen?" she says.

"I just mean she seems to be thinking private thoughts," Ritz says.

"Well, yeah, Brady. Like they would have to be private. Look, I'm in my car."

"Of course, I'm sorry."

"But I'm glad you called. I just don't like driving and talking."

"You're right, you shouldn't."

"So, you want to see me? I sort of gave up on you."

"I do, yes. Not, you know, for work, just for your good company. I'd pay, of course. I thought we might take Truman somewhere."

Duh. Ritz looks at the ceiling. *I don't want to get laid, I just thought we might take my dog on a family outing.* He's seated on the floor in front of the door wall, stroking Truman. The dog gives no evidence this means anything to her. What she is doing is missing Coda.

"I mean a picnic or something," he says.

"You can't take dogs to Naples beach," she says. "They make you leave."

"I didn't know that."

"It's pretty hot for a picnic. I'll call later. Give it a treat for me."

She hangs up. As he strokes the dog, Ritz imagines Sunshine driving her Sebring with the top down. She has on a summer dress, the kind worn in the fifties. A frock. She's wearing sunglasses, smiling. The image replaces snaggle-toothed Mrs. Graham, wig on crooked, holding a glass of gin.

28
'enry 'iggins

"You can tell a lot from how guys treat pets."

The following afternoon, they are walking on Broad Avenue in Olde Naples. Truman is between them. She always walks on Ritz's left, to keep her good right eye on him. They turn left at Third Street, lined with upscale boutiques, restaurants, art galleries. The original Tommy Bahama's is on the opposite side, Campiello's just ahead. Campiello's is Natalie's favorite restaurant. The Mole Hole is two blocks south.

"You meet a guy." Sunshine nods to herself. "Nice clothes, clean. Washes his hair. So you go home with him. You get out of the car, you see turds all over the yard. And his dog stinks. From that you know the guy doesn't care about anything but his own body. Other times, they don't care about anything *but* the dog. Or the car. That's the whole story with some guys."

She laughs. "A guy washing his car doesn't know you're watching? Totally revealing. Like they caress it. Talk to it like the car's listening. Complain about the boss. Bitch about an account they lost. All kinds. Rich guys, guys getting married next week. A guy works in a collision shop, his buddies chip in to show him a good time before he does the deed. A dog or car is like a shrink to them. Or a priest at confession. Older guys, too, where the wife died."

All this is too close to home. In most respects, Ritz's wife and friends *are* dead. When he tried again to reach Natalie, a new message told him she was at an Ohio amusement park with Jane and the girls. He feels his wife slipping away. She isn't a disembodied spirit, an invention like snaggle-toothed Mrs. Graham. But she is slipping away.

All of which has him talking much more to Truman, seeking to be forgiven for the ball incident. Last night he defrosted a large Delmonico. Ritz grilled it, medium rare, and served it with rice pilaf. As she always does, the dog lay on the deck facing her plate, waiting for him to finish his meal. He gobbled it down and hustled inside to wash up. Washing dishes seems to signal to her that he's done and she is now free to eat. He didn't like seeing her eating alone, poured more wine and went back out to sit with her. As she ate, Ritz talked about Grunwald's wife, and the gloomy prospects for Ace Foley.

Along with clothing boutiques and jewelry stores, the streets off Third are lined with art galleries. Mostly on display are works of knock-off Impressionism, or bad abstracts. Ritz and Sunshine pass a window filled with a giant painting of clowns in a Model T. This is followed by three women inspired by the work of John Singer Sargent. When he stops to look, Sunshine steps back next to him. Does the picture interest her? Maybe she's looking just because he stopped. Her sunglasses make it impossible to tell.

What's more important is her response to Truman. When she came to pick them up, Ritz stepped out with his dog. Sunshine crossed the lawn, and knelt before holding out her

Someone Better Than You: A Comedy of Manners

hand. Truman thought about it. But she then stepped forward, smelled, and bowed her head to be scratched.

That's why it doesn't matter whether Sunshine has any interest in art. She knew what to do, and Truman gave her the stamp of approval. Standing now before the fake Sargent painting, he is grateful. It's as though she read his mind. She is wearing an off-white summer dress, and a straw hat much like the one worn by the tallest of the Sargent women.

"Let's take Truman to the beach," she says.

"You said it's not allowed."

"Not here, in Bonita Beach. There's a place called Dog Beach. I saw it once from a boat. There's like this sand bar. When the dogs run, they look like they're running on water."

Ritz stops before another window. The picture here isn't a knockoff. It's an actual painting by Thomas Kinkade. In his second piece on cruise ships, he wrote about Kinkade's cottage-industry art auctions. "He paints pictures, then mass-produces them as prints," Ritz wrote. "He thereby makes 'cottage industry' into a pun." The paintings usually develop Kinkade's principal subject matter, idealized cabins and houses in natural settings. The houses are often draped in snow and moonlight, the interiors aglow with welcome. The one in the gallery window features a Wordsworthian cottage bathed in creamy morning sunshine. "His houses are too good for people," Ritz wrote. "That may be why they're devoid of life."

They move on, and now pass The Mole Hole. The gift shop's windows are full of tile hot plates, fancy nut crackers, cuckoo clocks from Germany. No slimy moles today, but Ritz stops again. Shining in the last window is a small molded Jell-

O salad made of green and red plastic. If he sent it to Natalie, she alone would understand.

The top is down on Sunshine's spotless Sebring. She pops the trunk and brings out a large striped beach towel. "To keep Truman off the hot leather," she says. Watching her snug the towel in the backseat convinces Ritz she mostly wants to protect her car, but he likes the gesture. Nothing about her suggests the sordid reality of big-city prostitution. If you exclude accounting fraud, medical malpractice, DUIs, and a little payday domestic violence, there isn't much of a crime scene in Naples. In other words, the right town for a nice working girl like Sunshine.

He wondered how Truman would react to riding in an open car. As they drove along Davis Boulevard, Ritz kept turning to check on her. She sat on the backseat, looking out with something like world-weariness. She bore no resemblance to the frantic dogs in other cars, heads wedged out half-open windows, ears flapping. None of that for *my* dog, Ritz thought.

Sunshine finishes working the towel into the crevice. "Maybe we should put the top up." She looks at the sky and shades her eyes. "We mustn't let anything happen to her."

"She seems fine with it down," Ritz says. "Come on, Truman." He holds open the door and folds forward the front seat.

They drive north on Gulf Shore Boulevard. Ritz feels energized. Revived. It is very satisfying to see that Sunshine likes Truman. He hasn't felt this good in months. Beautiful homes slip past. Chateaux, turreted manors, Honolulu-inspired verandas.

"Which kind do you like?" he asks.

"You want to buy me one?" Hands at ten and two o'clock, Sunshine smiles behind her sunglasses.

"If I could, why not?"

Expansive and revived, Ritz means it. In the moment, riding next to her in a convertible, he wishes he could set up Sunshine Urbanski in one the houses slipping past. Balmy air is scattering his hair. In no time he would have the neighbors eating out of her hand. A Henry Higgins for the New Millennium.

"Come on," she says. "You've got lots of money. Just do it. Buy me one like that—"

She points ahead to a gray-and-yellow clapboard, modelled after houses in Hyannis Port or Provincetown. It has a wraparound porch, with half-open shutters. Ritz studies it to learn more about Sunshine. It has window flower boxes, lots of tropical vegetation. Sure enough, it has a white picket fence. When he faces forward, she is still smiling behind her sunglasses, knocking her thumbs on the steering wheel. She is joking, but not. When she takes off her hat and hands it to him, dislodged strands of hair play about her ears.

"Come on, we'd be good together," she says. "We'd have the neighbors over for finger food and dirty martinis. The sharp older guy with the babe. It'd work."

She's all wrong about how much he's worth, but Ritz plays along. "It might," he says. "Do you play bridge?"

"I play poker."

"That's good, too, but you'd need to learn Bridge. And golf."

"I thought you hated golf."

"I do, but I think you could be good." He says this half meaning it, half Henry Higgins.

She turns east on Central Avenue, and Ritz again looks back at Truman. Is he seeking her approval on setting up housekeeping with Sunshine? He faces forward, and sees the three of them on the ninth green, his favorite hole. Bloated with envy, Tony Minetta sits in a golf cart, watching and chewing on his cigar. Bennett Trudeau sits next to him behind the wheel, equally glum to be watching the man they blackballed giving a putting lesson to a dish. A babe. Truman lies at the edge of the green, and looks interested.

It's fun. Except Ritz half thinks Sunshine might mean it. The dress, the Third Avenue boutiques and galleries. The convertible and gorgeous homes. The much older man in more or less good shape, with a border collie. No, the collie part is wrong. A one-eyed depressed dog doesn't fit the image. But otherwise, everything contributes to a new take on a well-worn story: making an honest woman of a hooker by teaching her to play golf and contract bridge.

* * *

At U.S.41, they head north. Ritz turns again in his seat. Truman is still looking out, leaning against the backrest. Her ears are up, her gleaming white chest and black coat flattened by wind. When he twists in his seatbelt to stroke her, she looks at him searchingly. Her black coat is very warm, and now she is panting.

"I think you were right about putting up the top."

"Is she getting ready to jump?"

"She's hot."

Sunshine looks at the hat on his lap and faces the road.

"Who are we talking about? What's that under the hat?"

She smiles, and angles right. At Mel's Diner, she swings into the parking lot. Mel's is the home of Mile High Pie, and highly regarded Early Bird specials. Since he stopped eating at the club, Ritz frequents Mel's at least twice a week. Once the car comes to a stop, Sunshine pushes a button. The roof pulls free behind the back seat and unfolds overhead. Truman stops panting and gives Ritz the same look he got for throwing the ball.

"It's all right." He strokes her head. "Relax." He wants to go on with more comforting words, but remembers johns with their dogs. The cloth top drops in place. Sunshine folds down her sun visor, clips her roof lock in place and points for him to fasten his. She swings behind Mel's, and stops for traffic. Ritz starts the air conditioning.

"We would, you know," she says, watching for an opening. "Be good together."

"Sure we would," Ritz says. "You and your grandfather, what a team."

He laughs to cover the anarchic little thrill her words give him. *We would, you know.* He understands perfectly what's going on. *Clever young sex worker seeks to improve station in life.* But she *is* clever. Sunshine reads him very well. The tact she showed proves it, first in the club bar, and later at the house. And how quickly she has understood how important Truman is to him. Never mind he knows all this. It's all part of the half-serious, half-comical thrill her words produce. In opposition to every cliché—no, *because* of clichés—Ritz thinks: what if we *were* good together?

"So what?" she says. "Girls need grandfathers." With an opening in traffic, she turns north and accelerates. "You're just afraid of what people would say."

"Why would I care? They hate me."

"So, what's the problem? Like your wife's been gone how long? Is it because I sell sex instead of toothpaste at Walgreen's? Really, I want to know."

"It's foolish," he says. "Vain. Egotistical. Some old sport dressed to the nines with his brand new girlfriend-hyphen-nurse. You see it all the time."

"What's 'dressed to the nines'?"

"Fancy, dressed up." To go along with other old-boy sayings, Ritz thinks. Like cloud nine, and nine days' wonder, and the whole nine yards.

"You mean like the old dude that married Anna Nicole Smith," she says. "Getting married just to have someone take care of you."

"It's a meme," he says. "You see it all the time in Naples. In restaurants, jewelry stores. A man my age or older with someone much too young. It's just vanity. Conceit."

"What's 'meem'?"

"Something we all recognize without explanation. *Born Yesterday* with Judy Holiday, William Holden and Broderick Crawford. The woman with a man much too old for her."

"That's a movie?"

Of course she doesn't know it. Why would she? Very possibly, Sunshine wouldn't know the actors, or what *Turner Classic Movies* is. When he looks over, she seems to be thinking behind her sunglasses. Could a comic cliché be serious for her? She seems to be turning things over. Ritz twists again in his seat. Truman is still facing out, but looks at him. The trouble about the roof seems over. Her confidence in him has been restored. Ritz turns back.

"That means you care what people think," Sunshine says. "If you believe you're like happy with another person, why would you give a shit what people think? So you dress up and go out with someone younger. Big deal."

Yes, she is making a case. Half-seriously defending May-December couples. Ritz amends this to late September-early October, but there's still no point in arguing. He *does* care. Even with her conservative appearance and good manners, he felt uncomfortable in the Donegal bar. Proud to be with her, but only for reasons of vanity and resentment. Exactly, Ritz thinks. You just like seeing yourself giving her a golf lesson in front of your foursome. Actually living the lesson? The main effect wouldn't be a fresh start, a new day. No, he thinks. It would just hurt someone better than yourself. And ruin whatever is left after September-early October.

Even so, the pilot light of his anarchic *what if* fantasy is still flickering. What if we packed up and went somewhere? he thinks. Just for a while. Mexico, Equador. Nothing to do with *leaving,* just running away with Truman. But "modest" would not fit with the dream house Sunshine pointed to earlier.

The pilot light blinks off. It lasted all of five to seven minutes, but it was fun. Ritz smiles. "You think I have money," he says. "I don't." He points ahead to the sign for Pelican Bay Boulevard. "*That's* money. That, and Port Royal."

"I've been in Port Royal."

She pushes back her hair. He sees her upper lip is marked by tiny beads of sweat. Again Ritz admires her dress, her smooth arms and thin-fingered hands on the steering wheel. He half wishes he *were* rich. Not to run off with her, but so he could buy Sunshine Urbanski a nice Naples house with flower boxes, a picket fence, and some bridge lessons.

* * *

Twenty minutes later, they are heading north on Bonita Beach Road. Wedges of aqua blink in the narrow gaps between houses. Sunshine has the radio on, and is humming to an easy-listening arrangement of "Let it Be."

"I bet you like classical," she says. "Highbrow stuff."

"That's me," he says "The Erik Satie type." He remembers Natalie next to him on her chaise, watching rain dapple the pool. Highbrow has nothing to do with it, he thinks. Dave Brubeck's *Time Out* is playing inside. He wishes Natalie were behind the wheel, sipping a Diet Coke and driving the three of them to Mexico.

"It's how you talk," Sunshine says. "Lots of educated words."

"'Dressed to the nines' isn't educated," he tells her. "It's an expression used by people my age. Actually, by people even older. I learned it from my father."

"You know what I mean," she says. "You're like a gentleman. Refined. So, am I right? You like classical?"

"Classical, and keyboard jazz. No pop music after the eighties."

"No Old Country? Johnny Cash or Tammy Wynette?"

"Johnny and Tammy aren't Country Western," Ritz says. "They're white soul."

Sunshine smiles. "Here we are—"

Ahead on the left, the road's shoulder slopes down to a parking area. About twenty pickups and SUVs are mingled with motor homes and campers. Behind the vehicles, a wall of coconut palms conceals the beach.

"Truman, get ready for heaven." Sunshine crosses the road and dips down the incline.

He looks back. His dog seems to be concentrating on what's outside. When Ritz faces forward, a pickup is exiting, sending up a plume of dust. The truck's windows are opaque. Two black labs are panting over the tailgate.

"She hasn't been friendly with other dogs," Ritz says. "She's stand-offish. Shy."

"Not here. I have a friend says his dogs love the place. He says it's the smells and freedom."

She parks. Truman is big on smells, but Ritz has doubts. She hasn't shown any sign of wanting freedom, or much else. Just walks, meals, and quiet. He brought along bottled water, a bowl and some leftover Delmonico steak. He snaps on her leash before getting out and folding the seat forward. Truman steps down, looking wary. Her nose starts working. She pulls on the leash, low to the ground and already using her tacking motion. She is searching, something she will do all her life. Knowing the reason, Ritz feels a pang.

They take a path through the palms. Protected from traffic noise, Ritz can now hear dogs baying, barking. The beach blinks through trees, the barking accompanied by shouted commands. Truman is still tacking left and right. She pulls him off the trail and noses under fallen palm fronds. Pools of standing water glitter in the shadows. For no good reason, Ritz is sure cottonmouth snakes are lurking in the pools, waiting to attack his dog. He pulls her back on the path and holds her close.

Fifty feet farther on, they step onto the beach.

The bright sand extends a hundred yards into Estero Bay. To the north, high-rise buildings mark Fort Myers Beach. Dog Beach is exactly as Sunshine described it. A dozen or more dogs are racing and prancing as if walking on water. One is chasing a Frisbee; another, very big dog is charging out, like a small horse. Left and right, dogs lie panting onshore or under umbrellas with their owners. Radios are playing.

Truman seats herself on his left. She too is panting, but Ritz sees she already knows everything she needs to. Coda isn't here. Like his own brief fantasy in the car, Dog Heaven holds no further interest for her. Ritz feels kinship. For a few minutes, looking at women in a fake John Singer Sargent painting led him to see himself running off to a new life. A young woman would rejuvenate him, and he would reciprocate by providing her with social tutorials. In the same way, he hoped coming here might in some way release Truman. Dogs in all sizes and shapes seem delighted with this doggie Grande Jatte. Not his dog.

"She doesn't like it." Ritz turns, but Sunshine isn't there. She may have gone to use one of the portable toilets set up on the trail.

As he faces the beach, a large dog is just now bounding out of the shallows. It's big, tan with a black mask. Possibly a Labrador-German shepherd mix. The dog is coming to them, a male, dripping and bounding, tongue out. He has seen Truman and is coming to meet her. He stops to shake himself—straighten his tie—and lopes forward. Truman doesn't move. Ears at twelve o'clock, she stops panting. The big dog reaches them and promptly jams his nose into Truman's muzzle. She does nothing until the dog moves to smell her hind quarters. At this she snarls, and the dog backs away. Seeking answers, he looks first at Ritz before ducking again to smell Truman. This time Truman gets up and turns away to protect her privates.

"Luther! Get your ass over here!"

A man in tank top and cargo shorts scuffs out from under a shade canopy. The woman with him turns to watch from her beach chair. Flapping overhead is a Confederate flag.

"Luther! Goddamn it—" The big dog gives up and swings away just as the man grabs his collar. "Bothering people," he says. "What'd I tell you? Get your ass out there—" He bangs the dog's hind quarters. Luther takes off, loping his good-natured, win-some-lose-some way toward the water.

"Sorry about that," the man says. "Big old dumb dog. I see you got a collie there."

"She's shy," Ritz says. "A rescue. She wasn't well socialized."

"I get that whole antisocial thing," the man says. "Same with me." He smiles and turns away, scuffing back to his canopy.

"What happened?" Sunshine is coming from the path, folding closed her flip phone. "Why don't you take off her leash? Give her a chance to let loose."

Truman is obviously done with the place, but Ritz reaches down and unclips the leash. The dog again looks at him, not this time with suspicion, but something like pleading. Perhaps she fears taking off the leash means he will leave her here.

"That's sad." Sunshine kneels and pats Truman's head. "She doesn't like it. She seemed interested when we got here. All that weaving back and forth."

29
Chez Sunshine

Back at the car, Ritz pours water into Truman's bowl. Why does it always move him to watch her lap this way? Any time he does something for her, it gives him a lift.

"Let's go to my place," Sunshine says. "I made something."

He looks up. "A meal? You made dinner?"

Her eyebrows rise above the sunglasses. "Don't get cute," she says. "Giving head is not the only eating people do in my line." She smiles to show she isn't mad. Ritz smiles back. Of course, he thinks. It's part of the fantasy, the hooker in a summer frock *and* an apron.

"Come on," she says. "It's a nice drive. We'll have some beef Stroganoff."

"Doesn't that take a while? My wife—"

"What's the matter, Brady? Rich people never heard of crock pots?"

Ritz smiles again. His own fantasy of a fresh start at sixty-six lasted six or eight minutes, but all this pre-planning is too designed. It bothers him. "I want to stop for some wine," he says. "I never accept dinner invitations without bringing something."

"Getting a lot of those lately, are we?"

Truman finishes lapping. Ritz spills out what's left, and the three get in the car. Sunshine doubles back along Bonita Beach Road. At the intersection, she turns north on 41.

"I don't know—" The radio is off, but she taps the wheel with her thumbs. "Why can't people just like leave people alone?"

"How do you mean?"

"What we were talking about before," she says. "This bogus age thing. Who gives a shit? Why should it matter? Say I have this thing for my daddy or something. Some kinky thing makes me attracted to older men. So what? If it works, it works."

"*Do* you have a thing for your father?"

Sunshine speeds up to make the light at Corkscrew Road. "He lives in Wisconsin," she says. "I see him maybe every couple years. No, I don't have a thing. I'm talking about a hypothetical, not me personally."

"It doesn't have to be kinky," he says. "It can just be psychological. You don't see much of him and that might make you miss him. Maybe that's why you like older men. They remind you of him."

Sunshine laughs. "See more of him—" The laugh builds. She pounds the steering wheel, shakes her head. She glances at the rear view. "Sorry, Truman....I really am....sorry… "

Ritz looks back. The dog's good eye is trained on the back of Sunshine's head. Then on him. Truman slowly turns to the window. Ritz faces forward as Sunshine pats her chest.

"Whooh. Okay, sorry."

"Did I touch a nerve?"

"My father's a bullshit Pentecostal minister," she says. "He calls the shit-for-brains dummies in his church his flock. A flock of sheep, no shit. Trust me, Brady, you don't remind me of daddy. I'm not looking for a sub. I told you what the whole thing is with me and older men. Manners and like being refined. And cash flow. That's the whole deal."

* * *

Fifteen minutes later, they pull into an apartment complex. Ritz is still processing what she said. Her use of language is good, even witty, but talk of *daddy* quickly coarsened it.

A trio of mustard-yellow buildings form a U around a large swimming pool. Sunshine parks in her carport. "I'm on three." Ritz gets out with the bottle of Bordeaux he bought at a convenience store. He snaps on the leash, and follows Sunshine. Two women in bikinis are sunbathing next to the pool. Both are wearing earbuds, and appear to be sleeping. Two men their age are waist-deep in the pool, smoking cigars. It will be mostly singles here. All he wanted was to share Truman with someone, nothing more.

She is again tacking left and right. Once Truman decides Coda isn't here, she will again lose interest. Music is blaring from speakers above the pool's bathrooms, rock from some era decades after his own. As they start up the stairs, it occurs to him that at his age, after comfort, good food and health care, the only major thing money can still buy is quiet.

"My lease is up next month," she says over her shoulder. "It's okay here. They fixed the mold problem, but I'm looking."

Is that it? he thinks. Her lease is up and she needs a place to stay? Maybe she figures your wife left you, so why not? No canopy covers the stairwell. As they climb, sunlight x-rays Sunshine's thin summer dress. Is that why she's leading him up this way, instead of using the elevator?

"I'd rather live in Naples, but rents are off the graph," she says. "You have to come north to find affordable housing."

"I imagine."

He is careful to keep Truman centered on the stairs. Watching the rolling movement of Sunshine's hips should interest him, but doesn't. They reach 3, and he follows her along the covered walk. He holds Truman close.

"Here we go—" She uses her key, shoves and steps inside. Truman hesitates before entering. Ritz drops the leash and follows. As Sunshine closes the door, he smells the beef Stroganoff. Everything in the room is white. Everything Sunshine has control of in her rented space—walls, dining and living room furniture, lamps—all white.

Ritz nods approvingly. "Nice," he says. "Light and airy." He sets the Bordeaux on her white pine dining table.

"Everyone says it's boring. They say I should add some color. I say, if it works it works."

She puts her sunglasses next to the wine, and turns to Ritz. She draws him to her with both hands, kisses him, and presses into his groin.

* * *

With or without pills, in the absence of Jamal or Iris making a sudden appearance, Ritz's lack of desire proves no match for the full range of Sunshine's work ethic. Mingled with her oral and other sexual techniques, he wonders what Truman is thinking.

Twenty minutes later, he lies gasping. "Is she in here?" he asks. "Did we bring her in?"

"Out in the living room."

Sunshine is now sitting cross-legged at the foot of the bed, holding a glass of water. The glass, her casually crossed legs and small, pert breasts make it impossible for him to link her to the humping, growling, pelvis-crashing demon of ten minutes ago. Even the sweat on her upper lip is missing.

Dazed, Ritz lies back in what is more aftermath than afterglow. He sees Ashley throwing herself back and forth in her father's arms, caught up in her role. If this audition was meant to demonstrate the workability of May/December arrangements, Sunshine has miscalculated.

That's the only way he can think of it: a make-or-break audition. Ritz's breathing is coming under control. If he could see any evidence in her of what just happened, Ritz might think differently. But there is no evidence. Here, in her own bed, Sunshine took command. She seemed to think something needed to be proved. Now, though, she is sipping from a glass, probably wondering when to turn off the crock pot.

"I made sure she had water," Sunshine says.

"Good."

"You're a nice lay, Brady."

"Thank you."

"You think I say that all the time."

The word *lay* is so unrelated to what just happened that for a second Ritz has no answer. "No, I don't think that," he says.

"Yes you do. You think I fuck for money, so part of the deal is I tell the guy how good he does it. How big his cock is. Come on," she says. "That's what you think, right?"

Lying drained of will or thought, Ritz would most of all like to lie silently enjoying the breeze wafting down from the ceiling fan. Either it was on when they came in, or she has since flipped the switch. The room's window is shaded with a Venetian blind. Restful yellow slats lie along the white wall. In his numbed state it would be peaceful to lie here, with Truman asleep and snoring at the foot of the bed. She does that now at home, a gentle wheezing or honking that comforts him.

But it's Sunshine at the foot of the bed, naked and sitting Indian fashion. He lies on his side facing her. "No, I really don't think that," Ritz says.

What he actually thinks he can't say. That what she likes about him is the idea of her lease coming to an end, just as refined-guy Brady Ritz asks her to move into his house. Instead, he says, "If you were just doing your job, you'd tell me you know guys half my age who couldn't make the team. But you didn't."

Sunshine half smiles. Glass in hand, she rolls off the bed and walks into the front. "*I'm* going to make rice," she calls. "Hi there, Truman, bet you wonder what that was all about."

30
High Crimes and Misdemeanors

He showers and dresses. Easy listening is coming from the front room. When he steps out of the bedroom she is at the kitchen counter in a white terrycloth robe, putting the finishing touches on the meal. Truman lies facing the door.

A cork screw is lying on the table. He sits and is opening the Bordeaux when she takes their plates to the stove. She ladles out the rice and Stroganoff, and when she comes back, he gets up and stands behind her chair. You've been cast as The Gentleman Caller, he thinks. "Thank you." Once she sits, he pours the wine before taking his chair.

The Stroganoff is easily good enough for him to pay an honest compliment. "Death Row delicious," he says.

Sunshine stops eating and looks at him. "That's where they keep prisoners sentenced to death," he says.

"What's that got to do with this?"

"It's a compliment. When Natalie eats something she really likes, that's what she says, 'This is death-row delicious.' She means it's good enough to be the last meal a prisoner asks for."

"Your wife." He nods. "Huh. Okay, I sort of get it."

As they eat in silence, he is grateful for music filling the void. Sunshine uses her napkin, gets up, and removes the dinner plates. She comes back and sets down a slice of pecan pie in front of him, then goes into the bedroom. The saucer of food next to Truman, leftover steak and a dollop of Stroganoff sits untouched. He had doubts about giving her something with sour cream, but didn't want to offend the chef. The shower is now running. He takes his wine, moves his chair and sits next to his dog. When Sunshine comes from the bedroom, she is dressed for work in tight black slacks, high heels, and a white blouse that reveals her bra. She announces her plan to go to Vergina after she drops him off.

As she scrapes what's left of the Stroganoff into a Tupperware bowl, the bra strap looks thick beneath her blouse. She scrapes the leftover rice into a second container, and knocks the wooden spoon. Ritz has heard the sound a hundred times. He has failed some test. Going to work is Sunshine's way of underscoring the message.

She goes back in the bedroom, and Ritz takes a last look around. No sign of a slacker boyfriend, or roommate who watches *Sleepless in Seattle.* He listens as she flaps the bedspread and plumps pillows. Everything being white is now oppressive. On the walls are gray rectangles where a previous tenant hung pictures. She comes out with her purse, and says "Let's book."

* * *

"Thank you."

When she doesn't answer, he looks again to the backseat. Truman is again staring out. Ritz faces forward as they approach Donegal. "For dinner, and everything else," he says.

"Thank *you.*" Sunshine pats the purse wedged next to her on the car's console. Not knowing what was in store, Ritz hadn't brought much cash. As he wrote out a check, she told him dinner was comped.

"I'll call."

"You do that." Her impatience tells him she knows he never will.

"Truman probably needs to go. Why don't you drop us here? It's a nice night, we'll walk."

She pulls in at the Donegal entrance. At the turnaround she swings left, and brakes to a stop. He thinks to peck her on the cheek, but she is back to tapping her thumbs on the steering wheel.

"Okay, then."

"Take it easy, Brady."

"I will. I'll call."

"You do that." She looks in the rear view. "'Bye, Truman, watch your back." He gets out, and folds his seat forward. The dog bounds out. Ritz slams the door, and bends to fasten the leash as Sunshine guides her car and completes the arc. He straightens and waves.

Dog and owner begin walking toward Donegal Boulevard. It's eight, still light out. Above the golf course, massive white coral heads float in a late-afternoon sea of pastels. A longing comes as Truman pulls him across the street. Natalie is coming back. Ritz can't explain why, but what happened has convinced him she will. Death row delicious. I know her, he thinks. Her voice and ways. Why she's taking so long makes no sense, but she's coming back. She'd be direct with you, he thinks. If she weren't coming back, she'd tell you. He wants to go on getting old with Natalie. Wants them to keep their knees and hips. Wants what hucksters are calling their "crepey skin" to remain melanoma-free. Their eyes free of floaters and solar eclipses. Most of all, he wants the impossible: that they cash out at the same time.

He and Truman reach the point where the sixteenth fairway flows between rows of condos. Ritz stops and faces the tunnel-like swath of grass. For the first time in over a year he feels something for golf. But not really. He and Truman move on. What he wants most is to be old with Natalie the way Murray and Esther Grunwald are old. The way they find ways to be happy with things the way they are. With things *as* they are.

Ahead, blue light is clipping out from the last house on his cul-de-sac. Ritz stops for Truman, and watches. When she finally leads him forward, the flashing turns out to be coming from a Collier County patrol car parked in his driveway. At the end of the street, more flashing comes from an EMS truck in front of Daisy Pruitt's house.

He reaches his drive just as Coco Ruiz steps through Grunwald's front door. "How you doing, Mr. Reetz?" He starts across the lawn. "'Youston, we got a pro'lem—" He smiles under the cowboy hat and watches his feet. "Mr. G and me reading. He take a nap, I hear somethin' next door."

Coco stops, and points at Ritz's house. "Some kinda noise," he says. "I don' hear if I not smoking outside in back. Like something heavy drop. I know you not there, I go in your pool cage and knock. I guess he run out the front. When I come around, it's open. Maybe something to do with that guy." Ruiz points to Foley's house. "I call the police."

Under no circumstances does Ritz believe Coco Ruiz would call the police. The story is meant to conceal something. "Thank you," Ritz says.

"No pro'lem."

He leads Truman inside the screen enclosure. The front door hangs open, and in the foyer the china cabinet is lying face down. A Collier County sheriff's deputy stands next to it, writing. He looks over as Ritz enters. You the owner?"

"Yes."

"Ritz?"

"Yes."

"I'm officer Nunez." The cop goes back to writing. "How long were you gone, sir?"

The Q & A that follows involves a highly edited summary of Ritz's day. "You mean the dog park," Officer Nunez says. "Off Goodlette Frank."

"No, the dog beach in Bonita Springs."

"So, you leave with this lady friend. This—" he checks the clipboard "—Sunshine Urbanski. You're on the dog beach in Bonita. Then what?"

"We went to her place."

As he writes, Officer Nunez nods for him to proceed. Ritz looks down at the china cabinet, then at Truman. How exactly should he go about it? "We had dinner," he says.

"In or out?"

"She made the meal."

"What was it?"

"Beef Stroganoff." These are the same commonplace questions asked by detectives Lenny Briscoe and Ed Green in

Law and Order. He and Natalie watch the reruns. "Over white rice," he adds.

"My wife does it with egg noodles."

"That may be better," Ritz says, wanting to form a bond.

"So, this friend. You know her how long?"

Ritz pretends this needs a moment of thought "Four weeks."

"You met how?"

"In Vergina on Fifth. I don't exactly see what it has to do with this."

"Maybe nothing, sir. Now, the party called this in.... A Doctor Grunwald. He says you're married, and your wife's in Michigan."

"Correct." Ritz is tired of answering yes or no.

The deputy waits, heavy-jowelled, just doing his job. How many times have Ritz and Natalie watched Briscoe and Green put adulterers through this same ringer? He is sweating and wants the episode to go to commercial.

"We're in a trial separation," he says.

"Trial separation. You went to court?"

"It's just between us."

"So, your wife knows about this Sunshine."

"No."

The deputy looks away with Detective Briscoe's exact same seen-it-all-heard-it-all expression. He turns back. "Okay, sir. You don't have to go into it, but some people had problems. People out to dinner or a movie came home to this type of situation."

"Do you know Miss Urbanski? I mean, in your capacity…"

"I'll check for a sheet, she could be new to the area. I'm just making you aware of the problem. Probably this is a standard break-in, but sometimes they work in teams. One person supplies the resident's movements, another does the break-in. Did she make any calls?"

Coco and Sunshine. That fast Ritz puts them together "No," he says, but now he remembers Sunshine coming from the path at the dog beach, folding closed her flip phone. He sees Coco smoking on Grunwald's pool deck, lowering his own phone.

The deputy flaps closed his notepad. "Donegal isn't far from an element," he says. "It would be good to do a little inventory. Find out what's missing. Do you video-record valuables for insurance?"

"I never have."

"It's a good idea." Officer Nunez stuffs the notebook in his hip pocket and hikes up his service belt. "To have a record when you file a claim."

Ritz puts Truman in his study and closes the pocket doors. As Officer Nunez helps him right the china cabinet, stemware falls and breaks on the marble floor. Ritz thanks the officer and sees him out. He goes to the kitchen for the broom. As he sweeps, his karaoke apology is drowned out by breaking glass. Dolores is Coco's aunt. Is she with them? No, not possible. Not Dolores.

The busboy's tray winds down as he sweeps up what was stemware given as a wedding gift. Natalie eloped the first time she married, and never owned matching anything. She will be sorry to lose these things. Mostly, she gets attached to keepsakes with private meanings. Small figurines she puts on the mantel, a blouse worn on a special night. "Their" chip monk munching on peanuts she leaves on the patio in Michigan. Memory Lane photographs.

He gets the vacuum, and works it in all corners to protect Truman's paws. How tempting break-ins must be at Donegal. When he rode his golf cart past a worker trimming hedges, Ritz sometimes thought about it. Say you're undocumented and working ten-hour days, six days a week in the Florida heat. Or in a clubhouse kitchen. Or grooming tennis courts. Every day you see people doing nothing but playing, eating, drinking. With or without a green card, what would be the effect? Why should so few have so much, just because they're old and white? Virtually all the workers at Donegal are Latino. At least a third of them aren't much younger than you, Ritz thinks. How many of them will ever be able to think of retiring?

He returns the vacuum to the utility room, and opens the pocket doors to his study. Truman looks up at him for permission. "Come on, let's check upstairs."

The master bedroom looks unchanged. In the walk-in, the shoebox still has cash. He puts it back and checks Natalie's jewelry box on the dresser. Looks in her study. In the guest and spare bedroom before going downstairs to check for messages. Truman is once again lying before the refrigerator. She looks wary again: first the stupid beach, then a strange apartment, and now an "element" allowed into our private domain.

"It's me," Natalie says. "I got your messages. I was with Janey and the kids at Cedar Point. I'm calling about the colonoscopy. Don't lose track, Buzz, mark it on your calendar.

And remember, nothing to eat except Jell-O the day before. Do all the prep the way you're supposed to. I guess that's it. How's Murray? Tell him hello, and ask him to give my love to Esther. 'Bye."

Her tone is less informational. Perhaps even tinged with something like regret. He's right, Natalie is coming back soon.

* * *

"Do you know the lady, sir?"

"I live up the street." Still under the interrogative spell of *Law and Order,* Ritz points. Yes, he thinks, lowering his arm. That would be up the street.

"Would you say she's a danger to herself?" The blond, twenty-something EMS technician makes a circular motion next to her ear.

"Not really."

"She sounded disoriented, that's why we came. She couldn't find her keys. She saw something on the Weather Channel about a tropical storm. She said she was on her way to her sister's house in The Villages. Because it's inland."

"Yes, her sister lives at The Villages." Ritz knows nothing about a sister, but the twenty-something's circular motion has aligned him with Daisy Pruitt. He doesn't want her put on a list of nuisance callers. "I'm sorry," he says. "She must have been scared. It's not a crank call."

Her partner is coming from the back of the house, followed by Daisy. "Behind the dresser," he calls. Daisy holds up the keys. "I told her she should keep a second set."

"This *is* the second set." Marching behind him, Daisy rattles the key ring. She is dressed for motoring in lavender, accessorized by a chain-mail arrangement of necklaces. "Dolores must've shoved them off while dusting," she says. "Where he put the original set I have no idea."

The girl tech looks at Ritz. "Her husband," he says. "He passed away."

"Okay—" With her back to Daisy, the tech winks at him. She makes a notation on her clipboard as her partner passes on his way to the door. He has dust on his pant leg from reaching behind the dresser for the keys. "We'll write it up as a false alarm," she says.

"Thanks. We all appreciate what you do."

"No problem." She winks again, and it annoys him. He doesn't like being invited by someone younger than his stepdaughters to share an eye-roll about his neighbor. "You'll take over now?" she asks.

Ritz nods. He follows her to the door and closes it. When he turns, Daisy is peering down into an open overnight case on the couch. She lifts folded clothes, looking for something.

"What is it? Let me help you."

"Never you mind, it's none of your business. Coming down here, interfering—" She drops the folded clothes, trying to remember where she put what is none of his business.

"Please tell me, Daisy, I'll help you look."

"My Synthroid."

"Your medicine?"

"It's not my sister's, that's for sure. Healthy as a horse all her life. Like you."

"Maybe it's in your purse."

She looks sharply at him before grabbing the shoulder bag off the couch. She unzips and spreads it violently. Rummages. She zips it closed, drops it on the couch and starts zipping closed her overnight case. "All right, you did your good deed for the day, you can leave now."

"Daisy, the storm probably won't develop. Even if it does, it's days away. They almost never come ashore here."

Done with the zipper, Daisy lowers the suitcase to the floor. "Please, Daisy, I'm truly sorry about hurting you. I was wrong, I had no business—"

She grabs up her shoulder bag and pulls out a terrycloth sweatband. "Give this to your jogger friend." She tosses it in his direction. "He dropped it in my bathroom." Ritz picks it up as Daisy slings on the shoulder bag.

"Let me help you." She shakes her head, but grunts with effort as she lifts the suitcase. "I'm pretty sure there really isn't---" She passes him, wreathed in designer scent. At the door to the garage, she waits for him to open it.

As he is walking home, Daisy passes in her white Lincoln Town Car. She doesn't look at him, still annoyed that Mister Smartypants knew where her Synthroid was. He remembers the breakfront. Nothing is missing, and Coco Ruiz pointed to Foley's house. Ritz hasn't seen Ace since the powder-room incident.

He nears the walkway, and hears auditory fallout seeping through Foley's stucco walls. All day every day, Ace keeps *Bang News* on. All day and night, the cable network delivers what its fiction writers keep ginning up. Ritz reaches the porch, and the voice grows louder. Foley is very hard of hearing, but won't admit it. Right up to the end, Deirdre Foley complained about it—at golf banquets, pool parties. I keep telling him to get tested, she said. Reading her lips, Foley always waved her off. I'm not wearing a goddamn headset, he told her. They aren't *headsets*, she insisted. They're the size of a peanut. I'm not screwing around with all those wires. *Ace!* (Deirdre died from a stroke, and Ritz remembers seeing her eyes cross more than once) *There are no wires!* Those present would shake their heads, drink their drinks, and pop in another coconut shrimp. They knew exactly why Ace Foley would never get his hearing tested. Deirdre Foley was a verbal powerhouse, as committed to high-decibel delivery as her husband was to his fitness mania. As a means of self-defense, Ace was sticking with his low-tech solution.

The symphony-grade chimes his wife had installed are trailing off when Foley opens the door. On the wall behind him is the water-skiing poster. "Brady! How they hangin'?" Foley is working a dumbbell with his free hand.

"I just saw Daisy!"

"Yeah? How is she? Want a beer?"

"Okay!" Still doing curls, Ace stands aside, then leads the way. He is limping. His big shoulders are straining under the seams of a woman's housecoat.

"So!" Ritz follows. "How are you doing!"

"Doing great. The country's another thing. This Muslim president, this African from Kenya running these death panels. I have Bud, I have Yuengling—"

"Anything is good!"

"Gin and tonic? Wine?"

"Beer is good!" When they reach the family room, Foley drops the free weight on a chair and steps into the kitchen. *Bang News* is at full volume.

"You can't believe the shit he's pulling—"

The refrigerator slams. "Health care my ass. What he wants, Brady—listen to this—he wants sterilization. Nationwide. You believe the guy? He wants government-funded sterilization. And legalized euthanasia. Nationwide. State-sanctioned murder, that's what he wants, all over the country." Bottle caps pop. Ace limps back and hands Ritz a beer. They clink bottles. Hand in the pocket of the housecoat, Foley faces the TV. "Unbelievable," he says. "A Kenyan in the Oval Office."

Eyes still on the TV, he grabs up the dumbbell and resumes doing curls.

After they moved to Donegal, moments like this one helped to fuel the attack-mode quality in what Ritz wrote. There weren't many of them, and until he decided it was futile, Ritz offered counter-arguments. Natalie wisely kept silent. She insisted the club had its share of moderates, but it doesn't matter. He now knows politics is not what drove his anger. Until puberty collided with the loss of his job, he had edited what *Bang News* refers to with contempt as the mainstream press. Almost all the people Ritz and his wife have met at Donegal are Republicans. They are generous, even kindly. But only to other Real Americans like themselves. People like Brady and Natalie Ritz. Until *Vanitas*.

"What's with the housecoat!"

"You like it?" Foley drinks. "Is it turning you on? You got me between loads. I'm doing my own laundry now. Everything's in the washer."

Ritz listens, but hears no machine. Even with *Bang News* on, he would hear and feel thumping and chugging. "What about Dolores!"

"I don't trust her, she's illegal."

"You *fired* Dolores?"

"I asked her, 'Let me see your green card, I'm not hiring people living here illegally.'"

"Ace! She has a green card!"

"Yeah, right, save me the liberal crappola. It's time people got serious before we lose the whole ball of wax."

Ace was dependent on Deirdre Foley for everything. Now he's dependent on his cleaning woman. Quite possibly, Ace Foley has never actually seen Dolores. He may just keep watching *Bang*, and raise his feet for the vacuum.

"What happened!"

"What do you think? She shouted something in Spanish."

"When was this!"

"Back when I still had clothes."

"Ace! Dolores has a green card! I've seen it! You need her! She's good people!"

It's pointless. Ace keeps working the dumbbell, staring at the TV. He switches hands, swigs his beer. Does he actually think he can manage to take care of himself? Do laundry, wash floors, spray for bugs?

"Do you even know how the dish washer works!" Nothing.

Ritz circles the kitchen island. In the sink, under precariously balanced layers of Styrofoam, cartons from Wu Fung's, McDonald's, Subway and KFC, he can see real dishes. All the detritus of Foley's world has heaped up like stratified rock. The floor in front of the sink is marked by the herringbone pattern made by a gym shoe. Ritz bends to see. Blood. Foley was limping when he came to the door, but the housecoat took center stage.

"What happened to your foot!" He stands.

"Hey, listen, buddy, whatever it costs, I'm good for it. I was going to tell you when you got back." Foley shakes his head, still working the free weight. "I came over to use the treadmill, I tripped on that hall rug. You should get rid of it. I reach out, boom! I was embarrassed, so I came home."

In the first-floor bathroom, he finds Neosporin and band-aids in the medicine cabinet. Wash cloths are stacked under the sink. He wets one and sees himself on his knees, trying to get Truman to forgive him. He comes back and motions for Foley to put down the dumbbell. "Sit! Take off the shoe!" Foley does as told. He leans back with his beer and watches as Ritz washes the gash on his instep.

"Does it hurt!"

"Nah, little cut is all. You do good work."

He squeezes on Neosporin, then peels off tape from a band-aid and sticks it to the end table. He needs three more. Ritz sticks them together to form a patch, and applies it. "Don't put your shoe on! Shake it out, there may still be glass in there!"

"Okay, doc." Foley smiles at him.

He looks under the sink for trash-can liners, opens kitchen cabinets. Stacked high are silos of canned peanuts, boxes of snack crackers. Seeing Foley in the housecoat is disorienting. Is he grieving like Truman? Is Ace Foley at last getting around to missing his wife? Or coming out late in life from Deirdre's closet?

A roll of trash bags is stored under the sink. Ritz tears off one and flaps it open. As he shoves in trash, Foley limps over to watch. "Hey, buddy, don't bother. Leave it for the maid."

* * *

"Never mind, I know what you going to say, you his friend. Don' bother, I got plenty of work. People calling here all the time wanting me to work for them."

"I know that, Dolores. No one knows that better than I do. But he's sick."

"He like that before he start losing it. Real nasty."

"Yes, but not like now."

"The missus shut him up is why."

"I'm not making excuses for him, he should know better." Spanish language programming blares in the background. "What if I got him out of the house? You could work without seeing him." She may be thinking it over. "It would be good, Dolores, you could schedule our street just like before. Daisy, me, Grunwald, Foley. I can take him to a movie, or up to the club. You'd have the house all to yourself."

At least she's taking a moment to weigh the idea. "I think about it," Dolores says and hangs up.

31
Revenants

He cradles the phone. Say Dolores forgives Foley, what then? Murray said he would call the Go-Cart son in Orlando, and he needs to do it now. Ace is in cognitive freefall.

Seated in his study, Ritz doesn't know why he cares. A retired financial planner fitness freak. A deaf, hale-fellow-well-met bigot and conspiracy theorist who jerks off in other people's powder rooms. *Why care?* Ritz suspects it has to do with his own guilt. Someone like Ace Foley serves you as a foil, he thinks. He makes it easy to seem *less bad* to yourself. Especially when you stick on Band-Aids. Especially when you were finally, actually unfaithful. But you weren't, he thinks. Not finally, not actually.

He begins working through the mail. The promotional flier from a charity called Smile Train makes use of a sweet child with a hair lip. Someone who actually needs your help, Ritz thinks. Doctors Without Borders (beseeching arms exposed above black hajibs), Right to Life and Pro Choice (fetal remains, angry women thrusting signs); glossy family photos in ads for small-business owners. In one, a dad kneels with his arms around twin boys grinning through orthodontia. They look identical to the boys in a *Post* ad Ritz sold to a Gutter Guard installer.

And a manila envelope addressed in Natalie's perfect handwriting. He snaps on the reading lamp and opens it.

Maybe she included a note. No one writes notes anymore, but Natalie is different. She has truly beautiful handwriting, close to what's under glass in the National Archives. He removes the obituary for Brubaker, and the death notice for his high-school English teacher. Then the reminder about his colonoscopy. But no note.

Ritz already knows most of what's in the obit for Alexander James Brubaker. They grew up in the same westside Detroit neighborhood, graduated from the same high school. Roomed together at Michigan before Brubaker went to State for his journalism degree. The list of Alex's accomplishments is long, beginning with top of his Journalism class. Then to the *Post*. There, he "early on distinguished himself as a tireless champion of factual accuracy." Brubaker had worked his way through the paper's food chain—city desk, features, the Sunday magazine—and ended his career as managing editor. On the board of the Detroit Symphony, advisor to the Capuchin Soup Kitchen. If anyone was *less bad,* it was Alex.

Ritz takes up the death notice for James Herbert Squires. That alone is new, Mr. Squire's full name. Ritz never knew any teacher's complete name. No student did. Teachers were figures of myth, their identities based on personal eccentricities. Mr. Dobbins' weird Frankenstein monster shoes (Civics), Miss Kaine's habit of pulling her dress out of her butt crack while writing on the blackboard (History). Outside the classroom, no honorifics were ever used. Teachers were just Dobbins, Martinelli, Kaine. But for Ritz, it was always Mr. Squires.

He learns his old teacher left teaching in the Seventies to sell real estate. Married and divorced, no children. Survived by parents still living in Michigan, a brother in Phoenix.

That's all, but it's enough. Ritz remembers himself and Mr. Squires leaning on a guardrail. Student and teacher are looking down at traffic on Interstate 94 during a field trip. The sky is overcast, gas fumes heavy. Ritz closes his eyes. Fifty years.

Before the spirit of litigation invaded every corner of life, teachers took students to places unthinkable in our time. Imagine a teacher today taking his high-school class roller skating. Imagine him risking his professional and financial future, and after being convicted for "willful neglect," being shanked in the prison yard or raped in the showers. For what? For something so whimsical and foolhardy as showing students a good time. If you can, try to imagine the folly of setting loose two dozen adolescents on a roller rink, on possibly defective skates, skates loaded with foot diseases, to stumble over a hardwood floor, fairly inviting his young charges to fall and sustain serious injury, this made almost certain because—shocking but true—not one of them is wearing a helmet!

Squires did that, took them skating. Writing about it forty years later, Ritz hadn't stopped to think more about his teacher. He sees Mr. Squires writing on the blackboard. He is dressed in a professionally laundered white shirt worn with a tie, like Ritz's accountant father. Teachers had not yet decided it would be pedagogically effective to dress and sound like their students. Always Squires' sport coat hung from the back of his desk chair. Ritz sees the cruel depression in his teacher's right shoulder, visible under the crisp shirt as he writes on the blackboard. It's the only evidence he was badly wounded in Korea. The rumor was that, after college, Squires had been invited to try out for the Detroit Tigers farm system, but the war in Korea led him to join the Marines. As a teacher, he still wore his hair Marine-short. In Ritz's memory, Mr. Squires is prowling up and down the rows in his classroom. Like a tiger they said of him, prowling and doubling back, demanding answers—*That's not good enough, think harder—*

The phone rings. He would like it to be Natalie, but prepares for a karaoke insult, and picks up. "I'm pleased to report Brady Ritz has agreed to set himself adrift with nothing but some kale and bottled water."

"Dad?"

"Jane! That wasn't for you."

"Kale and bottled water. Are you expecting a call from Anne?"

"No, Janey. I imagine she's still mad at me. I suppose she spoke to you about Captain Ahab."

"I haven't talked to her," Jane says. "Mom told me about the boat. She said you have a dog. How's that working out?"

The question surprises him. Jane has called again, and he wants to answer her truthfully. *I'm lost in love*, he wants to say, but mustn't. Letting her know how obsessed he is with a dog would make him sound too much like Ace Foley.

"Too soon to tell," he says. "She's afraid of thunder, and hates balls."

"They're like kids," Jane says. "You think you have a handle on something, then you don't."

Does the handle have to do with Ashley? Don't ask, he thinks. You know nothing about what Jane and Dan face every day. Or Anne. Nor will Ritz try making a case for himself. For a whole week he had his chance, and said nothing.

"Well, okay, then. I forgot to thank you for the week."

"You never forget."

"Okay, then. If there *were* a hurricane, you'd have plenty of time to leave. Right?"

"With the shutters down, I might be safer here than in a school gym."

"But if they said to go, you'd go."

"Yes."

"Okay, then, 'bye for now."

"Goodbye, Janey, give my love to the girls and Dan, I love you."

He hangs up before hearing the answer to his blatant appeal for her to say she loves him back. But he's cheered. She called him Dad. And it's true, she never forgets. Birthdays and holidays, Mother's Day. Even, in the absence of a Stepfather's Day, she remembers him on the day set aside for bona fide dads. Like her mother, all her life Jane has been like that, and will be for as long as she lives. Like her mother, she is one of the responsibles. Collectively, don't they help to hold civilization together? Don't they equal the little Dutch boy with his finger in the dyke? And she remembered their parting in the airport last month, her concern about his safety in a hurricane. Paradoxically, Jane's goodness is her inheritance from a neglectful, indifferent grandmother. Natalie has successfully done everything to not be like her own mother.

But aren't most of his right-wing neighbors nice? Conventional? Dutiful about those very same things? And you, Ritz thinks. Other than how you vote, and writing checks for The Smile Train and Doctors Without Borders, what good have you done?

He sees Jane in the airport, her weary look. He wants back every throwaway line that hurt or angered her. No mother raising a prodigy in daily rehearsal for the lead role in the first-ever pre-school production of *Tosca* can find time to paint anything. Except Neosporin on skinned knees.

32
Health Care Professionals

It's too hot for anything but short walks with Truman, but Ritz begins to see how smart she is about heat. And much else. Being hungry isn't why she lies in front of the refrigerator. The tile floor is cooler there. That's why she also lies in front of air-conditioning ducts. When he snaps on the light for the patio, she gets up and prepares to go outside. When he snaps on the front-porch light, she ticks down the hall to meet him. Any time he puts on shoes, same thing. It means she remembers. Has a form of consciousness.

Ritz has never been in Naples during the summer. The heat is truly oppressive. Besides, he wouldn't think of leaving Truman to face alone the short, almost-daily thunder storms. Every time she starts shaking he feels helpless. All he can do is sit next to her on the Aerobed, stroke her and talk softly.

For the same reason, he stops going to the library. He floats instead in his pool on a plastic raft. Pilot's owner is a creature of habit, and Ritz times his short walks with Truman to see the blue-legged man. He gives him the dog food Truman won't eat. They talk about their grandchildren, the weather. On two occasions, dog-walking women smile behind their sunglasses and tell Ritz he has a cute dog. They're renters and don't know they are talking to the Butcher of Donegal. Each time, Truman sits facing away, the least "cute" dog imaginable. But Ritz thanks the women, tells them their dogs are cute, too. He learns gender-neutral naming has spread to pets: Lindsey is a pug, Jordan a cairn terrier. Neither woman gives her name, nor does Ritz give his. Only on the fourth meeting does he exchange names with a tam-o'-shanter (Glen). He thinks of this in terms of upstairs-downstairs in British costume dramas: dogs have names, those who walk them are just "staff."

Back home, Truman lies inside the glass door wall, and watches him in the pool. By two o'clock, big, balloon-like clouds start to gather. When the first drops dimple the water, Ritz gets out and towels off, watching as Truman quicksteps down the hall and heads upstairs. She whimpers and trembles under his hand.

He finally asks Glen about local vets. "There's a good one on Davis," he says. "Just west of Airport Pulling. I took Pilot there first thing for her shots."

* * *

"I'm not Doctor Brown, sir. I'm the receptionist Denise."

Duh, Ritz thinks. What doctor answers her own phone? "I thought you could pass along the details," he says.

"Do you want to make an appointment?"

"Yes, preferably today." *Duh.* Of course you prefer to make an appointment *today.* "I mean an appointment for some time later today," he says.

"Let me check the schedule." Double *duh.* Later today as opposed to earlier in the day. The receptionist is replaced by *Baby, baby, where did your love go?*

At four that afternoon, he is seated in the vet's waiting room. But now he has doubts. What doctor with a solid reputation ever sees a new patient so fast? Truman lies on the floor at his feet, shaking. Ritz keeps stroking her. Except for Denise, and a woman three seats away with a small white dog on her knees, he and Truman are here alone. Ritz avoids looking over. When Diana Ross is replaced by Kenny Chesney, he wonders: could knowing the name of a country-western singer be a sign of cognitive decline?

"That's a beautiful dog you have there." Ritz turns. The woman is smiling at him, stroking her dog. She seems slightly familiar, but that's because, at a certain point, many men and women begin to look alike. He smiles back. "Is that a border collie?" she asks.

"Yes, mostly. A rescue."

"Well, she looks all BC to me." In shorts and glitter tee shirt, the woman tousles her dog's head. "This is Contessa, aren't you snookems? She's my babycakes snookems. What's your dog's name?"

"Truman."

"A boy dog. Snookems likes boys."

"Actually, Truman's a female. There's a story behind it, but I won't bore you."

"Contessa is named for a movie, *The Barefoot Contessa*. Know it?"

"I guess not."

"Ava Gardner and Humphrey Bogart, *Turner Classic Movies*. I really liked that one. I saw it the day we got the call from the breeder. It seemed like a sign. Contessa is a Maltese, she's three."

"She has a sweet face." Contessa is now studying him with small, glittery eyes. "Hi, Contessa." Ritz smiles at the dog, conscious of trying to make a Maltese friend.

"What's Truman here for?"

"She's terrified of thunder."

"Uh oh, that's too bad. Contessa doesn't mind thunder a bit."

Terrified sounds extreme, but that's what Truman is. Ritz wants the woman to go on. To add details about her dog's blasé attitude to electrical storms, and then tell him about owners she knows with dogs like his, and what they do about it. But she is back to scratching Contessa behind the ears. Seated and rocked by the motion, the little dog reminds him of Madison being primped by her mother. Gently swayed, Contessa is now studying the receptionist. Denise pays no attention. Absorbed by her phone, she is half smiling, slowly brushing the screen.

When he again reaches down to stroke Truman, other dogs start barking in the building. Truman is now half under his chair. It pains him. She hears them and must think she's being given up again. She'll be caged. Rejected over and over because of her eye, by people passing up and down the aisles in search of a new dog slave. Ritz feels for her soft, quaking head. Murmurs everything will be all right, that there's nothing to worry about. He thinks to slide her out and lift her onto his knees, but goes on stroking.

"Okay, Donna and Contessa, door 3." Denise looks to Ritz. "Door 1 right behind me." She raises up to see over the counter. "Can you get her out? I can call David."

"No need, I pick her up all the time."

Offering to "call David" must mean he looks too decrepit to pick up a dog. Ritz gets off the bench and kneels. Truman won't look at him. Rejected for trying to help, he thinks. For doing good. He reaches under and slides her out, heavy as a bag of sand. But when he stands and tugs the leash, Truman gets up and follows.

A woman Anne's age stands smiling in the entry. She has long blond hair and is wearing a crisp white lab coat. She opens the door wide and Ritz draws Truman into the room. Doctor Brown closes the door, introduces herself, and firmly shakes his hand. "So, this is Truman." She immediately kneels. After letting Truman smell her, she cups the dog's face in both her hands. She looks up, and asks about the blind eye. Is she studying him the way the nurse did at Naples Community Hospital? Scrutinizing him for "tells" of an animal abuser? Ritz explains that Truman is a rescue from Key West. He replaces "terrified" with "frightened of thunder."

First impressions matter, and Ritz does his own scrutinizing. What he most likes is how the vet is kneeling to examine his dog. How she holds Truman's face in both hands. She's unconcerned about her starched lab coat, as crisp and white as Mr. Squire's dress shirts.

"Do you know anything about her past?" He tells her about heart worm, the mats and pole barn. How Truman was fed only table scraps. He thinks about it, but decides that bringing up Truman's grief might erode Doctor Brown's confidence in him. The vet shakes her head. She gathers Truman in her arms, stands smoothly and sets her on a steel table. She clips on her stethoscope and starts listening.

"I don't think she's ever been to a vet," Ritz says. "The shelter staff took up a collection to treat her."

For more than a minute the vet listens. Moves the scope, listens. She clips it around her neck "They did a good job," she says. "Her heart sounds strong." She raises Truman's lips. "Her teeth look good, too, but they've never been cleaned." I will see to it, Ritz thinks. If you say she needs to floss, we'll floss. Dr. Brown feels the dog's belly. Truman is still shaking, but is now also looking at the vet with wary curiosity. "Does she scoot?" Ritz doesn't understand. "Drag her butt on the carpet or lawn?"

"I thought she was wiping herself."

Dr. Brown smiles with Detective Briscoe worldliness. She's not just close to Anne in age, but also has something of his stepdaughter's style. Including the small paw print tattooed on her neck.

"Usually, dogs scoot when the anal glands need to be expressed," she says. "Emptied. I'll do that, and get her weight." When Brown snaps on a surgical glove, Truman looks at him. Ritz's urologist snaps it the same way when he moves in for the kill. The vet raises the dog's tail and inserts a finger. Eyes still on him, Truman doesn't move. Her good eye tells him she will never trust him again.

"We'll need to do blood work," Brown says, "and run some lab tests. You'll need to bring in stool and urine samples." After emptying the anal glands, she uses a scope to check Truman's eyes and ears. She inspects her paws, then readies a syringe to draw blood. Ritz fights down the urge to speak

Someone Better Than You: A Comedy of Manners

words of comfort, but Truman gives no sign she feels the needle.

The vet recommends Ritz buy something called a Thunder Shirt. "It's a snug-fitting vest you fasten with Velcro straps," she says. "It's no cure-all, but a Thunder Shirt makes some dogs less anxious during storms. Let's start with that. You can get them at Pets Rock."

Knowing the store makes him feel worldly-wise. An experienced dog owner. The vet sends him off with Heart Guard to protect against heart worm, and something called NexGuard for fleas. She gives him a shallow tray to slip under Truman's rump to collect urine, and a small bottle for the stool sample.

* * *

He parks as close as possible to the Pets Rock! entrance, then cracks open all four windows. He leaves the locked car with the engine running to operate the air conditioning, and runs for the entrance. You never leave a dog in a car, not in such heat. Last week, he read a letter to the editor from a dog lover who smashed a car window to save a schnauzer. But Ritz has a sense of urgency about the Thunder Shirt. He must be ready for the next storm. Once inside, he asks where they are, and hustles down the aisle. The display offers three sizes, only one left in Truman's middleweight division. Ritz grabs it with a sense of triumph. You were right to come, he thinks. What if you delayed? Seconds later he is waiting impatiently behind a man in a wifebeater undershirt. Every conceivable accessory for a fish tank is in his cart. Ritz fidgets. He silently pledges never again to leave Truman alone in a car.

Back home, he discovers that whoever wrote the Thunder Shirt directions in China skipped half the translation classes. He leads Truman upstairs to her place of safety on the Aerobed. When he sits next to her and begins putting the thing on, his dog again turns herself into a sodden lump. Each of his failed efforts leaves her looking hung up in the rigging of a failed parachute jump. Eventually, Ritz starts to figure out the Velcro straps—up, through, around, under, across. "Over in a minute, Tru, hold on, girl, you're doing great, good dog." On the fourth try he steps back. Truman pretty much resembles the dog on the package. Or a stuffed cabbage. As he peels off the Velcro, she refuses to look at him, and runs downstairs.

The following afternoon, thunder begins rolling in from the south. He struggles to strap on the garment. Several minutes into the storm, Truman at last settles on the Aerobed. Muzzle between her paws, she faces him as he strokes her head. Seams of lightning flash through the guest bedroom drapes, followed by thunder. Ritz chooses to believe that Truman has decided he is clumsy, but well-intentioned. The sun comes out. When he parts the curtains, the emerald golf course lies dazed in mist and heat. He feels a sense of accomplishment, a wish to release energy. He has the treadmill in the garage, but instead drives to the club's fitness center. A hand-lettered notice announces renovations are in progress.

At noon the following day, he times his walk to see Pilot and Glen. Ritz thanks his fellow staff member for recommending Doctor Brown. He describes the Thunder Shirt.

"So it works, that's good," Glen says. "Now you're ready for July 4. Have a nice day."

"You have a nice day, too." The tam-o'-shanter quakes as the Amigo passes up the sidewalk. On principle, Ritz has never in his life asked anyone to have a nice day. Really, though, what's the harm? What concession have you made? he thinks. In what way have you diminished yourself?

33
Betty Brubaker

With lots of cooing and stroking—and the Thunder Shirt—Ritz successfully defends Truman during the July 4 Siege of Naples. He lowers all the hurricane shutters in hopes this will form a sound barrier. Muffled skirmishes break out during the day. That night, the final assault is staged five miles to the south on Naples Beach. Classical music might be too somber or jarring, so he puts on Bill Evans and turns up the volume. He feels pleased when his tightly bound dog plops down in front of a stereo speaker. Truman is listening, Ritz is convinced of it.

Sharing keyboard jazz with his dog in a cave-like house leads him back to Betty Brubaker. She too is alone now, he should call her. Putting it off seems selfish, even though Ritz still resists having to respond sympathetically to details about Alex's death. But if he doesn't call, his callousness will fit with what he wrote in *Vanitas*. That's what Betty and others will think and say as they ride down escalators with their phones. Or sit on the can. Or ream out their ears with Q-tips.

* * *

The following morning, he goes outside to fold back the accordion-like hurricane shutters. Back in his study, he faces brilliant sunlight on the front lawn. Whatever Alex said or didn't say, the point now is to take the weight off his wife.

"Hello Betty, it's Brady Ritz."

"*Brady.* I'm so glad you called."

"Natalie told me about Alex. She sent me the obit."

"I understand your delay," Betty says. "I know this isn't an easy call to make."

"I try to think about the good times."

"There were lots of them, weren't there? I have to hope you can at least be glad Alex encouraged you to write."

No, he can't be glad, but he will take his cue from generous Jane and her mother. "I had a career at the *Post* because of Alex," he says. "I'm grateful for that. But tell me about yourself. Did you have people there? How did the memorial go?"

Betty tells him the son and daughter came. "They flew in twice in the month before Alex died," she says. "We all knew it was coming. Well, as you can imagine, lots of people came to the service. People you would know from the three dailies. From the Michigan Chronicle, the Oakland Trib, the Macomb Daily News. The Mayor came. You newspaper guys really have a fraternity."

"The last of the old-time religion," he says. "Betty, if you can, I need you to explain it to me," he says. "If you can't, I understand, but I have to ask."

Betty sighs. "You want to know whether Alex ever told me why he pressured you to use your own name."

"It was my decision, not his. But yes. Just to close the books."

"I knew you'd ask. I debated what to say, if anything. I decided you should know. Even though it's embarrassing, you should know. Long ago, we were at a party."

"Which one?"

"At Christmas thirteen years ago." *Thirteen years?* "I had too much wine," Betty says. "I told you something personal I shouldn't have."

34
Mood Sick vs Sick Sick

"It seems wrong to be celebrating."

"It does," Ritz said. "A lot of people are missing."

"And we won't see them again. Not at a *Post* Christmas party."

Betty drank what was left of her chardonnay. Ritz sipped his champagne-brandy punch. They were in the Westin Hotel ball room, next to a table with punch bowls and platters of finger food.

"So many people we'll never see again," Betty said. "New Years, Boxing Day, Bloomsday, the Fourth, Labor Day. I held out hope all this time. Those appellate court pricks."

The court had reversed a decision made by the National Labor Relations Board. Betty was married to one of the paper's managers, but she had been sympathetic to the unions. Ritz reached out for her glass.

"Thank you."

He worked his way through knots of people. Many smokers had quit, and the cleaner air brought back the smoke-filled night in the *Post* lobby. What? Something like twenty years ago. A few people nodded to him. The strike had blown up lots of friendships. As an ad salesman, he hadn't belonged to either faction. Even so, union members who had managed to survive still resented him.

The party's mood of forced bonhomie called for more than a refill. At the bar he handed the bartender a twenty. She winked, uncorked a new bottle and handed it to him. Ritz started back, head bowed, unavailable to others. A burst of too-hearty laughter was followed by an angry shout. Those in management were drinking less to celebrate the court's decision than out of a sense of relief. Out of what people now called closure. When he neared her, Betty gave Ritz a wan, half smile. She was dressed in a yellow suit and matching blouse. Yellow suited Betty the way grays and whites belonged to Natalie.

"Thank you." Betty held out her glass and Ritz poured. He set the bottle on the table and took up his punch cup. "How's Natalie?" she asked. "I thought I'd see her. Is she sick?"

"No."

"Are you two having problems?" Betty closed her eyes. "I'm sorry—" She looked at him and shook her head. "That's none of my business, it just came out. I think it's called projection."

Projection must mean she and Alex had a problem, not the Ritzes. He didn't know Betty Brubaker all that well, but Ritz knew her husband, as well as he knew anyone.

"Natalie isn't *here* here," he said." "She's in Toledo."

"What's there?"

"Her father."

"Is he the one who's sick?"

"So he says."

"You don't believe him? You don't think there's anything wrong?"

"Oh, he's sick, but it's 'this long illness, my life' sick. What Natalie calls mood sick. Max Macintosh is a serial hypochondriac, and Natalie is daddy's little girl. When he wants her company, he 'falls ill.'"

"Complicated."

"Not really," Ritz said. "Max is firmly committed to his own self-interest. He made his money in slum apartment buildings in Toledo. His son phones it in from California, but Natalie does her duty in person." Ritz wanted off the subject. "Where's Alex?"

"I'm his proxy," Betty said. "He's in Miami."

"Ah, major policy decisions at the highest level."

"Miami" was code for the conglomerate that owned the Detroit *Post*, and Alex was now the paper's acting city editor. In recent years, Alex's over-achiever schedule meant Ritz saw less of his friend. Now, it was just lunch at the press club, or drinks at the Anchor Bar. Conversations no longer moved much beyond the boilerplate, catching-up stage.

"Well, you're his oldest friend, I might as well tell you." Betty sipped her wine. "The Miami trip is a cover story."

In the widening gaps between after-work drinks, something had happened. Alex didn't fool around. He wasn't a toker, or snorter. Wasn't even close to the cliché of the boozing newspaperman. "What's he covering?" Ritz asked.

"It's medical," Betty said. "A guy problem."

"Oh."

"It's not a big deal with me," she said. "Or wouldn't be, except Alex isn't being straight about it. He's blaming me. He doesn't say it, but I know that's what he thinks. There's no blame involved, but he won't see it that way. You know how he is, this hard-driving, take-charge type of guy. He's not the sort of man with 'that kind of problem.' He can't not perform for no reason. There has to be a cause."

The word "perform" was followed by a loud parody of "White Christmas" coming from the far side of the ballroom. It crowded out whatever Betty was now saying. Ritz got the wine bottle and motioned for her to follow. They passed through people balancing drinks and shouting. Once outside the open double doors, they were standing in the hotel's high-ceilinged lobby. It was quiet and empty.

"Good idea," she said.

"I missed the last part," Ritz said. "Does he hit you?"

"Alex? Of course not, nothing like that. It's just… in Alex's mind, his problem must have a cause. I think he's decided I'm it. Something about me must explain it for him. He's just cold to me. He acts as though I'm not there, but it's also like an accusation. When I ask him what's wrong, he gives me this look. Like, 'You know what's wrong, and you know why.' Yes, I know *what's wrong*, but I can't help if he won't tell me anything. He was never like this, Brady. He was—well, you know. Alex is good company. Fun to be with."

Betty looked to the broad staircase leading up to the hotel's mezzanine. "I think he's in Miami mostly to see a doctor," she said. "Someone not local. I hope he gets help." She turned from the stairs. "Tell me more about Natalie's dad."

"Please, Betty, he's my friend."

"Oh, all right. I asked whether he wanted to try this new pill. The FDA just cleared it this spring. I shouldn't have. It was a huge mistake."

Betty sighed again. "When I brought it up, he wanted to know if I was, you know, unsatisfied. I told him I wasn't, but I knew it concerned him. I saw what he was thinking. Why is she bringing up pills if she's okay with us not having sex."

* * *

Seated twelve years later in his study, Ritz sees them again in the hotel lobby. He rolls forward in his swivel chair and leans on the desk. "You told Alex you spoke to me about it."

"You two have known each other since high school," Betty says. "How could it be wrong to tell you? I just said you and I were talking—I never said anything about telling you he had a problem. I just said we were at the Christmas party and we talked about this... product. Well, four or five years later you wrote a *Vanitas* piece. You thought the ads were insulting."

Truman shoves her nose against Ritz's calf. She's never done this. He scratches her head.

"We used the pills, but then he was diagnosed," Betty says. "After they removed his prostate, I didn't care, but Alex cared. You were working out what essays to include, how to organize your book. In his last week, that's when he told me about meeting you in the Anchor Bar. He said by that time he knew he was dying. He thought Zeno Kowalski needed a bitter pill himself. But he now regretted pressuring you to use your name. He was going to dictate a letter for you, but ran out of time. He told me to tell you he was sorry. He said, 'Tell Buzz—'"

"It's all right, Betty. It doesn't matter. What happened is my doing, not his. But I'm sorry we didn't patch things up. Alex was a good friend. I'll call again." He hears relief in Betty's reply. They say goodbye and Ritz hangs up. He goes on scratching Truman's head, Brubaker's ravaged face inches from his own.

35
"Getting it on and on and on—
Brave New World 2004"

On your behalf, your reporter has in recent days surveyed the latest TV ads promoting treatments for erectile dysfunction. (Just to be clear: "on your behalf" means just that. Your reporter is no less functional than he is ram-rod relentless in the pursuit of truth.)

The survey was necessary because the initials ED have of late been drummed, or more accurately thrust into popular consciousness, to signify the medical crisis of the moment: flaccidity. Aided by ad agencies, Big Pharma now makes it possible for men with no previous way to feel aggrieved to declare "We're victims too!"

To this end, the initials ED have been pressed into service and the campaign has gained speed, saturating media with the promotional equivalent of a massive hormone injection. Both in intensity and repetition, the ad campaign suggests the pounding toward release in Ravel's Bolero.

But all this effort to lend a hand to men on the slippery slope of dysfunction—to help them, as Martin Luther King might have put it, off the molehill of flaccidity, up the mountain of sustained sexual performance, raises—introduces a question or two.

You've seen the ads: handsome men with good-looking women are presented on docks, beaches, dancing in the backyard. *My special favorite shows an alert, smiling couple looking over a brochure. Husband and wife have teamed up to educate themselves on the latest pill.*

The man is trim and fit, with a full head of hair tinted silver to lend gravitas to his youthful good looks. The woman is dusky-eyed, obviously a heavy breather. Although the director has told her to look interested, not carnal, there is a definite something about her slightly mocking smile and hooded eyes that says Good to Go. It won't be long now, she's thinking. Once he finishes lip-reading the brochure, we can get down to business.

Which of course is the operative term: the ED business. It's not unfair to say that what we are witnessing is the Sixties' sexual revolution dropping the second shoe instead of blotter acid. Chemistry has timed its latest "enhancements" to dovetail perfectly with the aging of the Baby Boomer generation. The same people who forty years ago copulated their way from rock concert to peace rally are starting to cash in their 401Ks. They make the perfect target for a campaign aimed at convincing both men and women that a full life, correctly lived, takes its meaning from orgasm. Not from spiritual enlightenment or intellectual growth or service, but getting off.

Curing cancer makes sense: living longer might give people the added time to discover a more enlightened appreciation of the human condition. But a bigger and better bang for people in their last trimester?

So, think about it, and have a sit-down with your missus or significant other. Are you both really that interested in upping the number of times you make the beast with two backs? Or have those sly boots admen done you again?

36
What Happened to the Stiff Upper Lip?

Ritz closes the book. A seasoned, worldly, big-city newspaper editor got angry enough at a magazine column to shame his lifelong friend. A friend from boyhood, a drinking buddy. A colleague.

Nonsense, Ritz thinks. Why can't you learn anything? *You decided to use your own name. You and your vanity were The Decider.*

Seated on the bed, he puts *Vanitas* back in the nightstand drawer. Aspirin is in here somewhere. Ritz rummages for the bottle, and for no reason he remembers the baby in the Carrier air-conditioner box. He would be about forty now. As he got older, did his parents go on putting him in bigger cartons? When he reached puberty, did he pay them back? Ritz finds the aspirin and pries off the safety cap.

Don't forget, nothing but Jell-O. Last time, you ate a Danish.

Ritz snaps the cap back on and drops the bottle in the drawer. No aspirin before they snake around your gut, he thinks. And no fish oil, or vitamin C, or E. Nothing that thins the blood and inhibits clotting. Unlike most men his age, Ritz hasn't been put on a statin blood thinner like Lipitor or Zocor. And no Ace inhibitors like Daisy Pruitt's Lisinopril. No arthroscopic surgery yet, or knee replacement. No shiny new ball joint in his hip or shoulder. No stents in his arteries, or shunts installed for drug administration. No ostomy bags, or Australian campaign hats with drop-down awnings to guard against melanoma. Or clodhopper boots following bunion surgery. No trips to the "vein clinic"—none of it. With varying degrees of operational reliability, he is still working with original equipment.

Maybe *that's* why Alex Brubaker said what he said. What were Daisy Pruitt's words? *It'll come sooner than you think, mister.* Maybe it had nothing to do with ED It was Alex knowing he would be dead soon as he sat in some oncologist's office with cancer drugs seeping into his arm. Drugs that would make him violently ill in a few hours. Maybe he decided then and there his healthy-for-no-reason friend needed a lesson. And went the next day to the Anchor Bar to have a drink.

Natalie says his own good health is part of the reason he is callous. That he dismisses the suffering of others as self-pity. Ritz answers that when the Big One comes, or the "diagnosis," he will take his medicine. But how can he know that?

You don't understand. Being mood sick can be just as bad as sick sick. Oh, is that right? Yes, it is. You lack empathy, even sympathy. I do not, Natalie. People who make themselves the only thing worth talking about don't deserve sympathy or pep talks.

When they got home from parties, he often complained about long-winded suffering. For them, Natalie countered, suffering *is* the most important thing. Why? he asked. What happened to toughing it out? People should buck up more. It's selfish to hold others hostage all through Happy Hour with blow-by-blow details about angioplasty.

* * *

"Well, hello, Buzz, how *are* you?"

Nothing of what happened three weeks ago is present in Anne's voice. That was then, this is now says her breezy tone. But holding the handset, Ritz realizes he is pressing it hard to his ear. He fears his stepdaughter. Because of Truman.

"I'm fine," he says. "Are you and the kids home?"

"Iris and Jamal flew back, Delta has this supervision thing. Well, you and Mom know all about that. I'm here another week, and things have gone *great*. We're in the review phase, like setting the hook. Ha ha, Captain Ahab, no pun intended. Seriously, though, what I've learned is totally applicable in Michigan. Iris and Jamal made friends with kids with moms in the class, you cannot believe the synergy present in this group. The energy. I'm telling you, Buzz, it's like being plugged into this psycho-emotional cross-pollination web, like being on speed without the cardio effects—"

Ritz tries to relax his grip on the handset. No mention yet of Truman. As usual, he can't quite follow his stepdaughter, but hearing the force and sonic range of her voice, he *gets* something for the first time. She has a gift. He can hear it. For the first time, he understands The Grid, her appeal for others. He gets how her crescendos and sudden drops in pitch, her beautiful smile must pump up her friends. Men who can't think of anything to say would buy plane tickets and much more for a woman like Anne.

"How's Truman?"

He covers the handset. Breathes in, breathes out. "Good, she and I—"

"Mom told me you two are bonding. She says that's good, she feels bad about you being down there alone."

"I suppose you'll—"

"Hey, don't worry, if you two are good together, she's yours. Me casa es tu casa, isn't that what you said? Okay, mi perra es tu perra. Like I say, Mom feels bad."

Ritz's sense of relief is followed by gratitude. Then skepticism. "Hold on," he says. "If your mother feels bad, why hasn't she come back?" When Anne doesn't answer, he says, "I feel bad, too, Anne. About not putting life vests on Iris and Jamal. I can see why you felt you needed to leave. And I know why your mother left, but please, Anne. Ask her to come back. Tell her the cold snap has warmed up some. She says she'll know when it's time. If you know what that means, please tell me. How long is long enough?"

Anne turns down music. "I'm not supposed to say anything," she says. "You shouldn't think you know everything. You do, you know. You're smart and you think you know everything. Mom says it's because you *did* know everything. When you were an editor."

"No, Anne, I don't. Not then, not now."

"Yeah, well, what's that saying you do about all God's chillen?"

"Got troubles."

"There you go, all God's chillen got troubles."

"You're talking about your mother." Relief over Truman is followed by more fear. Something is wrong with Natalie. Names of injuries and illnesses crowd forward. "What's *wrong?*" he says. "If something's wrong, you have to tell me."

"I promised not to."

"Promised *what*?"

"That's something else I remember you saying. 'Don't get your pantyhose in a knot.' It's not major, okay? If it was major, I'd tell you, but I promised. I mean it's big enough, but not *big* big, like the big C. But she's coming back soon. I have to go."

* * *

Natalie doesn't pick up, and her recorded message is unchanged. It's not *big* big, like the big C. What's that mean? What would major mean in Anne's world besides cancer? Ritz sees his wife pitching and yawing her way up the coffin-lid stairs in Michigan, wearing a foot-surgery boot.

The beep. "I just talked to Anne. She wouldn't tell me what's wrong, but something is wrong, Natalie. I know why you left, you had good reason, I know that. But I also know you wouldn't still be up there. Not out of embarrassment alone. Something else is keeping you from coming down. If you don't call back, I'm flying up. Right after the colonoscopy. You said you'll know when it's time, what's that mean? What has to happen first?"

* * *

Just before noon, he gets the plastic tray given to him by the vet. At the end of the paver walkway, Truman starts to squat and Ritz slides the tray under. Her urine is vivid, close in color to Betty Brubaker's yellow suit years ago. Clumsily Ritz decants it into the labeled bottle. On the other side of

Grunwald's driveway, Truman cooperates further by defecating.

He checks the morning paper for the day's forecast. No rain predicted. He leaves Truman alone and drives the samples to the vet's office. On his way back, Ritz passes a man on a bike, dragging a dog on a long leash.

It's tied to the post holding up the bike's seat. Too fat for a racing bike, the man is perched on an old-style Schwinn. His tee shirt is taut over his belly, and he is steering with his right hand, studying the phone in his left. Ritz slows and looks in the rearview—the dog is plodding to keep up, a big male mutt with lolling tongue and short, mottled coat. Ritz comes to a stop. When the bike catches up to him, he buzzes down his window.

"Look what you're doing!" Wearing sun glasses, the man looks over and peddles past. "It's hot!" Ritz yells. "Dogs can have heart attacks!" Still pedaling, the man gives him the finger. Ritz speeds ahead a hundred yards. He stops and gets out. As the rider approaches, he slows and stops ten feet away.

"What's your problem?"

"Look at your dog."

"Are you crazy? It's exercise. Benjy loves it, we do it all the time."

"Not when it's this hot. Look at him."

Balanced on the handle bars, the man looks back at the dog. Benjy is standing with his head down, panting hard. The man turns back. "What are you, some kind of dog whisperer?"

"I have a dog," Ritz says. "This kind of weather is hard on her."

"That's yours, not mine. Benjy loves it. My uncle is a Naples cop. You want to talk to him about something?"

"I don't give a shit about your uncle. Think of your dog. I want you to think of the dog you're dragging after you on hot pavement, when you're riding your fat ass around on a bike."

In his twenties, the man thinks a second or two behind his sunglasses. He sits upright and shoves down on the peddle. At the last second, he veers around Ritz. "If you weren't so old I'd whip your ass." The dog lopes after. Possibly, the rider is moving more slowly.

Back home, he tells Truman about it. "A fat tub of guts," he says. "About twenty-five, totally oblivious. I should have pushed him off his bike, but that might hurt Benjy. That's the dog. Or Fat Boy might take it out on Benjy later."

He is doing this more often: conducting dialogues with Truman. Ritz doesn't just talk out loud to her. He waits for her imagined response before answering. About his best friend Alex who died; about how his wife won't tell him what's going on up in Michigan. When he hears himself sounding like someone delivering a post-surgery debriefing at a pool party, he shuts up.

Walking Truman that evening on Donegal Boulevard, he waits for a passing dog walker to be out of hearing. Ritz now points to the bunker in front of the seventh green. "I used a nine iron, not a sand wedge," he says. "I pitched it into the cup for an eagle. One of two in my career." Minutes later, they pass the main drain in the golf course's irrigation system. Ritz points again. "Gators. They travel through the pipes looking for fish. If you ever get loose, steer clear of that."

But Truman getting loose and running off seems unlikely. She now appears to accept, perhaps even to like her new digs. She still refuses to eat until Ritz is done, but no longer spends the day upstairs on the Aerobed. Ritz has been educating himself with books from the library. *Dog and Man* by Konrad Lorenz, Patricia McConnell's *For the Love of a Dog*. In *The Intelligence of Dogs*, Stanley Coren describes his own dog Wiz, a Cavalier King Charles spaniel. One morning Wiz lay in a sunny square on Coren's kitchen floor. The dog got up and ran out. Moments later, he returned dragging a bath towel. He arranged the towel with his forepaws in the square of sunlight, then settled down for a nap.

When Truman comes into his study, Ritz closes the book. "Are you seeking me out? Do you need company?" More projection. When he wakes that night to pee, Truman is still lying on the floor at the foot of his bed.

He cooks for her more than for himself. Dices boneless chicken breast, squeezes ground sirloin into bite-sized morsels before sautéing. Always in healthy olive oil, not butter. She especially likes carrots, and sweet potato. Out on the patio Ritz quickly gobbles down his own meal to free his dog to eat.

He takes her to Cambier Park, just behind Fifth Avenue. A jungle gym and swings are set up for small children, with vapor jets to keep them comfortable. Sidewalks stay cool under big live oak trees. Ritz sits on a bench and Truman lies at his feet. In the next half hour, several women pass. Dressed to the nines, they are walking or carrying their small dogs. Teacup Yorkshire terriers and Pomeranians. A toy schnauzer. A tiny poodle made out of cotton candy—all of them serving as fashion accessories. Twice, a homeless man stops. There aren't many in Naples, but both men seem to be taking good care of their sympathy-prop dogs. *Say, would you have an extra fiver for Sam and me?* Ritz gives each man a ten, and feels guilty.

He and Truman circle the band shell, and sit again. On the greensward, a young dad is playing Frisbee with his little girl. After a minute, the dad curls his arm and whips the disk as hard as he can. "Dad!" The frustrated child turns and starts running. Her father watches a second before looking down at his phone. You are Modern Man 1.0, Ritz thinks. Watching Modern Man 2.0.

* * *

The day before his colonoscopy, Ritz eats nothing but the lime Jell-O made the night before. He swills jugs of a sports drink "with electrolytes," and is soon blazing a trail to the commode. Between trips, he sits in his lounge chair and toggles between *CNN*, and *Casablanca*. Truman comes from her post in front of the refrigerator to lie next to him. The first two times Ritz pushes up from the couch, Truman stands, thinking they will walk. But her staff member moves in the wrong direction, opens a door and disappears. As he sits splattering away, Ritz thinks how weird it all must seem to his dog.

Empty and sullen, he brings her with him to visit Grunwald. "Can you look after Truman tomorrow? I'm going in for a colonoscopy."

"Of course," Murray says. "Coco and I will take good care of her." Murray offers to have Coco drive him to Naples General, but Ritz says no thanks, he'll take a cab. Ruiz had nothing to do with the fallen china cabinet, but for some reason Ritz is still suspicious of Dolores' black-clad nephew.

Back at the house, he prepares Truman's food for tomorrow. The idea of Coco Ruiz having anything to do with his dog bothers him. It never happened, but he keeps wondering: Who was it she called at the dog beach? He microwaves a leftover pork chop and sweet potato for his dog's midday meal. He will be home in time to serve them a dinner of grilled salmon, white rice and steamed carrots.

* * *

Just after sunrise, he wakes from a dream. A Frisbee sails down the block as Deirdre Foley's chimes play the opening notes of *The Star Spangled Banner*.

A starving, evacuated Ritz walks Truman before taking her to Grunwald's. He brings a canvas Bean bag with her china dinner plate and matching water bowl. "There's boiled macaroni to go with the pork chop—" He taps the bag. "And Boars Head honey maple turkey for a snack. That's in a separate Tupperware bowl. Plus poop bags and toys."

"Brady, really—" Murray hefts the bag. "You'll be back in four or five hours."

And the Thunder Shirt. He doesn't like Ruiz being involved, but Murray won't be able to put it on. Ritz instructs Coco how to work the straps. Except for "lunchtime," and two short walks, Coco will be leaving Truman "in her own house." In case of an electrical storm, he will bring her back to Murray's and put on the Thunder Shirt. Ritz explains how his dog is accustomed to eating with her human, but for reasons of pack etiquette she always waits until he's done. Arms folded, Coco frowns and nods solemnly.

* * *

Half an hour later, his cab pulls up at the entrance to Naples Community Hospital. He stands before the Admitting desk and answers questions. A plastic I.D. bracelet is fastened to his wrist. He is directed to a lounge, and asked the same questions. Are they testing for cognitive function? Finding out whether he forgot his name and age between Admitting Lounge 1 and 2?

When he takes a seat, Ritz realizes he forgot to bring a book. TV now serves as the universal babysitter. He takes a chair under the set to avoid having to watch. Almost immediately a cruise-jewelried volunteer leads him to a dressing room. He puts on the humiliating gown, seeing Alex Brubaker in his hospital room. As directed, Ritz stuffs his clothes into a plastic bag. He *did* remember to bring the cell phone, and keeps it with him. A chatty pair of nurses load him onto a gurney, followed by another Q&A with a tween-something anesthesiologist. He's given a shot, then wheeled into a brilliantly lit room with many screens. After a second shot, Ritz is glad to close his eyes and start counting. His last thought is of Natalie and Truman in matching Thunder Shirts.

Awake an hour later, he learns he is "clean as a whistle." Have all the bald-headed or graying doctors died? The amazingly young gastroenterologist has found no polyps or suspicious cell growth, but tissue samples will be sent to the pathology lab. Left alone in the recovery room to drink orange juice, Ritz calls his wife. Nothing. It's not like her at all. Natalie knows what he's doing today, but isn't answering. Why? He calls his neighbor.

"Very quiet all morning," Murray says. "That's an incredibly passive dog you've got."

"But no storm."

"It's a lucky thing. I wasn't sure Coco understood the shirt thing."

"Thanks, Murray."

"Coco took her for a walk and they met up with someone else with a dog. Coco said Truman used him as a shield. Should he come get you?"

"Thanks, I'll take a cab. I appreciate your help."

"Your scope went well?"

"Based on the report, I have the bowels of an eighteen-year-old."

He calls Natalie a second time, and gets the same recorded message. *Why?* Why isn't she picking up?

* * *

In at seven, out by noon. Colonoscopy patients are supposed to be accompanied when they leave the hospital, but Ritz explains he's alone, and is allowed to sign a waiver and leave. The sliding doors roll open, and he is wheeled to the cab stand. A very senior male volunteer helps him into the first car and slams the door. It's been five years since Natalie drove him here for the procedure. As the cab pulls away, he remembers being wheeled afterward into the visitors lounge. Natalie looked up from her book. Smiled and said Hi. It's a small thing that isn't small, someone waiting for you, looking up and smiling. He feels weak and dull.

At Donegal, the driver pulls up to the keypad. Ritz lowers his window and enters the code. Once in his driveway, he pays and goes inside. Start to finish, the whole thing has taken five hours. Somehow, it should take longer. Involve an overnight hospital stay and another battery or two of questions.

"Truman?" No, Tru is next door with Murray.

He once more checks for messages. Again nothing. Natalie would at least call to ask about the procedure. She would call. And the Jell-O mold he sent her from the Mole Hole, she would call about that. He wants to celebrate his good report with her. With Jane and Dan. Anne and her children. Maybe he wants most to celebrate the moment with little diva Ashley. He sees her alone with grandpa in his study, opening and closing his file drawer. Her sister is upstairs watching *The Cartoon Network,* and Ashley and grandpa have each other all to themselves. Guess what? he whispers. Grandpa pooped all day. He kept pooping and pooping, until there was nothing inside his whole body. Then they put him to sleep and—get this, Ashley—they stuck this thing like the one your dad used. Remember? When you plugged up the toilet with a Beany Baby? That's right, all the way up Grandpa. Now, tell me what you did at Cedar Point.

But no one is here. Ritz feels a little unsteady, but he wants Truman, and crosses the back lawn to Grunwald's. As he packs up his dog's things, Murray tells him about Ace Foley. "I forgot to tell you," he says. "His son came two days ago and checked Ace into Aspen Afternoons. It was inevitable. Better he goes now before something happens."

At Donegal, Aspen Afternoons is both an actual place, and a synonym for having lost your memory. Not just someone went to Aspen Afternoons, but someone *went* Aspen Afternoons. Murray also tells him that Daisy Pruitt's storm shutters are in place. "But she's still in there," he says.

As he walks back with his dog, Ritz sees them listening to Bill Evans in his shuttered house on the Fourth of July. Daisy Pruitt is just now entombed up the street in the same way. He sees himself rehearsing in his closet for karaoke, and now Daisy is trying on her latest ensemble, bought at Chico's summer sale. Natalie described it for him, how Daisy modelled for her, turning before the mirror in her interior decorator's interpretation of Marie Antoinette's dressing room. After Reggie died, Daisy had the whole house re-done. She especially wanted me to see the dressing room, Natalie told him. It's her way of moving on.

Back in his own house, Ritz climbs the stairs. For some reason they seem steep, the air stuffy. In the bedroom he opens the French doors. The wind is picking up. Grunwald told him *The Weather Channel* reported that Tropical Storm Brianna has been down-graded. It will brush the keys and may cause some coastal flooding, but isn't expected to come ashore.

He lowers himself into a canvas deck chair. From up here, Ritz can see Donegal's gated entrance. A car enters; seconds later it schusses past. In the premature dark, Christmas lights still glow in the two condo door frames. Below, corrugations come and go in the pool. Trees on the fairway are bowing. Trying to straighten, bowing.

Truman comes out and settles next to him. She is needy now, in anticipation of what's coming. Maybe she already wants the Thunder Shirt. Ritz reaches down to stroke her head. It's become a small miracle to him. Round and firm, it slopes back to the slightly coarser hair of her outer coat. The inner coat is like cashmere. Tuffs of it gather on the staircase.

"She'd collect it," he says. "To save Dolores the trouble. That's Natalie, she keeps track of things. She remembers. She keeps a notebook full of food information—calories, good and bad cholesterol, fatty acids. She takes it with her shopping. When she has a big list, I go with her. She reads a label, consults her book. Every time we go, she points at the deli counter. 'Trans fats enough to kill off everyone in Naples,' she says. The book is for me, not herself. To keep the old boy going. And for 'the little ones.' That's Natalie. Never forgets a birthday, a holiday. I know you'd like her. Jane's the same way, so is Murray. Right now he's on his way to Esther, to close her drapes. Thunder frightens her, too."

A golf cart is coming along the gravel path. Mike Connolly, the head greens keeper. As always, his English setter Rowdy is riding shotgun next to him. Connolly is divorced, inseparable from his dog. Ritz stands to see better. The pin flags and sand-trap rakes Mike has collected clatter behind him.

"The luckiest dog on the property," Ritz says. "The only one who goes wherever he wants. I was playing with Minetta and Barney Rattle, we came across a turd on the ninth tee. Rattle was funny. He delivered a prosecutor's closing argument against Rowdy. 'Ladies and gentlemen of the jury, throw the book at the dog and the owner. They should be locked up, caged, disciplined.' All this over a dog turd on *his* golf course."

He waves, but Connolly passes without seeing. Ritz asks himself: why are you waving? He lowers himself into the chair. Why does he feel this small but real sense of disappointment as the greens keeper bounces up the cart path. Why does Glen, driving away on the Amigo, wave above his tam-o'-shanter? Ritz reaches down to Truman.

The sky is steel blue, streaked with phosphorous. Truman whines under his hand to signal she wants to go in. Last night, he woke to something like a bird chirping. When he got up, his dog was again sleeping at the foot of the bed. Ritz came back and lay watching her dreaming. At intervals, she made little yips. Her paws twitched. She's with Coda, he thought. Running with her cattle dog, chasing cars. Happy as dogs can get. No one will ever know how she's lived, what she's known. What disappointments, indignities, injustices, abuse, neglect. More projection, he thinks. A dog that came from nowhere, and is herself inscrutable. Why does that frighten you?

***

Rain on his face wakes him. Ritz pushes up and goes inside. He closes the doors and feels unsteady, but must go downstairs for the Thunder Shirt. Truman is on the Aerobed, looking at him. He holds to the railing going down. She passes him. He's gotten better at putting the thing on. Back upstairs, he gets down next her. She always goes limp, but he stuffs it under her, meshes together the Velcro tabs, and sits back. He will stroke her until she stops shaking.

He is sitting in the family room. Ritz has no memory of coming back downstairs. Outside, the sky has darkened. He gets to his feet, and steps to the glass. Vaguely, Ritz wonders how long he's been home and turns away. On his way back to the sectional, the lights go out.

37
In the room the nurses come and go Talking of Doctor Piccolo

A tube snakes from an I.V. pole up under his hospital gown. Next to the bed, Grunwald is sleeping in a comfortable chair. He is gently snoring, chin resting on his chest. His hands are pommeled on the cane between his legs.

"I did this already."

Grunwald snorts awake. "Hi Brady. You said you felt lightheaded and fainted."

"I was fine. I don't remember."

"It happens." Grunwald brings his hand up. His watch clicks against his glasses, and he lowers the hand to his cane. "Not very often," he says. "The prep for a colonoscopy depletes the potassium, but you're okay."

"I had a seizure? A stick-between-the-teeth seizure?"

"Relax, nothing like that. You never lost consciousness, but you fell and bumped your head. No concussion. It's called hypokalemia, You're on an I.V. loaded with potassium. You'll be fine."

Grunwald fishes in his breast pocket and brings out his phone. Ritz touches his forehead. A bandage is taped above his right eye. "Hi, it's me. Yeah, he's awake. Real good, I'll be down in five minutes." Murray pockets the phone and rocks forward. And again. He pushes down with the cane and stands.

"How did you know?"

"I was shaving, getting ready for Coco to drive me to Villa Bellissima. He was smoking on the deck, he saw the doors open on your balcony. I know you don't like him, so I went over. I tapped you on the floor with my cane, just inside the family room. You were mumbling but conscious. To be on the safe side, I called 911. But I need to go now to Esther. Heavy wind frightens her. I asked and they said you won't be kept overnight, you'll be released in a couple hours. Just take a cab, you'll be home before the evening news."

"Thanks, Murray." Grunwald finds the curtain. "What about Truman?"

"She's fine, She had the shirt thing on. Did I tell you Foley's son came from Orlando? He got Ace admitted to Aspen Afternoons."

"You told me. Thanks, Murray."

Grunwald leaves, and Ritz settles back. The tapping cane joins corridor voices and background music. He thinks it's the same easy listening that Sunshine played on her boombox. Along with potassium, what he feels spreading through his body is gratitude. Staring up at the ceiling, he examines his state. Its warmth and serenity. Grunwald to the rescue, he thinks.

And Truman is safe.

* * *

"You said Donegal."

"Publix first, then Donegal. I won't be long."

Ritz leans back from the Plexiglass screen. He's got on the same clothes Grunwald found him in. The shirt front is stiff with dried drool from his time mumbling on the floor. It fits with the taxicab, a Crown Victoria like the cop car. This one smells butt-funky, overlaid by a pine-scented deodorizer hanging from the rearview mirror.

The road ahead is dark, with bright patches of late-afternoon sun. The cabbie told him the storm was delayed, and this somehow fits with The Better Days Ahead pawn shop on his left. Now comes Olive Garden. Red Roof Inn. Red Roof ads always mention being pet-friendly. Something to file away for future use, Ritz thinks. We'll see the sights. Natalie, you and me.

"Change your mind?" The cabbie is looking at him in the rearview. "You said something."

"Sorry, no. Publix first, then Donegal."

The cab passes the marina where Ritz keeps his boat. Jamal is cradling his arm, looking at him through bleared Plexiglass. In half a mile, the cabbie swings up the drive at the King's Way strip mall. "Aw Christ—" Brake lights are shining ahead, outside the entrance to Publix. They belong to a huge SUV, a Cadillac Escalade. The cabbie pulls up behind. A minute or more passes. "Maybe it's medical," Ritz says.

"Nah, it's not medical. If I use the horn, they get out. They come back and yell, it takes even longer."

Still the Escalade remains in place. But now, very slowly, the passenger door is opening. Very slowly it inches further out. At last it pops in place. Seconds pass before a leg extends. A man's white shoe seeks and finds purchase. Several more seconds pass as more of the man emerges. Dressed in matching pink shorts and polo shirt, wearing a Red Sox cap, he now stands.

"It won't be long now," Ritz says.

"Don't count on it."

The man begins negotiating the curb. "Jake! Jake! The door!" In motion now, Jake is on his way to the entry with no intention of stopping. "JAKE! THE DOOR!" He stops and half turns.

"Christ." The Cabbie puts his car in reverse to swing around the Cadillac, but the driver's door opens and cuts him off. He sits back as a woman Jake's age gets out and quicksteps around the SUV. Knowing she will take care of the open door, Jake is again in motion. Ritz sees this often in Naples, the wife in charge of the driving.

"Just park, I'll find you," he says. "I won't be long."

"Uh huh."

He gets out and moves quickly to beat Jake to the door. But stops. The man's back is curved, shoulders sloped. He is scuffing his shoes the way Daisy scuffed her slippers. And like Daisy attired for motoring, Jake has dressed up to come here. Or his wife dressed him, coordinated his ensemble. In the seconds standing behind him, Ritz sees something self-contained. Even dignified. If you and Natalie have a future, he thinks, you are looking at it. You too will very likely go on and on, just like Jake and the missus.

Once inside, he grabs a hand basket and passes through a second set of doors, into the frigid market. Something overhead makes him glance up. It's immense to him, a cathedral with girders, like the Fort Myers airport. He passes

Someone Better Than You: A Comedy of Manners

quickly around shoppers lost in thought before pyramids of sale items. Others are waiting for sandwiches to be made. A woman picks up and puts down a rotisserie chicken. He hopes the deli counter won't be crowded, and aims for it. No such luck. Ahead, lunchmeat and cheese buyers shift and mill. They've taken numbers and keep looking down at the ticket. Truman needs more Boars Head honey maple turkey, but because the cabbie is waiting, Ritz will settle for pre-packaged lunch meat. He skirts the crowd and hastens toward the coolers. This involves passing bakery sample stations—cakes and bread, petit fours, sticky buns.

Between mounds of Tostitos and another sample station sits a boy. He is in Ritz's field of vision for not more than three seconds. Older than Iris, perhaps fourteen, he is bowed in his wheelchair, with round shoulders, shrunken arms. But in those seconds Ritz sees the boy has fine features, and as he passes, the boy sighs. Everything that follows drops into the vacuum left by a sigh identical to Natalie's.

Ritz has turned into the coffee aisle. Facing Seattle's Best, he still hears the sigh, like blood rushing in his ears. Packaged meat is one aisle over, but he came here out of fear. In his haste, he almost stepped on the boy's service dog lying next to the wheelchair. A panting yellow lab. The boy's hair was rich and black, his smile shining.

Ritz stands fixed in place with his hand basket. The broken body was not so much seated as contained by his chair, beside the softly panting dog. Handsome he was. Beautiful even. Torment and rage must accompany such a life. Someone so afflicted and so young but smiling. It's a warning. A sample station just for you, Ritz thinks. A gift of some kind, but of what? What is the gift?

He feels others watching. He doesn't need coffee, but grabs a bag to seem purposeful. Ritz is sweating in the frigid supermarket. Truman is safe, waiting at home. Waiting the way the boy is waiting. Ritz throws packaged turkey into his basket, and hurries toward express checkout.

* * *

"Got everything?" The driver turns down his radio.

"I need to make another stop."

"It's your nickel."

38

Aspen Afternoons

There are no aspens at Aspen Afternoons, but many of the residents hail originally from aspen country in the upper Midwest. That's what they would say of themselves, they hail from somewhere.

Behind the reception desk, a giant photo shows yellow-leaved aspens stepping down a mountain slope to a sapphire-blue lake. A flannel-shirted couple sits fishing in a rowboat, and overhead soars an eagle. At the shoreline, a buck keeps watch as his doe drinks.

Never to be conquered—not by epiphanies in supermarkets or anything else—an automatic resistance to cliché leads Ritz to see jet skiers terrorizing the deer. Drunken duck hunters are blasting away at the bald eagle, and under the soaring bird, the L.L.Bean couple in the rowboat is replaced by a boy falling out, his elbow dislocated by a snaggle-toothed park ranger.

Ritz steps to the counter and the receptionist looks up. "Albert Foley."

She smiles and takes up a clipboard. "You mean Grace Foley." Again she looks at him without a hint of condescension. She's about thirty, but clearly knows her geriatrics.

"Everyone calls him Ace, but he would be listed under Albert."

As a courtesy, she looks again at the clipboard before slowly shaking her head. "No, he'd be on this list. Do you know when he arrived?"

"Three days ago. His son checked him in."

"Ah..." She flips pages. Of course they would keep a list of those who have moved on to Even Deeper Memory Care, or have died. She holds back the pages and runs her finger down the column. "Okay, here we go. I was off yesterday, but they told me what happened. Mister Foley wasn't happy here."

"He left?"

"Well, yes. His son came back yesterday. With an attendant and a van. It says they took him to The Reef in Orlando. We own that, it has closer supervision." She looks up from the clipboard. Closer supervision means Ace Foley punched someone.

"Anyone else?" Of course, he thinks. That's how it is. When a friend or family member turns out to no longer "be available," the visitor holding a melting ice cream sundae is given a Plan B. Maybe even C. There is something terrible about coming here and not seeing Foley.

"I live at Donegal Country Club," he says. "Does your list include home addresses?"

Eyes on him, the young woman gives Ritz a slow nod to acknowledge his sharpness of mind. "Yes, it does," she says. "Would you like me to check for others from Donegal?"

"Please. Anyone."

What's he doing? Why is he still here, waiting for her to pull a name out of a hat? A Bingo number? She flips back to page one, and scans down. "Rita Lane, on Pomfret Place." Ritz shakes his head, he's never heard of Rita Lane. The receptionist looks again, involved now, wanting to reward his sharpness of mind. "Trent Sanger—no, he went to Phase Three last month. Okay." She nods. "Barney Rattle, Cambridge Court." She looks up and smiles. "Funny how the names go in spurts," she says. "We have three Barneys with us just now. If he hasn't gone to dinner, his room is 110." Only one hall leads from the lobby, but experience must be why she points.

"Thanks."

"Thank *you*, sir. We know what it means to our residents to have visitors. If he hasn't eaten, you can join him for dinner on us. That's our treat for visitors."

Ritz smiles, but she is already back to her laptop. He glances again at the giant photo. The scene now strikes him as insensitive. *That time of year when yellow leaves, or none or few do hang upon those bows that shake against the cold.*

He starts down the wide, well-lit hall. On the walls hang more calming images. Cascades, smoky forest interiors, sea oats against a gulf sunset. Parked under the images are wheel chairs, some occupied, others empty. As he nears her, a woman studies his face. Two other women are slumped in sleep. He eyes room numbers, and begins to feel panic. How long has Rattle been here? Before coming, did he join the posse? Has a visitor told him about the book? Will he raise his index finger?

He approaches a man trapped in a grooming ritual. It's wrong to look, but Ritz can't escape seeing him scratching and pulling his hair. The yield lies on his shoulder, below a bloody place above his ear. Everything is becoming literal. Yellow aspen leaves *are* death, people *are* pulling out their hair.

Coming here was a mistake, but Ritz keeps moving. Go see Barney, he tells himself. Do the hard thing and see Barney.

He stops short of the open door. You're lying, he thinks. You're here for the same reason you came to see Ace Foley. Because you hope to see someone who will see you, not the author of *that book*. But still he hesitates. The other real possibility is that Barney Rattle no longer knows anyone named Brady Ritz.

He enters as a horn blares from the wall-mounted TV. Barney is watching the set, propped against the bed's headboard. He is dressed in golf shorts and a white polo. Ritz realizes he has never seen Barney wearing anything but white polos. Rattle's hands are folded defensively over his crotch. He looks from the set, frowns, then smiles.

"Look what the cat dragged in."

"Hi Barney."

"Did you bring a cheeseburger?"

"I didn't, I'm sorry."

"Next time."

Ritz steps to him, relieved when Rattle shakes his hand with a firm grip. A jokester, that's Barney. A born politician, always cozying up to the ladies at dinner. "Go on, sit." He points to the TV. "Red Sox kicking New York's ass, I love it." He tilts his head at the curtain separating the two beds. "He's deaf as a stone," Barney says. "Sleeps through anything."

"That's good."

Seated now, Ritz takes in the room. A clean, well-lighted place. Hanging above Barney's headboard is an aerial shot of mansions along the Newport, Rhode Island coast. Rattle was a fire chief in Providence, and the poster seems to suggest knowledge of his background. Was it put up to make Barney feel at home, or just coincidence? Aspen Afternoons could have a garage full of regional posters, changed to fit each patient's background. The nightstand has a water pitcher, and a framed photo of grandchildren. Slippers are lined up on the floor. A wheel chair is positioned on the other side of the bed.

"How's the food?" Barney's mouth turns down and he waggles a hand. "You doing physical therapy?" Mouth still turned down, Barney nods. He's short and stocky, still powerfully built, but his nod says Why ask? PT is for people with a future. What you see is my future.

"It's dinner time," Ritz says. "I'm not a member of your Donegal harem, but do you want me to be your date?"

Rattle smiles. "Why not?"

Ritz gets the wheelchair and positions it as Barney works himself to the edge of the bed. Ritz kneels and wedges the slippers over toes at odds with each other. "Okay, big guy, get me out of here." Ritz holds Barney's elbow and eases him off the bed. Once standing, with tiny steps Rattle turns himself into position. Ritz locks the chair, pats the seat. Barney drops with a sigh.

"What'd you do with my seatbelt?"

Ritz laughs, relieved and grateful. Barney Rattle is done for, but not done. "You don't need one with this model," Ritz says. "It's got airbags."

"*You're* the airbag."

As he starts pushing, a woman's voice blares from the TV, pitching a luxury golf development. Once in the hall, Ritz shoves past the hair ritual without looking. "Watch for drunks," Barney says. "Lots of DUIs in here."

"Do they have drinks? Happy hour?"

"You kidding? Not a chance."

"Why not?" Ritz feels purposeful pushing the chair. Worthy of having an opinion. "What could it hurt?"

"I said the same thing. 'What's the problem?'" Ahead, people are seated at tables. Ritz smells food, but can't tell what it is, or whether the smell is good or bad.

"What did they say when you asked them about Happy Hour?" *They,* Ritz thinks shoving the chair. *Them.* Barney Rattle and Brady Ritz against all odds.

"Insurance," Barney says. "Liability. It's the meds in here. One drink and kaboom. I said okay, I get it, the lawyers. So, why not give people a waiver to sign? You got people here can still sign a waiver. Nah, they won't do it."

Adjacent to the dining room, people sit in wheelchairs and folding chairs before a huge TV. A game show. Some are watching, others sleep. Everything Ritz sees, whatever his eyes pass over makes him feel callous. A voyeur. It's the boy in Publix, so young, so denied. How could Ritz see this, and not remember the boy, the bookend opposite, but not? Whatever he sees turns instantly into an exhibit, a diorama. Children in *Brave New World* will be brought here to condition them to death. Ritz feels like that, a peeping Tom. He pushes the chair, careful of slippered feet. The game-show theme explodes, the studio audience applauds and cheers. He pushes the chair around plastic rubber trees, and Barney points ahead to an empty table. They pass a seated woman next to the wall. Very small but looking crowded in her wheelchair, she is hunched to protect a baby in the crook of her arm. For an instant Ritz stops pushing. It's all wrong, leaving her alone with an infant, a newborn.

    A doll. Technology has made it that lifelike. Perhaps the same doll Ashley Vanghent pointed to last Christmas. He pushes past a couple bowed in prayer over wedges of bread pudding. Another doll, then a lifelike beagle puppy wedged companionably next to a man reading a brochure. Ritz reaches the empty table, locks the wheel chair and sits. Within seconds a server sets down plates, fills water glasses and is gone. Barney begins eating and doesn't talk—pork tenderloin, bread dressing and mashed potatoes, green beans. Conversations are taking place around them, but Barney just eats. Ritz follows his lead and keeps silent. Did you offend him in some way? he wonders. Commit some breach of nursing-home etiquette? Or, Rattle never speaks at meals here. His big voice and laugh figured often in the Donegal dining room. Here at mealtime, he has fallen silent.

    In what seems like one practiced gesture, the plates are taken away and replaced by peach cobbler. As Ritz starts on his dessert, a man sits across from him at the table. In a blue suit and black tee shirt, he looks in good shape. He is quickly served the dinner, and starts eating. After a moment, Ritz asks how he likes the food. Deaf like Ace Foley? The man says nothing and keeps eating.

    Back in Barney's room, he helps Rattle back onto the bed, then sits again in the visitor's chair. Truman is the only news he has, so he recounts information in the latest Donegal newsletter. In the fall, an assessment will be made to set up a driving range behind the equipment barns. A new sous chef has been hired by Chef Gordon; the acting club manager has been made permanent. "They do it every summer," Rattle says. "Approve a lot of changes when no one's around to make waves. You watch. She was okay as acting director. She knew enough to do what she was told to keep the job. Now? A women in charge? That fatso running the board will figure out a way to get rid of her."

When Barney reaches to his bedside table for the TV remote, Ritz knows it's time to leave. He stands. "Say hi for me to the guys," Barney tells him.

"I will." Ritz shakes his hand.

"Next time, don't forget the cheeseburger." Barney winks, and presses the remote.

39
It was a dark and stormy night

"Good dog, Trumie, don't worry, it's me, I'm home—"

The cabbie pulls up the driveway. He flips the flag on the meter and looks in the rearview mirror. The eyes of someone dealing every day with people who keep remembering more stops, Ritz thinks. People all alone in the backseat talking to Trumie.

He hands his credit card over the Plexiglass and gets out. The rain hasn't started, but the air is still heavy. He takes back his card, and tips generously in cash. As the cab backs down, massive clouds are shifting slowly. He hustles up the walk and lets himself in.

"Truman!"

No, not here, next door. He trots down the hall, pulls open the slider and crosses to Grunwald's pool cage. Inside, he finds the door wall locked. Ritz cups the glass. The bridge lamp is on. He bangs the glass. *Think!* Because of the coming storm, Grunwald has gone to be with his wife at Villa Bellissima. He will close her apartment drapes and turn up the TV to muffle the thunder. Yes to cats at Bellissima, no to dogs. Murray would not be allowed to bring Truman with him.

He runs back. Once inside his own house, he calls Murray's cell. "Hi Brady, I'm sure you want to know about your dog. I had to get here to beat the storm. We brought Truman with us."

"They let her in?"

"Coco has her."

"Ruiz!"

"Take it easy, she's all right. He has the thunder shirt."

"Ruiz owns pit bulls! Two pit bulls!"

"Please, Brady, really, it's okay"

"It's not okay! I read it, Murray, they steal dogs for pit bulls to tear apart! How could you do it! Where's he live!"

"Brady, really, calm down. He's at Dolores's. His own place has a mold problem."

Ritz bangs down the handset.

40
Chekhov's Gun, Act 3

Rain in sheets is rocking his SUV. He will pay Ruiz any ransom. Tru is quiet, no fighter. He keeps seeing a YouTube video made at a dog-fighting club. Small strays or stolen dogs are used as bait, pit bulls shake and tear them apart, revving themselves up for the main event. Pit bulls not considered tough enough are hanged. Pro quarterback Michael Vick ran something called Bad Newz Kennels. Ritz sees Vick in handcuffs being perp-walked out of court.

In ten minutes he brakes in front of Dolores's bungalow. Ritz gets out and runs through the downpour, up the walk. He slaps the frame, opens the screen and bangs on the door. At last Coco swings it open. "I'm not here to make trouble, just to do business. You have my dog, I'll pay you, name a price, show her to me so I know she's all right, that ends it, no questions asked, end of story."

"Dottor G call to warn me. I don' got your fucking dog." Water is pouring out a gutter downspout on Ritz's left. "Jou got a lot of nerve, know that? Telling lies to Dottor G, saying I steal shit from him. I don' steal nothing. You one crazy old man. I hear about you singing karaoke, make all kind of people hate you. Man, you some kind of crazy, no shit."

"Give me my dog you fake cowboy! You thief! 'Truman! Here Truman! Come on girl!'"

Ritz tries to shove past into the house and Coco kicks him. "Aiee!" Kicks into his right shinbone, so hard that Ruiz has to yank his foot free as Ritz falls on the front walk.

In agony, Ritz holds his shin. "God—"

Coco looks down at his steel-tipped boot. The rushing downspout is splashing on Ritz's neck. "I take your dog to that greenkeeper like Dottor G tell me." Coco slams the door.

On his side, Ritz is rocking in pain, gripping his shin with both hands. He squirms away from the gushing water. The pain is a dagger jabbing down to his foot, up to his groin. But Truman is safe. "Coco, I'm sorry, thank you…" You deserve this, he thinks. You deserve everything.

A full minute passes before he can brace himself and sit up. Ritz groans in agony. Competing with the pain is something like gratitude. A strange, peaceful agony. What's wrong with you? he thinks. How can you be like this?

Kept in the glove compartment with extra golf gloves is a bottle of Advil. Dolores' front porch has a wrought-iron railing. In the next minute, Ritz uses it to pull himself up. When he tries putting weight on the leg, he falls on his side. The pain is overwhelming. He rolls from side to side. "That's you… lose your balance… Lose puppies. Jobs, your wife… you're a loser—" He thinks of Glen's blue legs.

When at last he manages to roll on his side, Dolores is looking at him through a parted curtain.

"Help me!" The curtain falls. The door opens.

"Why you don't go home now, okay? Is late, you all wet, just go home."

"He stabbed me!"

Dolores makes a clucking sound. "He give you a little kick is all. He save your dog for you." She steps back inside and eases the door half shut. The throbbing is worse. He does not know what to do. Doesn't know where the greenskeeper lives. You are responsible for her and she's gone, he thinks. Lost. The thought means too much, out of all proportion. But the idea of his dog, terrified of thunder and running from a strange house into traffic... No, he must not think that.

"Which one you want?"

Dolores is holding open the screen door with her foot, and now flaps open a Calloway golf umbrella. Hanging over her arm are four canes. "From customers." When she steps down, rain batters the umbrella. "They give me the old canes! And the walkers! I sell them on eBay! Which one you want!" She holds out her arm.

It's distracting. Tormented about his dog, his leg, Ritz lifts off a cane made of Lucite embedded with glitter. "Thank you."

"Coco take your dog to the green keeper, he got your dog. You got no reason to make trouble for my nephew. His dogs ain't even here. I see you next Tuesday." Dolores turns away and steps under the porch roof. She flaps the umbrella free of rain, goes in and closes the door.

Truman will be safe with Mike Connolly. Ritz remembers the Advil. Once more he drags himself to the iron railing. After a moment, he pulls himself up. This time, using the cane, he is able to stand. Very slowly, using Barney Rattle baby steps, he begins gimping his way toward the street. Rowdy, that's the name of the greenskeeper's dog. A big English setter. Friendly with everyone, a great runner. What if Rowdy reminds Truman of Coda? What if Tru wants to live at Connolly's?

Once inside the Explorer, he uses his sodden shirt to wipe his face. The walk has made the right leg develop its own thudding pulse. He reaches and opens the glove box. Ritz fumbles off the cap, counts out four pills, and tosses them in his mouth.

41
Final Words

Whenever lightning strikes the golf course, a siren is triggered. It goes on wailing as the Donegal gate swings open.

Left and right, shallow pools of casual water gleam on the fairways. As he sat in his Explorer waiting for the Advil to take effect, the rain slowed and stopped. When he drove off, Ritz buzzed down all his windows. Washed now by fresh air and the dashboard's colorful lights, he feels his wound pulsing but less painful. He raises and gently lowers his injured right leg in the passenger-side footwell. It's clumsy, but he is managing to work the accelerator and brake pedals with his left foot.

The siren stops as he nears his street. Ritz turns. Parked ahead is a small trailer.

"Anne. She changed her mind. She wants Truman."

The throbbing grows as he creeps toward the U-Haul. He must get in the house and call Connolly. *Please bring her here, Mike—* But what if the storm made his worst thought come true? What if his gentle, terrified dog *did* run away from another strange house? The dog is dead, crushed in traffic after her master failed her. He reaches the U-Haul, and stops next to the silver Chrysler Sebring.

His heart is thumping hard from too much Advil. Sunshine, not Anne. "I am sorry, I am truly sorry for wasting your time."

The convertible top is only half raised. He parks in front of Grunwald's house. Ritz delicately brings his right leg over the transmission hump. Gets the cane, opens his door. Once out, he rocks his way to the Sebring. Beads of moisture glisten on the leather seats, on the steering column and dashboard. Water has pooled in the folds of the half-open cloth top. She was driving and stopped to put it up, but something went wrong. A fuse, a mechanical glitch.

"Please, Sunshine, you must know I can't fix anything."

The trailer's aluminum is dull, the U-Haul logo peeled in places. At the back, a heavy padlock is hanging loose, slotted in the twin holes to keep both doors closed. A forgotten combination? Ritz balances with the cane, and pulls out the lock. One door swings open and as he pushes back the second, the streetlamp reveals her white furniture. Mattress and bedsprings, end tables, a padded rocking chair.

On the left, a sheet is draped over what look to be picture frames. The frames are almost vertical, held in place by two-by-fours laid flat on the floor. Snugly wedged against the trailer's opposite wall, the boards have been cut to an exact length for just this purpose.

Ritz hops and sits on the edge of the trailer. He reaches up and hangs his cane on the open door. Now he begins working to dislodge a two-by-four. And another. Their careful, intentional placement makes him feel a sense of violation. He hears a bark and stops. Tru barks in pairs, but there is no second bark. Turning back, Ritz dislodges the last two-by-four, and again hears the sound. The board scraping the trailer floor, that's what he heard.

He slips off the back deck. Ritz pivots, hops on one foot, and reaches to the first frame. It's solid and heavy, a picture professionally mounted with glass. As he gently rocks the frame forward, Ritz feels its weighty importance to the owner. Hopping back, he draws the picture with him. It starts to fall, but he catches the top with his free hand. He lowers it, and rests the frame carefully against the open trailer door.

"What did you expect, Elvis on black velvet? That's not her style."

Neither are sea oats or sunsets. Bluish in the streetlamp's beam, a house rests on a hill in winter. Chimney smoke rises, the windows glow; the painting's night sky looks pure, not cold. Pine boughs hang heavy with snow. Ritz can almost hear corn popping inside, people laughing. Like all Thomas Kinkade pictures, this one hails from a dream that people choose to live with.

Being careful, he hops back and tugs out the next picture. Another Kinkade house. And a third. Ritz stares in poor light at Christmas carolers in front of a Georgian colonial. Snow is falling as the family inside waves through the window. All houses. Places of peace and refuge. No, Ritz thinks. Edgar Guest was right, not houses, *homes.* In the moment, he is sure of it: Sunshine read his essay on Kinkade. The blank walls in her apartment bore marks where picture frames had knocked the paint. In the call she made at the dog park, she asked someone to take down the Kinkades.

As Ritz begins carefully returning the pictures in the right order, he is reading with ten-year-old Jane; snow is sifting down in the windows, logs popping. He replaces the two-by-fours, and floats the sheet back in place.

***

Truman stands in her Thunder Shirt, looking up at him.

"You're supposed to be with the greenskeeper."

He closes the door, turns and hobbles to her in the dark foyer. Bends and strokes her head. At the far end, the pool gleams in the wedge of light coming from Grunwald's deck. A Florida Thomas Kinkade. Water is running upstairs, traveling through a pipe in the wall.

He snaps on the foyer chandelier, hops over and grabs the handrail. After a moment, Ritz turns to his dog. She is studying the strange glittery thing in his hand. "Stay—" he gestures with his palm. "I might fall on you." Deciding it can be done, he shoves on the cane and steps up with his good leg. Then the right foot. Painful, but doable. He continues this way, glad for the carpet runner cushioning the dulled stabbing in his shin bone. The sound in the wall takes on familiar specifics. It's coming from the bath in the master bedroom.

He pauses at the last step before shoving up. The water stops. Only now does Ritz wonder how Sunshine got in. Or Truman. He stands in the hall, balanced between his good leg and the plastic glitter cane. Sixty-six, he thinks. Your only concern is where to place your feet.

After loading the U-Haul, she came here. Sunshine is pulling up stakes. Taking her furniture and what matters most, professionally framed Kinkade pictures. A door opens with the rush of an exhaust fan. Why should that be touching, the sound of the fan in his bathroom? Rocking forward, Ritz tries to focus. Why is she here? The broken convertible top? To steal? He remembers a long-ago story in the Detroit *Post*. A moron burglar arrested while taking a shower in the homeowner's bathroom. But Sunshine Urbanski is no moron. At the open bedroom door, he sees the panels to the walk-in closet are folded open. Clothes hangers are being scraped. He rocks forward and now sees her in the walk-in, dressed in his terrycloth robe. Hair wrapped in a towel, she replaces the lid on the shoe box, and looks over her shoulder, shiny-faced. His black camp shirt is draped over her arm.

"What's up, Brady?" She stuffs the wad of cash in the robe's pocket. "You learned Brianna wasn't coming here? I thought you'd be in a school gym."

"I decided to wait it out here."

"Bullshit. You didn't close the shutters."

"Something came up."

"Yeah, same here, I have to leave Naples. I called but you weren't here. I decided I underbid the last date."

"I'm sure you did."

Sunshine glances at the cane before she turns and reenters the bathroom. The door closes halfway. The fan shuts down. "You're good about the money?"

"I'm good about it."

Faded movements slide over the wedge of mirror he can see. "I was curious, I checked with a realtor. She said houses here go for about what you said." If he could, Ritz knows what he would buy for her. Thomas Kinkade has designed an entire village in California. I'd get you a home with a thatched roof, he thinks. Better than anything in Naples.

She comes out in bra and panties and tosses his black camp shirt on the bed before sitting. Sunshine starts pulling on jeans.

He's never seen her in jeans. She takes the camp shirt off the bed and shakes it out. "What's with the cane?"

"Coco." She slips on the shirt. "With his boot," Ritz says. "I couldn't find Truman. I thought he took her."

"Who's Coco?" She starts on the buttons. "Okay, I get it. You thought this Coco took your dog for ransom. Dognapping does happen."

"He knows how I am about her. The way you know."

Still buttoning the shirt, Sunshine smiles at him. "That time in my apartment? How I did a number on you? I was jealous of the dog."

She finishes buttoning the shirt and puts her hands on her knees. "You are a case, know that? The funny thing, it's hard not to like you. Difficult, true. Ex*ceedingly* difficult. Taxing. Challenging. Remarkably, ostentatiously, enigmatically—whatever. That's you, *Buzz*. You aren't fake, but you don't understand yourself. You're a softy. You really are, no shit. All that hard-ass stuff in your book? After dinner that first night, I Googled you and read some reviews. Okay, that's you, too, but really. Take it from me, you should like talk your wife into coming back. You need… structure."

She starts lacing up running shoes with stripes like Ace Foley's. Finished, she straightens, hands again on her knees. "Like supervision," she says. "Another set of eyes and ears. She left a message, your wife Natalie."

Sunshine smiles again. "When I came in, I don't know why, I checked for messages. That's how I learned Buzz is your nickname. That time I was here, first thing we walk in the door, you checked for messages. Maybe to see if the estranged thing was over. 'It's me. I've been wrong, I should've come back weeks ago, but I was wrong. It was vanity, Buzz, don't fly back, I'm flying down.' Something like that, you can play it for yourself. She said she's coming in two days with Iris and Jamal. Hi there, Truman. Nice threads."

His dog has come up and now sits on his left. "Someone must have a pass key," Sunshine says. "When I let myself in, she was here." Sunshine returns to the bathroom. Seconds later she comes back stuffing the cash in her jeans pocket.

"Where are you going?"

"Wisconsin. Never mind, it's related to my asshole father."

She snaps her fingers, and goes back in the bathroom. He has had sex with her, eaten and drunk with her, shared Truman with her, and knows nothing about her. She comes out holding a wad of wet clothes. "The top on my car wouldn't go all the way up," she says. "He got bitten by one of his snakes during a midnight service. Snakes are part of his flock thing."

"You can't drive with the roof like that."

"It's not what you think. The trailer gets in the way when you try to put the top up. I can fix it, but U-Haul was getting ready to close.

"So." She looks at him, remembers something. Laughs. "'Death Row delicious.' She sounded nice. After I Googled you, I went to Barnes and Noble. They let you sit and read. Pretty funny, Buzz. That's how I learned why Natalie left and people are pissed at you."

And read what you wrote about Thomas Kinkade, he thinks. And forgot to take down his pictures before plugging in the crock pot.

Holding the wet clothes away from her, she steps around Ritz and starts down the hall. But Sunshine stops to look at the first painting. "What did you say? Beauty lies in the eye of the beholder? To each his own?" Sunshine shakes her head. "To me, this is gloomy, but okay, your kid painted it, it matters to you." She continues down the hall.

"Please wait," he calls. "Tell me again what my wife said. I can't go downstairs with this leg."

"Right. She said she's on her way the day after tomorrow. With Iris and Jamal." Sunshine starts down the stairs. "She said The Weather Channel said Brianna won't come ashore at Naples. And she asked how some test went." Her head slips out of sight.

"Sunshine—" He hears her stop. "Please call when you get to Wisconsin." A moment passes. He hears movement, and now her face appears between the railing supports. "And call me tomorrow from the road."

"All right."

"I'd just like to know."

"All right."

She turns away and heads down. Seconds later, the front door clicks open. "I'll leave your key back under the flower pot. Everyone hides it under the welcome mat or a planter. *Duh.* By the way, my name's Charm. Sunshine works here, but not so much in cheesehead country. 'Bye, Truman!"

42
Natalie, take us home

Riding on sticky-sounding tires, the security guard seems to be aiming for us—talking, rolling. Bluetooth-equipped to leave her hands free to work the Segway.

I'm in the boarding lounge with Iris and Jamal, waiting to see them off for their flight back to Michigan. No to metal joints or other replacement parts, no to a pacemaker. Then TSA scanned me up and down before letting me take them through Security check-in.

Buzz says I brought grandchildren with me the way terrorists use civilians as human shields. He's half right. But since she got back, Anne's been very busy with co-op business. That makes me *her* shield: since Iris and Jamal are with Grandma, their mother won't need to worry about detectives digging up more of what Buzz calls intel.

As the Segway passes, a woman's dreamy, tranquilized voice is asking whoever left a suitcase unattended at Delta baggage to please report to the ticket counter. The voice is fear wrapped in a fuzzy blanket, and somehow it and the Segway are connected to news we heard on the way here: another Improvised Explosive Device. Or was it a suicide bomber? Making such connections must have to do with Grandma being worried about Iris and Jamal flying home alone.

"I wish I had one." Iris is standing next to me, watching the Segway pass down the aisle between boarding lounges.

"Why would you want a Segway? You're a wheelie already."

"Heelys, Grandma. Hee-lees."

To be sure Grandma *gets* it, Iris shoves off, balanced on her heels. That's what I want for Christmas, she said last fall. Nothing else, that's all I want, Heelys *period*. This was followed by a diagonal slicing motion of her right hand. Buzz and I use that gesture almost on a daily basis: a sharp hacking motion for emphasis. His boycott was still in effect, but he ordered the Heelys in time. As a result, I retained my status as Best Grandma Ever for another Christmas.

Gliding silently, arms extended, Iris seems to be riding a wave. She dips in a graceful arabesque left. Right. She wants me to see how good she is at it, how right she was to want Heelys. Knowing Iris is doing this just for me draws something out of or into my chest. All at once the wide sweep of terrazzo floor in front of her seems guaranteed to end in a bad fall. When I asked where her helmet was, she said helmets were too nerdy for Heelys. If I call her back, I'll hear Buzz whispering in my ear: *TSA forbids helicopter grandparenting.*

Seven Christmases ago, Iris and her mother were the first to visit us here. We hadn't yet finished the move, and our new house was still spartan. All we had were some director's chairs, inflatable Aerobeds, and two TVs. Plus a few things purchased at resale stores to make do until we could shop. And Jane's paintings. Buzz had insisted on shipping them down right away. He got a local framing shop to gallery-wrap them and hang them. That's what kept the place from looking like any other just-completed house still smelling of tile grout and drywall. But the pool had been completed, so we flew Anne and Iris down for Christmas.

My husband would tell me I'm sidestepping. Talking about drywall and home furnishings to avoid getting to the point. He would be right.

Jamal is on my left, watching his sister. He now regrets not asking for shoes with wheels. He wanted some expensive game gizmo, a thing you point at the TV and wave around. I open my purse and unfold my wallet. "Here—" I hand him a twenty. "Go over to the gift shop and pick out some snacks for the plane. Just two kinds, Jamal. And a *New York Times* for Grandpa. Please don't wander off."

"I won't."

He says "won't" with an audible T. I watch him walk away with the twenty gripped in his hand. Anne says his pronunciation is getting better every week. Soon, Iris will no longer need to translate for her brother.

I have given him the economic power to choose what candy to take on the flight home. And I've also bought myself a moment alone, which makes me something like the dad in Cambier Park. Buzz told me about him yesterday, playing Frisbee with his little girl. As Jamal nears the gift shop, I look again to Iris. She's still at it, sweeping her hands left and right.

Like a lounge-act chanteuse. Last night, he also described Jeremy's reaction on seeing "Mister Ritz at the start of his ill-advised flirtation with show business." Gina Buskirk had broken the code of silence and called with the story, but his version brought it to life. I remembered the ugly aloha shirt and pants. The whole idea of my husband on stage was truly unthinkable. Even so, I could see him there, the line dancers, the breaking glass and spinning tray. I laughed very hard, until he got to the man with no voice box.

That story led him to what happened with Ace Foley and the china cabinet. I prized those wine glasses. My mother had no interest in china or stemware, and that helps to explain why finally having my own nice things represented a kind of long-delayed coming-of-age. I'll get others. Deirdre Foley I always liked. I thought she deserved better than Ace, but I'm sorry for him. Buzz says the worst thing is Foley losing his mind without ever coming to his senses. When he told the story, the inflection in his voice suggested to me that Buzz has come to his own senses. What that means I have yet to learn.

I hear him saying "More evasion, more sidestepping. Just like a Lipizzaner."

Iris has reached the end of the concourse, and is now doing figure eights. Jamal is studying the candy rack above the newspapers. Having left my purse open on purpose, I look down and rummage for my compact. I find it, look up once more to check on both children, and snap it open.

It still looks like a prisoner's or soldier's haircut, but it will have to do. At least it's my own hair. I knew it was petty, but I could not come back wearing a wig. I just couldn't. I had left him alone for two months. I knew it was wrong, and I went out three nights in a row to shop for wigs. I went to a custom shop with photos of myself with hair. They showed me computer-aided designs of wigs that could be made with human hair. Looking at the screen, I remembered the girl in one of his columns, on a bicycle pulling one of the rickshaw carts. She was talking on her phone about shaving her head. I knew it was wrong, but I still just couldn't come back. Not after rereading his column on "rugs, wigs, buzz cuts, heads prepped for the electric chair, novelty-shop toupees, cribbage-board hair plugs, falls, extensions, streaks, Rainbow Nation colors on the same head, tribal designs, third-world knockoffs." Every time I went out after dark to shop for groceries, his words came with me.

It was eight weeks to the day after I'd left Naples. I had bought my plane ticket that morning. I was finally ready to face "the angry villagers with torches and pitchforks." I was brushing my teeth, working out a speech to use for the encounters I knew would be waiting for me at Donegal. I stopped brushing to remove a hair in my mouth. I looked in the mirror, touched my scalp. When I tugged at it, a clump of hair came loose. Not one or two hairs, a small clump. I pulled again. With no more force than it takes to pull out a jammed sheet of paper in my printer, I pulled out another clump. I went into our bedroom and snapped on the overhead light. Hair lay matted on my pillow. I thought: ringworm. Jane had ringworm when she was twelve. But it wasn't ringworm.

Over the years, I've often told Buzz he is insensitive to other people's problems. He defends himself by saying people are too self-involved about their feelings. Too self-absorbed. I tell him being mood sick is often no less serious than being sick sick. Now, I was both kinds. I was sick over seeing myself bald and walking toward familiar faces at Donegal. Or, more honestly, sick at imagining people walking toward me, focused on my head. Even as a healthy me, I would need all my self-confidence to walk into the dining room with my husband. Or shop with someone, or meet for bridge. But now I was going bald. When I confided the story of *Vanitas* to our family doctor, he said research argued against stress as the cause. I told him I knew better. Being mood sick was what had caused my hair to fall out from alopecia.

Alopecia totalis. I was losing my hair from guilt over leaving Buzz down here alone, and from fear over what it would be like for me when I faced the pitchforks. Anticipating what was waiting in Naples had joined my anger and disappointment over Buzz keeping his *Grumble* column a secret for years. What his silence said about our marriage discouraged me. With the inevitable ups and downs, I had always thought ours was a good marriage. Now, I began to think we might have stayed together out of convenience. Many women I know have done that.

But it wasn't true, and I knew it. We never stopped being glad to see each other coming from the garage after work. We liked too many of the same things. After almost thirty years, we still genuinely appreciated each other's jokes. That can't be true if you don't still belong together. Over time, we'd developed a glossary, a lexicon of gestures and words that had meaning only for us.

I was just *angry*. And when I calmed down, I went back and re-read *Vanitas*. It was often funny and inciteful about what he called "these days." But it was also full of anger and bitterness. He had always been a glass-half-empty man, but until now I had never stopped to fully consider what it had meant to him to lose his job as a copy editor.

He loves words. He often says he fell for me because I do too. And he especially loved being in charge of words at the *Detroit Post*. Loved knowing what writers had first written, and seeing those stories in print the next day, seeing how much better his editing had made them. But then he was forced to dumb himself down for ad clients. I thought my failure to see this had to do with my worry over Anne's rebellion. And it did. But my blindness also had to do with my own work as the office manager for a group of lawyers. To me, what I did was just a job, not a vocation. If I lost my job, I'd get another. It wasn't *me*, it was *work* work, but that hadn't been true for Buzz.

On our anniversaries, we often reminisce about our first meeting at the *Post* New Year's party. Just before he gave me his book, we talked about the swizzle stick, and Buzz spoke as he often has about how "disarmingly candid and direct" he thought I'd been. Now, I was being anything but candid. I was the one doing the concealing. I was being small-minded and vain, and the worst thing was that I resented Buzz for forcing me to see this aspect of myself.

I lost my sense of humor. I badgered him when we talked on the phone. And I went on keeping my own secret about why I hadn't come back, my humiliation at looking in the mirror. That in a true sense was my own *Vanitas*. I think in my own mind I was punishing Buzz by not sharing it with him. I let him go on assuming that embarrassment over his book was the only thing keeping me away. Within three weeks I was almost bald. I swore Anne and Jane to secrecy. My doctor said there was no actual treatment for alopecia. All he could suggest was that I go to a health-food store and look into dietary supplements.

Anne's co-op sold them. When I explained what the doctor had said, she called back an hour later. The bioflavonoids in fruits and vegetables are supposed to help, she said. Go to a health-food store and get quercetin, it's all bioflavonoids. And drink green tea. I began taking massive doses of the supplement. I drank gallons of green tea, and took Valium to sleep. After dark, I shopped for groceries wearing the Tigers baseball cap Buzz bought me at a game. I kept the drapes closed, avoided the neighbors. Anne, Jane and Buzz were the only people I spoke to. The whole thing was secretive and humbling, but slowly my hair started to grow. As a trial run before coming back to Florida, I wore my Tigers cap and took Jane and the girls to an amusement park in Ohio. Otherwise, I was pretty much alone, like my husband.

Because of his leg, he couldn't pick us up at the airport. He elevates it on a hassock with a bed pillow, "like Richard Nixon did with phlebitis." He says only people our age or older would get the reference.

We took a shuttle bus from the airport to Donegal. I saw Buzz watching from his study window, and he opened the door to greet us. He smiled, but then his eyes were taking in my hair, my still-missing eyebrows. I said nothing, but I saw he already knew why I'd been gone so long. We kissed, Buzz with one arm around me, balancing with his cane. Later, he explained the really nasty, deep wound on his shin. "I lost my head over Truman" is how he put it. He had gone to Dolores' house and made crazy accusations against her nephew. Coco kicked him with that boot of his, something Buzz says he completely deserved. He called Coco the next day to apologize. A doctor friend of Murray Grunwald's came to the house and gave Buzz a tetanus shot.

After the hug, he introduced me to Truman. Iris and Jamal knew her already, and were on the floor to scratch her head and let her sniff. As we watched, Buzz said there were no bad dogs, including pit bulls. Inconvenient dogs, and sometimes dangerous dogs, yes. But that had to do with bad masters, or breeding, or vicious training. He said the best thing about dogs was how easy they made it for you to believe you were being understood. The second best thing was how good it made you feel to be kind to them. I don't think that was aimed at me, but it registered.

What Buzz says about dogs is true for me, with children. It's a great pleasure to think I am doing right by them. Jamal's curly blond head is now nearly up to my shoulder. Iris will soon be much taller than my five-six, probably even taller than Buzz at five-ten. We will do what we can to limit their tall father's influence to that.

As we went up to bed that first night, all this was still tumbling out between us. I was behind him on the stairs, keeping an eye on him as he worked his way up with the cane. As he often does, Buzz slowed to look at Jane's paintings. It occurred to me that truth-telling should include the two pictures he most admires—the African violets without blooms, and the drowned peony bush. He thinks they're ironic, but Jane painted those before Madison was born, in the year following her miscarriage. We seem to do a lot of swearing to secrecy around here: Jane demanded that Anne and I not tell her stepfather. It's past time he knew the truth: grief inspired those two paintings, not irony.

I am also wondering whether truth-telling will apply to the message he got from someone in Wisconsin. The second night, we were on the deck watching Iris and Jamal in the pool. I went in to check on my latest vegetarian concoction (I keep the faith when they're with us), a cauliflower-curry-cheese casserole. The phone rang. I didn't like the thought of answering an insult comedian trashing my husband, and let the call go to voicemail. "Hi, Buzz AKA Zeno Kowalski, it's Sunshine AKA Charm. You asked me to call when I got home. So I got home. I fixed the top, it worked okay. My father's dumbass flock is praying like crazy for him, but that's what they are. Crazy. Nothing's wrong with daddy-o a bolt of lightning couldn't fix. Take care of yourself."

When I get home, I'll say there's a message from someone named Sunshine. I will know a lot about who and what she is from his face, but whatever he tells me I will probably accept. I was gone much too long, and not for high-minded reasons.

Jamal is still picking up and putting down cellophane packages. Mints, Hershey's Kisses, gum balls capable of sucking the fillings out of his teeth. Buzz would insist the majority of Gummy Bear stockholders are dentists. When Jamal finally makes his decision, he will come back and again watch his gliding sister. I want Heelys too, he'll say. Jamal worships Iris. He almost always follows her lead. Her bursts of passion and need.

Someone Better Than You: A Comedy of Manners

I took a photo of the plastic Jell-O mold Buzz sent two weeks ago. When I show it to him, I'll again make my case for his actually carrying the cell phone I put in his car. He probably won't. He refuses to be "tethered 24/7." The Jell-O is propped up on the fireplace mantel in Michigan. Between the soapstone faun he got me on our wedding trip (Paris), and the cherub standing on a globe (Vienna). We must have the cherub, he said. A baby angel straddling the planet, made in Nazi Germany. A plastic Jell-O mold doesn't really belong with such keepsakes, but the mantel is its permanent home.

It's a quote, courtesy of Ashley Vanzhent. From her visit here last Christmas, right after her show-stopper performance in a children's play. We were all swimming and eating pizza after dark. Trailing water in her darling little bathing suit, cutie-pie Ashley came inside. She insisted her mom and Madison and Grandma come out to watch the pool finish making Jell-O. That's how it was supposed to work on me, the way 'lo referred to the cockatoo in Stratford, Ontario. It did work on me. At some point, you reach an age and come to see that it's now mostly about words. How they fix moments. If you're still paying attention, and don't suffer Ace Foley's fate, words save the moment to share with everyone who was there. I think of it like metal shavings drawn to a magnet, a pattern that keeps gathering. Buzz told me once that Saul Bellow said memories are what keep the wolf of insignificance from the door. True, that.

At last, here comes Iris. She's looking down at her rolling feet, and almost runs into a man working a floor buffer. She stops to apologize, but his back is turned, and she keeps coming. The worker looks to be in his seventies. Still in the trenches, Buzz would say.

"I know I know—" Iris rolls to a stop. "Slow down."

"That's right." I point to the gift shop. "Please get your brother." She starts to go. "Iris? I told him he could do the choosing. Please don't tell him what to buy." She nods, and shoves off.

They're remarkably good kids, considering. Not just during the custody battle, but in spite of the nomadic nature of their lives. To say Anne and Buzz haven't often seen eye to eye is like saying a teller and a bank robber work in the same field, but have differences. And I think they always will. But I know Buzz is finally going to let Tushy go. Anne told me he apologized about the life jackets.

She wondered whether Truman had something to do with it. Today or tomorrow, I'll tell him Anne is the one who deserves the credit for his dog. Not just for bringing her to him, but the whole idea. At first she was mad about the nurse's elbow business, but she still intended to leave the kids with him and go back down to Key West alone. Then she realized taking them with her would be her best chance to leave Truman with Buzz.

It's so obvious how much she already means to him. How he dotes on her. She's not a very conventional source of doggy good cheer. He says there's a story behind that, but it's easy to see his attachment isn't a one-way street. Whenever he lifts his foot off the hassock and rocks out of the room, Truman follows. A man skeptical all his life about *feelings* is head-over-heels gaga for a dog. But there's a kind of logic to it:

someone who resists showing his emotions to people, but not to a border collie.

The four of us were eating two nights ago on the patio—correction, the five of us—when he explained "their" mealtime ritual: the timing and the plating, pouring himself another glass of wine and going back out "to keep Tru company" while she ate. It touched me. I felt guilty knowing how loneliness lay behind monologues spoken to a dog at Happy Hour. But at the same time I just managed to keep a straight face. Iris and Jamal listened carefully. Treating a dog as a person made perfect sense to them.

Passive and sad-looking, yes, but Truman is easy to like. That soulful right eye of hers is eloquent. And her beautiful, lustrous coat, her perfectly shaped head he keeps reaching down to stroke. With a smidgeon of jealousy, I am already losing my own head over Truman. Falling under her sway. I love watching her fine-tuned ears collecting intel from all directions.

When I tell him she was Anne's idea, that's going to register. I know it. How the two of us were talking about what to do until my hair grew back, and that he needed someone. He used to talk about his dog, Anne said. When we were growing up, Tunnel, a dachshund. Buzz said he rolled a ball under the couch, and shoveled snow for him to do his business.

True. Over the years, he had talked about Tunnel. There's a photo in my study, seven-year-old Buzz between his parents, a puppy on his lap. We couldn't have pets due to allergies that Anne eventually outgrew. I knew in the moment she was right.

All kinds of shelter dogs down here, she said. All through the south, and many of them kill shelters.

Something to occupy him. To take his mind off being alone with his mood sickness. And to ease my conscience. But not just any dog. It was Anne who decided against a grinning, public relations glad-hander dog, in favor of a sad, one-eyed Key West collie she would save from being destroyed, and take to her stepfather. A dog in need of TLC, in need of being taken care of. A dog given a new name, a fresh start. Anne has her faults, but she *is* generous. And no fool. After I adopt her, I'll figure out a way to leave her with Buzz, she said. If it doesn't work, I'll take Truman back to live with me and the kids. She didn't say it, but her meaning was clear: as penance for Tushy. She said it bothered her to drive off the way she did, using Nurse's Elbow as the reason. It was the only way I could think of to leave her with Buzz, she said.

Here they come, perfect timing. Coming as well from the Delta counter is the representative who sees to children flying alone. The rep will take them down the jetway and hand them off to a flight attendant. Jamal gives me the *Times*. I hand Iris the plastic bag with her sandals, and kneel to hug him. His sister sits on the floor to unlace the Heelys, and I stand.

"Busy?" I ask the rep.

"Very," she says. "You wouldn't believe how many grandkids are flying in and back out by themselves. I see them coming and going."

"I promise you, their grandmas and grandpas are grateful." She smiles, a woman in her forties, probably someone with grandchildren in her own future.

Iris finishes putting on her sandals, and gets up. I hug her hard. "Okay—" I step back and cup her elbows. "You're in charge, you know what to do." Iris nods. "You have my number if mom's late. Got the candy you want?" Jammy nods. "Share, and don't kick the seats in front of you. And have mom call as soon as she picks you up. Don't forget."

I fold the *Times* under my arm. The Delta woman and I smile again. We know each other from previous visits. She reaches out for the Heelys and Iris hands them to her. Now she takes the woman's hand, takes her brother's hand, and the three move into the jetway tunnel.

I can't be sure, but I think we'll be leaving pretty soon ourselves. Even without *Vanitas,* I don't see us staying. Our lefty point of view has never fit well with life at Donegal. We bought without thinking it through, without doing our social due diligence. It's one thing to fly down for a couple weeks, very different being here for months. Buzz did his regular-guy impersonation, and unlike me he quickly adjusted to the humidity. As for getting along with my bridge friends, "Family and Consumer Science" and grandchildren have served as small talk instead of politics. Now and then something would trigger a burst of Tea Party nonsense ("My husband has a bumper sticker on his golf cart, 'I'll keep my guns and freedom, you can keep the change'"). But when that happened, the others mostly shook their heads without pursuing it. Probably because they know I'm a liberal.

When the Delta rep and the kids reach the dogleg, Iris and Jamal turn and wave. I wave back, blow them a kiss, and they're gone. Time to take a taxi back to Naples.

After dinner at the club, or walking home from parties, we have often felt mood sick. Especially since the '08 election. Buzz would come home from golf and report on what had been said about The Darky President. He spoke up for Obama, but got lots of blowback, and stopped. What was the point? At the end of April, we're always packed and ready to go *home* home to Michigan.

I reach the escalator and head down. Maybe it's the *Times* under my arm, or watching the kids leave that makes me think again of that first winter in the new house. It was late January. Jamal hadn't been born, and Anne and Iris had flown back to Michigan. The annual Naples Wine Auction was going on, and Buzz was reading to me about it from the *Naples Daily News*. The Auction is a big deal here. Celebrity chefs are flown in to prepare gourmet banquets in the homes of the uber rich. People bid thousands on single bottles of wine and other luxury items. One year, someone wrote a check for a million dollars for a "gently-used" Rolls Royce.

Stepping off the escalator, I'm still caught up in the memory. I move aside for the person behind me. Most of the money raised by the auction goes to aid Hispanic children, but Buzz wasn't having it. A society with real social justice doesn't need rich people's charity, he said. Besides, charity from the rich costs them nothing. So what? I said. If it helps kids, who cares? I care, he said. Patriotism is the last refuge of scoundrels, and philanthropy serves the same purpose for the rich. Real good, Buzz, I told him. Spoken like a true gated-community golfer with his own pool. That shut him down. He sometimes needs reminding that sticking signs on the front lawn in Michigan and writing checks does not a better person make.

On my left, passengers are watching, waiting, grabbing suitcases off the luggage carousel. I turn away and move toward the exit. Outside, the air is sticky, the sky overcast. It's too soon for the plane taking off above me to be carrying my grandchildren. People are crossing the street to the parking structure. I move to the cab stand, and get in the first. The driver looks in the rearview mirror. "Naples, Donegal Country Club." He pulls away.

It was after dinner. We were sitting in the kitchen at the resale butcher-block table we still use. The wine-auction article Buzz was reading to me ended with the menu and wines being served at one of the fancy dinners. Ten separate wine glasses would be needed. I hadn't shopped, and we were eating what was on hand: tuna fish salad with a baked potato and sour cream. This is Chef Natalie's version of Surf 'n Turf, I told him. As Escoffier confided to me long ago, this dish must always be served on paper plates. Buzz liked that. Our own dishes and stemware hadn't yet arrived, and we were drinking our screw-top chardonnay out of plastic beer cups. So now you know where you stand, I said, and raised my wine.

He liked that too, and gave me a high five. After he poured what was left into our cups, we went into the family room and sat in our canvas director's chairs. I got the remote and turned on *Turner Classic Movies*. Buzz moved a packing box, and we put up our feet as the credits began for *Born Yesterday,* with Judy Holiday, Broderick Crawford and William Holden.

When the airport shuttle arrived today, he walked us out. Truman sat on his left as Buzz hugged the kids. I kneeled down to check his wound. When I stood, he placed his hand on my head in mock benediction. He pantomimed *sorry* and I replied with *me too*. He hugged me hard and kissed me. I have an idea, I said. Let's you and me think of this as our gap year. Buzz laughed. I was quoting from "Arrested Development." In that one, along with cell phones, he mocked today's college students for taking a year off for "me time."

The kids climbed in the van. I followed, and began fastening their belts as the driver closed the panel. All of us waved as we backed down the drive.

"Love means never having to say you're sorry." That's the tagline from a Sixties bestseller, a real tear-jerker. What a smug catch phrase that is. It figured with us four years ago, the day Buzz opened his first Social Security check. I told him love means never forgetting to tell your spouse to take his Metamucil. Or to use her anti-fungal foot ointment, he said. Or low-dose aspirin, or the once-a-day pill for brain maintenance. This is great, he said. A Happy Meal for seniors.

I watched him still waving as the van turned onto Donegal Boulevard. Iris and Jamal already had their new books open (a family tradition: whenever they visit, we go to Barnes & Noble). As we neared the seventh hole, I saw three men at the edge of the green watching the fourth.

I've driven past this tableau so often it's visual white noise for me. But I sensed myself already saying goodbye to Donegal, and I studied them. Hunched over his putter, the fourth man was tenderly, delicately picking up and putting down his feet. He was wearing saddle shoes. As he kept glancing to the cup, I saw his partners were striking what Buzz would call a classic pose of golfer insouciance: one leaning on his putter with a toe upended, one with a hand in his pocket using his putter for balance, the third with the putter behind his neck, both wrists hanging from the shaft.

The club's a nice place, and the people here want to have a nice time. They don't want someone making them feel bad about it. What's the point? they'd say. We're out of the loop now, and we know what we know. We don't need some smartass easing his own conscience, his own doubts and guilt by making fun of us. Most of them would forgive me. They would see me as the wife of *Vanitas,* a woman in need of kindness.

But not my husband. What he wrote isn't going away for them. I was sure of that after re-reading the book. The wife, yes, the smartass, no. And it's not just a guy thing—all that talk of cruise jewelry and cosmetic surgery. I will miss some of the people here (the Grunwalds of course, and Gina Buskirk), people who are decent, not just nice. But Donegal is a throwback, a Fifties-era time capsule of what Buzz would call white suburban *roots.*

So, we'll sell, and head back to Michigan. Other than not being able to walk around in shorts all winter, I won't mind. I'm not a beach person, and I hate the humidity. Bridge is played everywhere.

But one thing I'm sure of: we'll be driving north, not flying. He's read how terrified dogs are when forced to travel in the baggage compartment. No dog *on my watch* is flying steerage,

Buzz will say. And this will be followed by Iris's diagonal slashing hand.

END

BIO

After a career of college teaching, Barry Knister is now focused on writing fiction. His first novel, a thriller about Vietnam Vets titled *The Dating Service* was published by Berkley. More recently, Knister's psychological suspense series follows the career of journalist Brenda Contay. *Someone Better Than You* is a distinct departure from his crime novels. Knister lives north of Detroit with his wife Barbara.

Thanks for reading. Like all writers, I am grateful to those who still enjoy the magic of turning words on the page into meaning. I hope you will consider writing a review, and that you visit my website, www.barryknister.com, I welcome emails at bwknister@sbcglobal.net